Sisters in White

Snow Sisters Trilogy, Book Three
Love in Bloom Series

Melissa Foster

"*Sisters in White* is a steamy romance infused with solid reflections on complex, evolving interpersonal relationships."
—*Midwest Book Review*

A Note to Readers

Prepare for a wedding full of bliss, blunders, and so much love, it jumps off the page. As with all of my novels, Sisters in White may be enjoyed as a standalone novel or as part of the larger trilogy. The Snow Sisters stories are ripe with emotions and funny, flawed, and easy-to-relate-to characters. I hope you enjoy them as much as I do.

The best way to keep up to date with new releases, sales, and exclusive content is to sign up for my newsletter.
www.MelissaFoster.com/Newsletter

About the Love in Bloom Big-Family Romance Collection

The Snow Sisters is just one of the series in the Love in Bloom big-family romance collection. Characters from each series make appearances in future books, so you never miss an engagement, wedding, or birth. A complete list of all series titles is included at the end of this book, along with previews of upcoming publications.

You can download free first-in-series ebooks and see my current sales here: www.MelissaFoster.com/LIBFree

Visit the Love in Bloom Reader Goodies page for downloadable checklists, family trees, and more.
www.MelissaFoster.com/RG

Be sure to check out my online bookstore for pre-orders, early releases, bundles, and exclusive discounts on ebooks, print, and audiobooks. Ebooks can be sent to the e-reader of your choice and audiobooks can be listened to on the free and easy-to-use BookFunnel app.

Shop my store: shop.melissafoster.com

For my Bauer Drive girlfriends. May we always remember pig orgy underwear, condom earrings, *It's not his fault!*, and Assawoman Street.

I miss you every moment of my life.

Chapter One

"I thought they were going to do a cavity search," Danica joked as she and her fiancé, Blake Carter, finally passed through security at the Nassau Airport. After six hours on an airplane, she felt like she'd been folded, packed tight, boxed, and shipped. The sooner she stepped out those glass doors and into the sunshine, the better. "Maybe we should go walk around a bit."

"Don't you want to wait for your sister?" Blake asked, holding the doors open for Danica to pass through. Her sister, Kaylie, and Kaylie's fiancé, Chaz, were not far behind. His consideration of Kaylie and his gentlemanlike manners were just two of the many reasons Danica had fallen in love with—and finally agreed to marry—Blake.

"I guess. Then maybe we can take a walk after we get to the hotel."

Blake set their bags down and pulled Danica in close. He lowered his voice to a sexy, sleepy drawl. "If you think I'm gonna let you out of our room any longer than to attend our wedding, you're wrong."

She playfully pushed him away as he made a show of nibbling on her neck.

A few minutes later, Kaylie breezed through the doors with

Chaz, who was weighed down by two enormous suitcases. Her hair blew in the warm breeze like thick, shimmering strands of gold. "That took for-e-ver!" She took a deep breath and drew her arms open wide. "So this is what freedom feels like."

"If you call six hours on a plane freedom," Chaz joked. His blond hair was slightly disheveled, and still, in his ever-present khaki shorts and smart linen shirt, he and Kaylie looked like Ken and Barbie.

Kaylie shot him a flirty smile.

"Oh, you mean as in no-children freedom," he said.

Kaylie and Chaz had met three years earlier, and Kaylie's unexpected pregnancy, and the surprise birth of their twins, had kept them running at a frenetic pace ever since. Chaz Crew had proven himself as not only a loving and involved father, but he was the calm to Kaylie's dramatic storms.

"I love my babies, but after two years of chasing the twins nonstop, I need this little break. Three whole days before they come with Mom. Three. Whole. Days. And two whole nights. It feels so decadent to be here in the middle of the week."

It had taken Kaylie two years after Lexi and Trevor were born to feel like herself again, and as Danica watched her sister's face light up at the prospect of time alone with her soon-to-be husband, she was glad they'd waited to have the wedding. At first, a double wedding had seemed like a bad idea. Danica had been sure Kaylie would want to be the star of the show, and wasn't it just as much Danica's day as Kaylie's? But Kaylie had proven her wrong time and time again; from choosing flowers to bridesmaid dresses, Kaylie was agreeable, and even deferred to Danica on several occasions. At times, Danica still had trouble processing just how much Kaylie had changed since she'd met Chaz. She was no longer a party girl, but a mature mother of two…who just so happened to have a flair for drama at times.

"Two whole nights," Chaz repeated.

"Now, that's what I'm talkin' about." Blake picked up their bags and hailed a cab.

Although the others thought he was teasing, Danica saw the gleam in his eye and recognized the hunger that had yet to abate between them. She felt a flush rush up her neck and ducked into the cab so no one would notice. Each time they made love, it left her wanting more, like a hormone-infused teenager. *Or a sex addict*, she mused. Lately, in the darkest hours of the night, when Blake lay sleeping beside her ravished and sated body, she found herself wanting more, thinking about new and different things she and Blake might try. Things that, in her pre-Blake years, she'd never have even entertained. But she'd never—ever—say such things out loud. Not even to him. She'd learned that from her parents' divorce a few years earlier. Danica knew that no matter how much she loved, and how much she trusted, sometimes life kicked you to the curb, and all that love—and all those promises in the dark—could be forgotten just as quickly as they'd slipped from her lips. A partner could walk away at any moment, taking the dirty scenes of their intimate moments with them and sharing them with God knew whom. She wasn't having cold feet, and she trusted Blake explicitly, but some lessons were engrained too deeply to simply forget.

"Oh no. I'm talking about sleep, my friend." Kaylie linked her arm through Chaz's as they climbed into the cab. "My man needs to rest."

After Chaz had taken over full ownership of the Indie Film Festival his father had started, he'd planned on taking the business to a whole new level. He'd been working night and day to ensure that he would never be desperate for sponsors again, and he'd succeeded. The bags under his eyes, and his slow pace, revealed the stress of working twelve-hour days and then coming home to late nights with the toddlers.

Danica and Kaylie both gasped as they entered the elaborately decorated hotel. The incredibly high ceilings, and the widely sculpted, artistically weathered pillars, were highlighted by salmon-colored granite floors speckled with flecks of black, white, and gold, dramatically reflecting the crystal of the chandeliers.

Kaylie took Danica's hand. "Oh my God. This belongs to Blake's cousin?"

"Yeah. Treat Braden," Danica said in a breathy voice. "This is too much."

Blake put his hand on the small of her back. "He was happy to comp us the venue. It's his wedding gift to us."

"He must be loaded," Kaylie said.

"Kaylie!" *Maybe Kaylie hasn't changed that much after all.*

Kaylie smiled, and covered her mouth with her hand. "Oops. Sorry."

Blake took it in stride. "He is loaded. His entire family is well off, but you'd never know it. All five brothers, and his sister, too. But they're good people. Very humble, generous to a fault."

"And from what Blake told me, each one is more handsome than the next, and yet they're all single. Even Savannah, their sister."

Kaylie furrowed her brow. "Are they all gay? I mean, women

must flock to them, and guys to her."

Blake shook his head as he checked in at the registration desk.

"They're not gay; trust me, they all play the field. A lot," he said as they headed to their separate rooms, agreeing to meet for a quick bite once they were settled in.

Danica brought her wedding checklist to the café to go over it one last time.

"Everyone arrives Friday. Sally and Max are bringing our dresses with them; the flowers and food are all set, and Treat has reserved an entire island for the ceremony. Oh, and of course a boat, too, to get to the island." Danica let out a relieved sigh, wondering what she might have forgotten. She still couldn't believe that they were really getting married. She grabbed Blake's hand, and when he turned his green eyes toward her, the yellow specks that had always intrigued her were dancing in the light.

He put his other hand on her cheek and said, "Yes, we're really doing this."

He'd been reminding her every chance he got that she would soon be his wife. Danica found it funny. He'd been the player when they'd met, not her, and yet he was the one afraid she'd leave him at the altar. "Yes, we are," she assured him.

"Oh, please. Get a room." Kaylie set the menu down as the waitress arrived and took their orders.

The waitress's pearl-white teeth contrasted against her deeply tanned skin, and colorful beads were weaved through tiny braids in her long dark hair. Danica expected some sort of island accent, but when the summer beauty spoke, she was as American as apple pie. "I'll be y'all's waitress today. What can I get ya?"

They ordered tropical drinks, salads, and sandwiches, and Danica watched Kaylie survey the young waitress as she sauntered away, her hourglass figure expertly defined beneath the long, tight skirt and slinky tank top. She waited for Kaylie's snarky remark.

Kaylie moved her chair closer to Chaz and said, "Wow, she is gorgeous. If that's what the tropical sun does to a girl, then I'm never leaving."

"Who are you and what have you done with my sister?" Danica was only half joking.

Kaylie swatted the air. "I'm old now, sis. I'm almost thirty, with two kids to boot."

"If that's old, then what does it say about me?" Danica asked.

"You're right. At almost thirty-two, you are old. I'm still a spring chicken."

The waitress brought their drinks and meals, and Blake raised his glass. "To two marriages. May they last forever." They all clinked glasses.

Chaz took a drink, then asked, "What time does your father get in?"

Kaylie groaned.

"Play nice, Kaylie," Danica said. Kaylie hadn't seen their father since right after she graduated from college, when she'd found out about his long-term affair and he'd moved away and married his mistress. "He, Madeline, and Lacy get in today around six."

"Madeline is coming, too?" Kaylie asked with a long sigh.

Of course, Kaylie already knew their father's wife was coming. Danica shook her head at her sister's penchant for drama.

"Please tell me why he's coming on Wednesday when our wedding isn't until Sunday," Kaylie said. "I'll need more of these, please." Kaylie sucked down her drink and held up the glass, indicating to the waitress that she wanted a refill.

"Slow down, girl. You should at least be coherent when he arrives," Danica said. "He wants time with us, and he knows we'll be busy the day of the wedding. I told you all of this, and you agreed."

"I didn't agree," Kaylie said with a vehement shake of her head. "You just didn't listen to me when I said it would ruin my week. And that girl is coming, too. At least I don't have to be nice to *her*," Kaylie said.

Blake and Danica exchanged a worried glance. They'd anticipated how Kaylie might react to meeting their half sister, Lacy—their father's love child—who was born just a few years after Kaylie, while their parents were still married.

When the twins were born, Kaylie had refused to call her father. Danica had taken it upon herself to give him the news about his grandchildren, and through her father, she'd made contact with Lacy. Although Danica had yet to meet her in person, they'd been exchanging emails, phone calls, and even a few handwritten letters over the past year and a half. Kaylie had been livid at her for weeks about contacting their father, so Danica decided to keep her relationship with Lacy a secret…just until Kaylie settled down. And by her reaction, it appeared that the subject of their father was still an open wound.

"Kaylie, I let you make most of the decisions, and you won on the dress decision. You were worried about Chelsea and

Camille forgetting the dresses, or something happening to them, and practically demanded that Max be in charge."

"She's Chaz's work wife. She gets everything done perfectly," Kaylie said with a wave of her hand.

"Work wife? Whatever. Listen, whether you like it or not, Lacy is our blood relative," Danica said carefully.

Kaylie pointed at Danica. "Half. If even that. I mean, how do we know she's really his? We don't know this Madeline woman. Maybe she's a slut. I mean, she has to be to break up a marriage, right?"

Chaz had heard this from Kaylie dozens of times. He pushed back from the table. "Do you mind if I go lie down for a bit? I'm beat."

Kaylie touched his thigh. "Do you want me to come with you?"

"No, babe. I'm fine. I'm just gonna rest a bit so that I'm awake when your family arrives."

So, Chaz has learned the art of escape.

They kissed, and Kaylie turned back to Danica and Blake. "Sorry. He's been working a lot."

Danica had given up her therapy license almost three years earlier, when she'd realized her feelings for her new client— Blake—were not therapist-client appropriate. Even now, so many years later, she still could not ignore the therapist's voice inside her head. Danica tried to hold back the worry that nipped at her nerves, but as she watched Kaylie suck down another drink, the words tumbled out.

"Kaylie, is something wrong between you and Chaz?"

"What? No, of course not. Why?"

Danica shrugged, trying to downplay her concern. "He just seemed to take off awfully fast when we started talking about

Dad."

Kaylie rolled her eyes.

There's the old Kaylie.

"He thinks I'm being childish about the girl."

Danica saw the pleading in her eyes; *Support me. Tell me I'm right.* She'd decided, after almost turning down Blake's proposal because of her sister's relationship drama, that she would play things straight from then on. She was done putting her own feelings aside in order to save Kaylie's from being hurt. Danica was sticking to her guns and allowing her true feelings to be known; she was determined to no longer placate Kaylie's needy side—*too much.* Her relationship with Lacy, however, was excluded from that straightforward deal. That subject had to be handled with kid gloves.

"Well…" Danica said.

Blake kissed her cheek and stood. "I'm gonna check out the gift shop. I'll meet you back at the hotel?"

"Sure." She watched him lazily, sexily saunter away, his thick, muscular back swaying with each step, and her favorite pair of jeans hugging his—

"What are you, fifteen?"

Danica hadn't realized she was licking her lips until Kaylie's voice interrupted her thoughts. She snapped her attention back to Kaylie. "What?" *Oh God. I've turned into one of those sex-crazed girls.* She made a mental note to tame her libido. At least in public.

"You look at him like he's a Chippendales dancer and you're made of one-dollar bills." Kaylie crinkled her nose, like she was disgusted at the thought.

"Don't you look at Chaz like that sometimes?"

Kaylie shrugged. "I guess. But once you have kids, you kind

of put all that stuff aside."

Uh-oh. "Kaylie, now that the guys are gone, can we talk about Dad and Lacy? Just you and me?" She'd tried to bring up her father at least once each month since the twins were born, and each time, Kaylie had refused to discuss him. Danica had to try, just one last time.

"Why do you do this? Why do you feel the need to ruin a perfectly beautiful day? Isn't it bad enough that he's coming to the wedding?"

No need to beat me over the head with a stick. Lesson learned.

Chapter Two

Blake and Danica hashed out every scenario surrounding her father's arrival, and in the elevator on their way to the lobby, her muscles were pinched so tight she could hardly breathe. She had little faith that Kaylie would actually show up, and even though she and her father had been exchanging emails, letters, and phone calls, she knew that seeing him in person might do all sorts of painful things to her mind and body. Was she dressed okay? What would he think of her? Should she have worn more makeup? Would he be upset with her for giving up her practice? He hadn't seemed to be upset, but Danica knew that face-to-face meetings could bring out all sorts of emotions.

Blake took her hand as they crossed the lobby to the plush chairs beside the windows. "Relax. It'll all be fine."

She wished it were true, but she had known Kaylie too long to think tonight would be an easy reconciliation. She watched the elevator like a hawk. "She better get her butt down here."

"She will. Don't worry. It's not like we're going anywhere. We're meeting him here, so even if she's late, it's okay." Blake picked up a magazine and leafed through it.

Twenty minutes later, Kaylie still hadn't come downstairs. Danica stood in her too-high heels and paced. She'd put on her favorite royal blue wrap-around dress, the one she felt most confident in. She'd tried to tame her mass of curly hair, which she'd cropped back to shoulder length after the twins were born so her niece and nephew would stop pulling at it, and it had freakishly obeyed. She'd won the battle of Afro versus curly chic, and still, her heart raced within her chest.

She thought she was ready to see her father again. Out of support for her mother and Kaylie—at least that's what she told herself—she hadn't seen him since he moved away. *If I'm this nervous, Kaylie must be petrified.* She opened her purse and pulled out her cell phone, texting Kaylie.

U coming?

Her phone vibrated a minute later. *Not yet.*

"Damn it, Kaylie," she said under her breath. Her phone vibrated again. *Ha-ha. Just joking.* "She's such a fool," Danica said with a terse smile. She was glad to see Kaylie was in good spirits. Maybe that would bode well for their impending meeting.

At six thirty she texted her father's cell phone. Ten minutes later, when he hadn't responded yet, she texted Lacy. *Where r u? Can't wait to meet u!* Her cell vibrated a few minutes later. *Flight late. Stuck in immigration line. Go eat. Be there soon.* A few seconds later it vibrated again. *Me 2!!*

"They're going to be a while. Let's get Kaylie and grab a bite." She texted Kaylie as they headed for the restaurant. *Meet us in restaurant. Dad's gonna B late.*

Kaylie and Chaz walked into the restaurant forty minutes later, bright-eyed and slightly flushed. Kaylie brushed her hair from her shoulders. Her black minidress accentuated every perfect curve of her body. She clung to Chaz's arm like a groupie, looking up at him with something in her eyes that Danica didn't recognize. It wasn't just lust or love. It was a look that bordered on need.

Oh God, really, Kaylie?

"Sorry we're late. We were—" She looked at Danica and winked. "Napping."

"Napping, my ass," Danica said, relieved to see that whatever strife had been present before seemed to have subsided. "Did you talk to Mom?"

"Yeah, the kids are great. She said they barely miss us." She frowned as she sat in one of the cushioned dining chairs across from Chaz. "It feels so weird not to have them here. I kept expecting to hear *Mommy! Daddy!*"

"Not me. I was out like a light. I miss them, but whew." Chaz shook his head. "I think I could sleep for a week and still not catch up." He looked at Kaylie and smiled lazily. "Of course, she'll have no part of my sleeping all day."

"Oh stop." Kaylie swatted him. "We have no time together, so I'm just gonna take advantage of the time we do have."

They nibbled on appetizers and had a few drinks. A half hour later, Danica broached the subject of her father again. *I'm a glutton for punishment.*

"Dad's so late. They must've been hung up in immigration." She turned toward Kaylie with a serious gaze. "Are you gonna be civil tonight?" she asked.

"What do you think I am, a monster? Of course I'll be civil." Kaylie looked around the table for support.

Chaz's eyes were trained on the stuffed mushroom at the

end of his fork.

"Well, I'll be civil," Blake said. "I'm actually looking forward to meeting the man who raised two independent, beautiful women."

How does he always know just what to say?

"That would be my mother," Kaylie said.

"Kaylie, that's not true. Dad was there the entire time we were growing up, and he was a good father, regardless of what he did to Mom."

Kaylie downed her third drink. "Whatever. All I know is, everything I thought was true when we were growing up wasn't true. I mean, he wasn't on business trips; he was with *her*. And all those birthdays that girl and that woman had, you know he was with them instead of us then, too. So—"

She was right to some extent, but Danica's therapist brain saw both sides of the argument, and she had no interest in starting World War III right then and there, in the midst of a lovely evening with a stunning view of the water.

"All I'm asking, Kaylie, is for you to be kind to them. Try to tolerate the situation without making snarky remarks and making everyone uncomfortable."

Kaylie's eyes were locked on the entrance to the restaurant. "Oh. My. God."

An almost mirror image of Kaylie—tall, blond, with innocent baby blues—nervously fingered a black clutch purse as she scanned the restaurant. Her skin was the same fair shade, and the oval shape of her face was a replica of Kaylie's, just a few years earlier. The familiar Snow long and lean legs ended in—Danica cringed—the same black sling-back heels that Kaylie had on her feet. The only difference between Kaylie and Lacy, as far as Danica could see, was the corkscrew curls tumbling to

Lacy's shoulders. While she possessed the body and face of Kaylie, she had Danica's and their father's kinky curls.

Her hopeful eyes landed on Danica's and caught. And in that breath, so did Kaylie's.

"Wait." Kaylie's eyes shot back and forth between the young girl who was headed directly toward them to her sister, who was now rising from her seat with a wide smile across her mulberry-colored lips and taking long strides toward the interloper.

Danica felt Kaylie's stare piercing her back as she crossed the restaurant. The sight of Lacy there in the flesh, the sister she'd secretly longed to meet, caused her heart to increase in size, filling her chest. She opened her arms, and the blonde fell comfortably into them, like she'd always had a spot right there against Danica's chest. Danica heard the competitive click of Kaylie's heels as she approached from behind.

"Danica?" Kaylie tugged on her arm.

Danica reluctantly pulled away, holding on to Lacy's forearms for just a beat longer. She wanted to hug Lacy even longer, but she was painfully aware of the hurt it would cause Kaylie. Over the months, their emails had shifted from cordial topics like work and hobbies to more intimate subjects, and eventually, they'd each slipped into the sisterly role of offering support and guidance. Guilt shrouded Danica like a woolen shawl, heavy and unmistakably present, as she realized that she'd shared things with Lacy that she'd never shared with Kaylie. *What have I done?* She didn't have time to ponder the whys and hows of it all. Lacy already felt like a sister to her, someone she loved, and by the look on Kaylie's face, Lacy was a living, breathing threat. A betrayal. Danica was quick to react to the brewing storm behind Kaylie's stare.

"Kaylie, this is our sister, Lacy." She regretted the words *our sister* as soon as they fell from her lips.

Kaylie feigned a smile, while Lacy's warmth was true and real. Eye to eye, with the same shade of buttery blond hair and identical full, sensuous lips, their familial connection could not be denied.

Danica had warned Lacy before she came to Nassau that Kaylie might not be as welcoming as she might hope, but to wait it out, and surely Kaylie would come around.

Lacy opened her arms and leaned in toward Kaylie. "You're even more beautiful in person," she said sincerely.

Kaylie pulled out of reach and crossed her arms, her eyes darting back to Danica with a *you're in so much trouble* look. "Nice to meet you." Kaylie's efforts at even the simplest of pleasantries were soiled by the tension surrounding her like a shield.

Danica knew all too well that she'd be in for the wrath of Kaylie later, but she had to save the moment. "How was your fl—"

"Lacy, so nice to meet you. I'm Blake."

Danica hadn't heard him approaching. She breathed a sigh of relief when Chaz appeared as well, both welcoming Lacy with warm hugs and kind words.

"Dad and Mo—my mom—should be here in a sec. They just wanted to get the room keys first." Lacy dropped her eyes. "I wanted to come right in. I couldn't wait to meet you in person. I've been waiting for so many years for this day."

She looked from Danica to Kaylie, and for that quick little eye shift, that feigned indication that said she didn't recognize Danica any more than she did Kaylie, Danica was thankful. Maybe Kaylie wouldn't realize that they'd been in touch after all.

Please be nice. Please be nice. Danica prayed that somehow Kaylie would feel her vibe and make the evening a little easier.

As they sat around the large round table, Lacy waved toward the entrance. Her eyes lit up. "There they are."

Danica held her breath. She hadn't expected the tears that welled in her eyes or the force of the lump in her throat at the sight of her father. He'd gone gray around the temples and his thick hair had thinned. His shoulders and chest showed the thinning and loss of muscle that every year over fifty seemed to take with it. But there was no mistaking the underlying current of happiness in his dark eyes as he neared the table, one arm on the small of Madeline's back. Danica stole a look at Kaylie, who had steeled herself against the table, her eyes silently screaming, *Get me out of here!*

Lacy, Danica, Blake, and Chaz all stood to greet their father and Madeline. Lacy took her father's hand.

Her father. My father. Oh God, our father.

"Dad, Mom, this is Danica, Kaylie, Blake, and Chaz," she said sweetly, then caught her own error. "Oh, sorry, Dad. You know Danica and Kaylie, but Mom doesn't. Gosh, this is awkward."

Dad. She called him Dad.

Kaylie still hadn't moved from her seat or so much as lifted her eyes. She was falling apart right before Danica's eyes, and Danica's heart ached for her. She couldn't just watch Kaylie cling to the table, her jaw clenching so hard she might break her teeth. Before greeting her father, and before greeting the woman who would be her stepmother, she went to Kaylie's side and whispered in her ear, "Kay? You all right?"

Kaylie's nod was so slight that had she not been watching her every movement, she would have missed it.

"Do you want to stand up?" Tears welled in Danica's eyes, and she forced them back. Seeing her father for the first time in years brought memories, both good and bad, but seeing Kaylie struggling with the reunion was what made Danica's emotions raw. If she allowed her own tears to fall, it would be that much more difficult for Kaylie to make it through the evening. She forced the lump in her throat to subside and put an arm around her sister, while Blake and Chaz came to their rescue, making a show of greeting their father and Madeline. Drawing the attention away from Kaylie.

Madeline's hair was the same buttery shade as Lacy's, framing her face in natural waves.

As Danica stood beside Kaylie, she watched Blake pull out a chair for Madeline. *Great. She looks just like a short, heavy Blythe Danner. I love Blythe Danner. Damn it.* She hadn't expected to want to dislike Madeline as much as she did, but the loyalty to her mother and Kaylie—and even herself—was palpable. She surveyed Madeline, looking for something to dislike about her, beyond the obvious betrayal of her family. There was a kindness that lay behind Madeline's nervous blue eyes as they flitted from person to person.

"Don?" Madeline reached for their father's hand, then dropped her hand to her lap as she trailed the path of his gaze— a path thick with love, leading straight to Kaylie's pained face.

"Kaylie." His voice cracked, and a tear slipped unabashedly down his cheek.

Kaylie trembled in her seat.

"It's okay, Kaylie." Danica rubbed her back, then looked at her father and softened a smile. "She just needs a minute," she said.

He nodded, but remained standing.

Sit down. Please sit down.

Didn't he know that it was even more difficult for Kaylie when he was standing? That somehow he emitted a more familiar, fatherly presence while he stood?

Kaylie reached for Danica's hand and squeezed. She nodded, sniffling back the tears that Danica knew she was praying wouldn't actually fall. She kept nodding until she touched Danica's hand with her other hand; then she looked into Danica's eyes and nodded one emphatic final time before releasing her.

She let go.

She let go of my hand.

I'm alone.

Danica looked at her father, then back at Kaylie. She was alone on a tightrope, with the world far below. When had Kaylie become *her* safety net? When had she started needing her so much? *Take a deep breath.* Danica inhaled deeply and blew it out slowly. *You can do this.*

"Babe? You okay?"

Blake's comforting voice broke the panicked spell. She managed to smile. "Yeah, I'm fine." She touched Kaylie's shoulder, more for her own comfort than Kaylie's. Then Danica went to Madeline's chair and extended her hand in a formal, awkward fashion. "I'm Danica. It's nice to finally meet you."

A shy smile pulled at Madeline's pale pink lips. She covered Danica's hand with her own, then whispered, "Thank you."

Without any conscious thought, Danica scrutinized her, taking in her light flowing jacket, smart skirt and top to match. She wanted to draw comparisons between her mother and Madeline, to pull the pieces of Madeline apart, if only to protect the mother who raised her, but she stifled the urge. She'd spent enough years as a therapist to know the millions of ways marriages deteriorated and how little it took for a lonely person, or a person who felt as if they were being taken for granted—or even for a person who was simply too bored with their own life to function—to fall into the arms of another. Whatever happened between their parents happened between them, and she knew that no matter how hard it might prove to be, she and Kaylie had no business judging either of them. They hadn't been in their bedroom when things went wrong. They weren't privy to the trials and tribulations of their marriage as it crumbled and deteriorated until there was nothing left. Even if this quiet woman had coerced their father into her bedroom, it was his choice to return, and in the end, his choice to leave his family and remain with her. She might have been holding the apple, but he was the one who took the bite and swallowed, letting his other family—their family—fall away.

With that acknowledgment circling her neck like a noose, Danica went to her father's side, trying to keep that noose from strangling her efforts. The man who had taught her right from wrong and how to be a strong, secure person, the man who brought her a giant lollipop when she got her first period—as if that was even the slightest bit appropriate—this was the man she had once adored. Why, then, when she looked at him now did bile rise in her throat?

She bit back the desire to tell him how awful he'd been by leaving their mother—and her and Kaylie. She squelched the words that vied to spew forth: *bastard, cheater, liar, thief.* She reluctantly eased out of the protective armor that she'd carefully formed around her and Kaylie like a cocoon and gave in to her tears.

"Dad. I've missed you." She couldn't breathe, could barely

think as she returned to her seat beside Blake. He took her hand and held it tight, and finally, after what felt like a lifetime had passed in the previous three minutes, Danica was right back where she belonged. She let out a loud breath and felt the armor slowly slipping back into place.

Chapter Three

Danica had been lying awake since the wee hours of the morning, worrying about Kaylie. She'd been silent during dinner, tossing a feigned smile here and there and answering their father's questions in clipped, terse snippets. She hardly looked at Lacy, who'd been sweet and kind to everyone and so very protective of their father and Madeline. *Want some butter, Dad? Mom, is your dinner okay?* What must it have been like for Lacy growing up? Danica knew from their emails that Lacy had grown up knowing she had two sisters whom she'd one day meet, but what would that feel like? Danica wondered. And at twenty-six years old, how did it feel to know you were the product of an affair? How brave do you have to be to face the family that you've been dying to meet, knowing they weren't really yours to claim?

She was just about to jump out of bed and head to the shower when she felt Blake's body sidle up behind hers. His arms wrapped around her; his hips pressed into her backside, firm and warm.

He kissed the back of her neck, then kissed the peak of her shoulder, sending a shiver down her back.

"Couldn't sleep?" he whispered.

She shook her head, closing her eyes and reveling in his touch as he caressed her breast. She turned onto her back, and he slid his hand down her belly, splaying it across her abdomen as he moved closer to her. She felt the heat of him as his naked body slithered alongside of her, the hair on his thighs tickling her. He brought his right hand under her hair and grasped the base of her skull, using his other hand to turn her body toward him as he settled his mouth onto hers, gently kissing her at first, then harder, his tongue pushing the worry right out of her mind. She moaned as her body gave in to his touch, arching toward him, wanting him to love the memory of Kaylie trembling at the table right out of her mind.

Heal me.

Blake pulled back, leaving her hungry for more, the taste of him lingering on her lips. He arched over her, trailing his fingers along her side, then grasping her waist and holding tight. He looked into her eyes with a sultry, yet sorrowful gaze, his dark eyes hurting right along with her heart.

How was he able to reflect her pain so perfectly? she wondered, and sucked in a sharp breath as he gripped her tighter.

"Tell me what you want," he said huskily.

The strength of him elicited fire in her veins, and she leaned up toward his lips. He closed his eyes and drew away.

"Tell me," he whispered.

"Love me," she said, wishing he'd take her in every way possible and make her forget the look in Kaylie's eyes when she'd seen Lacy across the room.

"Be more specific, baby," Blake urged. He'd been trying to get her to be more verbal when they made love, to let go of her fear and trust him completely. Although Danica knew exactly what she wanted, she still held back. She'd never let go with anyone. Not the boyfriends who talked dirty to her, or the guys who tried to coax her into doing the same. She couldn't trust that much, because, thanks to her father, she knew what lay ahead.

"How?" he pushed.

She closed her eyes, unable to make herself say the words. She grabbed the back of his head and drew it to her breast.

He licked the tip of her nipple—one quick swipe of his tongue, just enough to send her pulse soaring, then again, a long, slow lap around her areola.

"Words, baby. Tell me *everything* you want."

Her chest rose and fell to the beat of each heavy breath. She arched toward the warmth of his mouth, ready for him, wanting him inside of her. She thrust her hips toward him, trying again to guide his mouth to her breast.

"I want to hear it from your sexy mouth," he coaxed, running his index finger along her lower lip.

She bit her lip as he rose above her, settling his warm palm on her cheek, and gazing deeply into her eyes. "Baby, it's just me. Let me love you. Tell me what you need."

Oh, how she wanted to scream it from the rooftops! Everything about Blake proved his love for her, from his gentle touch to his constant consideration, and yet the fear remained. *What if one day…?* She'd come a long way, sexually. She'd become playful and had learned how to tease and taunt. Her sex drive was ten times what it had ever been before, but saying what she wanted—what she craved? Out loud? Asking him? No, begging him? She didn't know if she could do it. No, she couldn't cross that line. She wouldn't cross that line.

He ran his tongue between her breasts, then lapped at the curve of her collarbone. Looking at her with those incredible eyes that seared sex into her mind, he took her lower lip between his teeth, then licked at the tender spot, ever so lightly, until Danica's body trembled beneath him.

She closed her eyes tightly, wanting to please him, wanting to trust him, and wanting, more than anything, more of him. She gathered her courage and tried. "Lick me," she said.

He licked her lips again.

"My breast." Was that her breathy voice? That sexy, wanting, throaty voice? "Lick my breast." It wasn't as difficult as she thought it might be, and as he followed her command and lowered his mouth to her breast, nipping at her nipples with his teeth until they stood erect, she ached even more for the wetness of his mouth. He circled her nipples with his tongue.

Yes! Oh God. Yes! "More. *Harder.*" She clutched his hair in her hands and pulled him down. His tongue pushed hard as he suckled her breast until she was moaning in ecstasy, on the verge of peaking.

Then he drew away slowly, and she reached for him. "No, don't stop. Touch me. *Touch me,*" she pleaded, her shyness lost amid the desire that pulsed and swelled within her. She took his hand and drew it down between her legs.

"Uh-uh," he said, and held her hand there.

Danica felt a rush of titillation. She'd never touched herself in front of anyone before, and she could barely believe she was doing it now—but, *oh my*—this felt so naughty, so forbidden. A rush of excitement set her hand in motion.

His tongue moved back to her mouth and he thrust it in, exploring in a way that sent shivers right through her. She found the spot she knew would carry her over the edge and moved quick and hard against it. She felt his hand move away and she opened her eyes. He was quick to plant a kiss on each lid, forcing them closed.

"No," he whispered when she drew her hand away. "Keep going."

She felt his eyes on her as she moved swiftly and skillfully along the moist folds of her sensitive skin. Every muscle in her legs tightening, heat rose within her to a fever pitch—one final stroke and she knew she'd be there. Blake's fingers found hers, and he worked her into a frenzy until her body bucked and rocked against him. Her flesh throbbed and pulsated against his fingers as sensations tightened every nerve in her body, then slowly dissipated, leaving her body limp, her mind foggy, and her heart full.

"That's my girl," Blake said, kissing her cheeks and her neck and pushing her hair from her forehead.

Every touch was so tender and loving that she melted into the safe and sated feeling. Their bodies were slick with sweat as he pulled away. Then his massive thighs were pushing hers apart. She gasped, not sure she could take any more. He leaned on his elbows, holding her head between his hands.

"Look at me," he said, staring into her eyes as he slid into her, until she could feel every blessed inch of him. Then he drew himself out slowly.

No. Don't stop!

Danica felt her eyes fluttering open, closed, then open again as she fell into his rhythm, her body responding again and again, in ways she didn't think possible. He moved faster, harder, and she grabbed at his back, and when he hit just the right spot that stole her breath, grabbing wasn't enough. She clawed at his back, forgetting whatever had held her back when they first began and pleading for more.

"Faster." To her dismay, he slowed his movements.

"*Fast…faster*," she pleaded.

He pulled out from between her legs and slid down her body until she felt the heat of his tongue upon her, lapping, sucking, making every nerve in her body tingle and burn. His hands slid up her body and he took her nipples between his index fingers and thumbs.

She couldn't take it. Her loins were on fire, aching for more of him. She clutched his hair as her body finally found its release. She clawed at the sheets as aftershocks rocked her insides, like bolts of lightning searing her again and again, until she had no more energy to give. Her body fell limp, shuddering against him. And his sweet voice found her ears again.

"Tell me."

She shook her head, unable to think, much less speak. She couldn't take any more. There must be a sin in experiencing that much pleasure in such quick succession.

"Come on, baby. Tell me everything you want," he urged again, drawing his tongue up the center of her belly, to the undersides of her breasts, until she was pulling him into her, ravenous for his love.

"More. Now, *more.*"

"More what?" he teased.

Her eyes flew open. "*Really?*" Her voice was throaty and raw.

"Really," he said, and began to pull away from her.

She grabbed him and pulled him back toward her. "Aren't you? Don't you need to…?"

"I will. After you tell me everything your pretty little heart desires."

"Take me. *All* of me. *Love* me. *Fuck* me." She couldn't believe she'd said the words.

Blake's eyes darkened and he took her hard and fast, his hands gripping her shoulders, his hips fueled by as much love as need. "Oh, Danica. I love you so much."

She wanted to say it back. God knew she felt it down to her very core, but she couldn't stop gritting her teeth, willing her body to ride out their heated wave. His motions took her right up to the peak again, and she rode out the unexpected crescendo along with him as he arched into her, moaning his pleasure, gritting his teeth, and pumping slower, slower, until they both collapsed, side by side, their fingers intertwined, their breathing filling the space between them.

Later that morning, Danica felt Blake's eyes on her from the moment she came out of the shower. How could she have said those things? What had she been thinking? Now she was too embarrassed to look at her fiancé. She dressed in a pair of capris and a peach sleeveless shirt, keeping her back to him as he sat on the edge of the bed.

She dried her hair while he showered, then put on a pair of amber earrings and slipped into a pair of peach sandals while Blake zipped up his shorts and pulled a T-shirt over his head. She couldn't ignore his stare any longer.

"What are you staring at me like that for?" *Oh God, he thinks I'm a fool. I made a fool of myself. I did it all wrong.*

"I can't stop loving you. You're the most beautiful woman I've ever seen, the most sensual woman I've ever met. I just—" He shook his head, like words couldn't express what he was feeling.

Danica's cheeks warmed. "I'm so embarrassed. I've never done anything like that before."

"Yes, you have," Blake said with a laugh. "We make love all the time."

She spun around. "Not that. You know what I mean." She watched him for signs of mocking, but there were none. And when he took her in his arms and kissed her so passionately that her body instantly responded, she knew he was not mocking her.

"I want you to trust me. We're going to be husband and wife. You don't ever have to be embarrassed in front of me." He sat down on the bed and put on his shoes. "Danica, anything we do in the bedroom, it stays between us, and anything you don't want to do, we won't do. Ever."

She nodded, unable to speak. How could she tell him that she loved what they'd done? How could she tell him that she actually liked touching herself when he watched her? That it was probably one of the most erotic things she'd ever done. She couldn't tell him those things, and she wouldn't, because the memory of the evening before settled in, reminding her that even when you think you're safe, life can slip you a mickey and turn your safe and happy life upside down.

Chapter Four

"This is going to be so awkward," Danica said as they rode the elevators down to meet everyone for breakfast. "I texted Kaylie, but she didn't answer."

"She's got a lot to take in. It's not just your dad. I mean, dealing with her feelings toward him is enough to send anyone back to bed, but remember, Danica, you've had time to adjust to Lacy and Madeline. You've spent a year and a half getting to know Lacy, and through her, you got to at least become familiar with Madeline, too. To Kaylie, they're still strangers. Strangers who stole your father."

Danica realized that she'd been so focused on Kaylie, she hadn't even taken the time to see how Blake was doing. His father would be at the wedding, and he hadn't seen him in quite some time either. There were no hard feelings between Blake and his father, who'd raised him as a single parent, working two jobs and doing the best he could. Life and distance were the only things that separated Blake from him. Still, he deserved the same care and tenderness that she and Kaylie did.

"How do you feel about seeing your dad?" she asked as they came to the entrance of the restaurant.

"I'm good. Actually, I can't wait to see him. It's been too

long." Blake ran his hand through his thick dark hair and scanned the tables. "There they are."

Danica followed him toward her father and Madeline, who were sitting at a table. Lacy met them on the way with a plate from the buffet.

"Good morning," Lacy said cheerily.

She reminded Danica of Kaylie so much that it almost hurt. "Have you seen Kaylie?" she asked.

Lacy shook her head. "No, she hasn't been down yet. Do you think she's okay? Should we check on her?"

We. Lacy's empathy only further endeared her to Danica. "She's probably talking to my mom on the phone. I'm sure she'll be down soon." *Like hell I am.*

They sat down at the table. Danica plastered a semi-fake smile on her face. "Dad, Madeline, did you sleep okay?"

"Perfectly," her father said.

His voice stirred memories of when she was younger and they were still a family. Danica pushed the nostalgia away and turned to Madeline. "I really like that skirt. It suits you perfectly." Madeline was only about five foot three, and while Danica remembered seeing the photographs of her as a younger, thinner woman, which Lacy had sent of the three of them from the years when her parents were still married, she now looked more like her age: early fifties, with a mildly thick middle and gentle lines around her eyes. Danica silently thanked God that Madeline wasn't a trophy wife. That would have made the whole situation much more difficult. Kaylie would find competition with two women instead of just one.

"Thank you. How's your sister? I was so worried about her last night. We're a lot for her to digest."

The pain in her voice was palpable, and Danica rode the

fine line of not wanting to say anything that might make Kaylie look immature. "She's okay. I'm sure she'll be down soon."

"I'll get us some breakfast. Can I bring anyone anything?" Blake offered.

"I'll come with you." Her father stood, patting Madeline's shoulder on his way.

Danica watched them walk away and suddenly felt like there was a little more breathing room at the table. "I'm sorry about Kaylie. This is all very difficult for her."

"We know," Lacy said with a tentative smile. "I wish we could have at least gotten to know her before today, with phone calls and emails, maybe even passing a few old photos through the mail, like we did with you. She seems like she'd be nice, from what you've told me."

"Danica, I appreciate how kind you have been to Lacy, and I know this is hard for you, seeing me and your father together—"

"It's fine, really," Danica said, cutting Madeline off mid-sentence. She swatted the air like it was no big deal, even though her stomach clenched so tightly she thought she might be sick.

"No, it's not okay, and it's not my place to discuss that whole thing with you. That's your father's place. You deserve to know what happened all those years ago, and I'm sure he will find the time to tell you, but for now, between us women, I just wanted to thank you for your kindness toward Lacy."

Danica took a drink of water, hoping it would settle the twisting in her gut. "I really like Lacy," she said honestly. "But I also love Kaylie, and I think we have a rough road ahead of us. I'm not sure if this was a good or a bad idea." She watched Madeline's smile fade and felt even worse for being honest. "I don't mean not a good idea for you to be here. I mean talking about Kaylie. I can't talk about Kaylie without her here. She's a really great person, and I know you'll love her once you get to know her." Why was she selling Kaylie to them? *Kaylie get down here!*

Blake and her father returned with plates of food, and the smell turned her stomach.

"I have to…I need to go to the ladies' room. Excuse me." She escaped the restaurant and headed up to Kaylie's room. She'd need to be quick, or her father's family would think she'd lost her mind, too, disappearing during breakfast. Although Madeline seemed to take Kaylie's absence in stride. She even appeared to understand it. *So why can't I?*

She knocked on Kaylie's door twice, and when no one answered, she texted her.

Where r u? She paced the hall. *Damn it, Kaylie.* Her cell vibrated.

Pool.

Danica cursed under her breath as she headed back down the elevator and outside into the warm, morning sunshine. The pool was behind the hotel, built high enough to give an extraordinary view of the Bay. She found Kaylie and Chaz lying on lounge chairs. Chaz's arms were folded over his chest, his lips pinched into a hard line.

Her anger spewed forth. "Kaylie Elizabeth, what are you doing?"

Kaylie looked like she'd never had one baby, much less two. Her stomach was taut between the tiny swatches of her bikini. She lowered her sunglasses and peered at Danica over the frames. "Getting a little sun. Want to join us?" She righted her sunglasses on her nose.

"Listen, I know this all sucks for you, but that was really rude of you to skip breakfast and not tell anyone."

Chaz sat up and leaned his elbows on his knees. "Just for the record, I wanted to go, but Kaylie nixed it."

"I'm sure she did," Danica said. Kaylie made no move toward joining them, and Danica was not going to spend the next two days running between her father and Kaylie. She sat down on Kaylie's chair, pushing her over with her butt, and took her glasses from their perch on her nose.

"What?" Kaylie said, exasperated.

"You know what. Come on, sit up."

"No."

"Kaylie."

"Why don't you go hang out with Lacy? God, Danica, couldn't you have reminded me when I started calling Alexandra Lexi? The names are so close. I can't believe I didn't think of it before."

"Kaylie, really? That's ridiculous. Come on. You're my sister. I want to hang out with you."

"So is she; you said it yourself." Kaylie folded her arms across her chest and turned away just like the stubborn teenager she'd once been.

Danica took another, softer approach. "Kay, Lacy could never take your place. You know that."

"Well, you apparently got to know her really well at some point, because she walked right over to you in the restaurant."

Danica dropped her eyes. "We've been writing to each other."

"And?"

The hurt in Kaylie's eyes stabbed at Danica's heart. "And I'm really sorry. I should have told you, but you were so mad at me when I told you about telling Dad about Lexi and Trevor that I was afraid to."

"Afraid? You're not afraid of anything. Everything you do is well thought out. You probably told Lacy not to tell me, and you had this little conspiracy going behind my back."

The ugly trust monster rises again.

"You know what? I'm gonna go catch up with Blake," Chaz said as he rose to his feet.

"Chaz!" If looks could maim, Kaylie's would have amputated a limb.

"Kaylie, this is between us. Let him go." Danica turned to Chaz and said, "I kinda left without explaining anything. Can you please tell them that I'll be back shortly?"

"Sure." He looked at Kaylie.

"Ugh! Fine. Go ahead."

Chaz walked away, then turned back and said, "Danica? Thank you."

He nodded in Kaylie's direction, and Danica understood that he was doing his best, but he wasn't sure how to handle her when she was like this. Then again, when it came to Kaylie, Danica was often shooting from the hip, too.

"Kaylie, I made a huge mistake. I should have told you about Lacy, but honestly, I knew that you'd never accept me talking to her, and I kinda wanted to see what she was like before we all got together. I mean, if she was bitchy or mean, or entitled or whatever, I would have made an excuse for her not to come, but she's not any of those things, and you can see that she idolizes you despite your bitchiness."

"Well, she shouldn't. I'm not her sister."

"Jesus, you're stubborn. Okay, you're not her sister. That's totally fine, but you are someone she just met, and even if you treat her like a stranger, you should at least be cordial."

Kaylie held her hand out. "Glasses, please."

"You're so frustrating!" Danica said and tossed her the glasses. "Well, I tried. I know this whole thing is weird, and hard, and even kinda icky, but we really need to find a way through this, and no matter what you think, you're my number one sister and you always will be."

Danica found her family leaving the restaurant.

"There you are!" Lacy said with a wide smile. "Blake said that you were thinking of going into town today. Would you mind if I tagged along?"

"Actually, I thought we'd all go together. We lined up snorkeling lessons for later this afternoon, too. I'm so sorry. I thought I told you this the last time we talked."

"You did, but given the circumstances with…well…I didn't want to assume," Lacy said.

"Don't be silly. She'll get over all of this, and I'm looking forward to spending time with you guys." Danica looked at her father and Madeline. "I hope that wasn't too presumptuous of me to set this up. Lacy said that you both had talked about wanting to try scuba diving, so I thought this might be a nice introduction to it, without all the risk."

Madeline squeezed her father's hand, and her eyes lit up with anticipation.

"That sounds perfect," her father said. He slung an arm casually around Madeline, and she leaned in to him.

Danica found herself staring at the ease in which they interacted, like they'd been doing it for years. And, she realized with a start, they had been together since Kaylie was at least three. They'd been together longer than he and her mother had been together.

"Kaylie's not coming, is she?" Her father's words fell heavy with disappointment.

"I don't know, Dad."

"Would you mind if I talked to her?" Lacy asked.

Danica shot a look at Chaz, who shook his head. "I'm not sure that's such a great idea."

"I'll talk to her," her father said.

"I'm not sure that's a good idea right now, either," Danica admitted.

"There's never going to be a good time for this discussion," he said. He kissed Madeline's forehead. "I'll be right back."

Madeline grabbed his hand as it slid from her shoulder. "You're a good man, Don. Don't you doubt that. Be gentle, but be honest."

He nodded, lowered his eyes, and walked out the doors.

Chapter Five

"You had to go and sic Dad on me?" Kaylie seethed as they rode the jitney bus into town. Every seat was taken, and even though it was early in the day, the smell of perspiration and suntan lotion was already thick. They sat in the rear of the bus, Chaz and Blake in the seats in front of them, and their father, Madeline, and Lacy were forced to sit in the only other available seats, toward the front of the bus.

"Calm down. I didn't sic him on you. He said he wanted to talk to you. What did he say, anyway?" Danica was glad their father was so far away. She'd be mortified if he heard the venom in Kaylie's voice, though she couldn't imagine that she'd gone easy on him out by the pool. When they'd returned, her father looked defeated, as if he'd aged ten years during their ten-minute conversation. Kaylie's face had been stoic as she'd disappeared into the elevator.

Now she had the same stoic look on her face as she shrugged in response to Danica's question.

"You won't tell me?"

"I didn't listen." Kaylie turned toward the window, her lips pressed tightly together.

"You're such a child sometimes," Danica said. She tapped

Chaz on the shoulder. "Swap seats with me?"

Chaz lifted his mouth into a half smile. "My turn for the silent treatment?"

Danica held on to the sides of the seats as the bus rumbled over the bumpy roads. She slid in next to Blake, and he reached his arm around her. She settled against his chest and closed her eyes and began to count. *One, two, three, four…* There really was something calming about counting to ten.

"Just give her some time," Blake whispered. "She'll come around."

"I know my sister, and this is just the tip of the iceberg." She turned in her seat and gave Kaylie an icy stare, which Kaylie expertly ignored. She leaned back against Blake and thought about how quickly the day had changed. She'd been so safe and warm with Blake in the hotel room. She'd felt so loved and happy, and that happiness had seemed so easy. But as she mulled over the events of the morning, she realized that she'd brought this on herself. She *should* have told Kaylie about connecting with Lacy sooner, but she also knew how painful that would have been. Once again, she had to get herself out from in between Kaylie and everyone else. How did she keep ending up in this middle place? At least their mother would be there tomorrow. *Oh God. Mom.* If seeing them was this hard for Kaylie, it would be pure torture for their mother.

Awkward didn't begin to describe their walk through the town shops. Chaz kept his gaze trained on the sidewalk, and Danica felt like she was walking a tightrope between Kaylie and their father. Only Blake and Lacy tried to pull the others into their attempts at light banter, and even those fell on deaf ears. Tension had sealed everyone's lips, resulting in an uncomfortable silence. Danica desperately wanted to get her father alone to hear what had transpired with Kaylie, but every time she hung back, Kaylie dragged her off in another direction. Finally, while Kaylie texted their mother about the kids, Danica was able to corner him outside of a souvenir shop.

"Dad, how did things go with Kaylie?"

He shook his head.

"Oh no, that bad?"

He turned to her with hurt in his eyes, and it was a look that Danica recalled from the one time she'd ever failed a test. He had that same look of disappointment in his eyes—disappointment in himself, like he had failed as a parent—and it incited the same sinking feeling in the pit of her stomach.

"She wouldn't even talk to me," he said.

"You know Kaylie. This will take her a while to navigate, but give her time. Don't give up on her."

"Give up on her?" Her father took her arm and guided her farther away from the others. "Danica, I would never give up on her, or on you. Is that what you think of me? That I gave up on you?"

"Dad, no. That's not what I meant." *Is it?* No sooner had she gotten the words out of her mouth than she knew the damage had already been done. Her father was already walking away, his head hung low, his thin shoulders curled forward. In his dress pants and short-sleeved button-down shirt, he looked much older than his fifty-eight years. And that, even more than the disappointment, tugged at Danica's heart. Time was slipping by like sand whisked away in the wind; each year they missed seeing each other was another year lost.

Her father disappeared into the back of the shop and Kaylie came into view. She felt Blake sidle up to her.

"Sweetness, I saw a little alcove over there that we can slip into for a quick make-out session." Blake's eyes were lit with mischief.

She was too busy watching Kaylie stalk Lacy to respond.

Chapter Six

"What did Mom say about my favorite niece and nephew?" Danica walked with Kaylie into a small boutique next door while the others lingered behind.

"They're excited to see us tomorrow. Lexi didn't sleep well last night. Mom said she got up and was just fidgety, so she finally put her in bed with Trevor, and she fell right to sleep." Kaylie watched the others approach. "I just hate letting them sleep together."

"A few nights won't hurt. Besides, I remember you climbing in bed with me when we were little."

Kaylie's eyes remained trained on Lacy. "Yeah, it's just that Lexi needs to learn to self-soothe."

"You sound a little like a therapist. Ferberizing?" Danica teased. It had been a few months since Kaylie stopped seeing Dr. Marsden, a therapist who had helped her to deal with her anger issues surrounding their mother and her careening career while she was pregnant, and now Danica wondered if she might do well talking with her again—about their father and Lacy.

Lacy passed with a smile and went into the store.

Kaylie followed. "I read everything I can on kids; you know that. I don't want to screw them up."

That's my in! "Then maybe you should read about dealing with divorced parents."

Kaylie rolled her eyes, and while she pretended to lift and inspect a shirt, Danica knew she was really watching Lacy's every move. Lacy moved easily from counter to counter. She turned, looking past them to her mother, and waved her over. Danica watched as Lacy put her hand on her mother's shoulder and spoke animatedly into her ear, while pointing at something inside the glass cabinet. Madeline put her hand to her chest, then leaned closer to inspect whatever they were looking at. Their father came up behind Lacy, and Kaylie's body went rigid. Madeline pointed into the cabinet, and he touched Lacy's shoulder. As Danica watched the scene unfold, she remembered what it had been like to be the center of her father's attention for so many years and was surprised that she felt a twinge of longing.

He withdrew his wallet and handed it to Lacy, at which point Kaylie suddenly stormed deeper into the store, glancing quickly at the cabinet that held their attention, then stalked to a corner and rifled through a bin of purses.

"She's really having a hard time."

Danica startled at Chaz's deep voice. "Yeah, she is." He watched Kaylie with a worried look in his eye. "I'm sorry that I invited them. I probably should have left well enough alone, huh?"

"No." Chaz shook his head. "I don't think so. Lex and Trev are his grandchildren, too, and if we can mend this broken fence, I'd love for them to know him, and Madeline, who, by the way, seems lovely, despite…"

"Yeah, she does." Danica blew out a breath. "Look at Kaylie staring at Lacy. I know she's jealous, but I'm not sure what to do about it."

Chaz turned his back to his wife and leaned against the table where they stood. "I'm even more lost than you. Seems everything I say leads to a fight, and it doesn't help that she misses Lex and Trev something awful."

"She does? I guess that's good that she misses them, as long as all of this doesn't come between you two."

"Between us? No, we're fine. Don't get me wrong. This is tough, and Kaylie's emotions are all over the place right now, but we'll be fine."

"She's having a hard time…She's distracted by the whole Dad, Lacy, Madeline situation." Danica worried about Chaz. She knew that Kaylie would lash out at anyone in her path when she was upset; no matter how much she'd changed, everyone needed an outlet. And Chaz was an easy target; he was so loving and gentle.

"It's everything, not just them, but they're a big part of it. I feel bad for her," Chaz admitted. "I know it doesn't seem like it, but she's trying. She just goes about it differently. She has to deal with the muck and mire before allowing herself to release it all."

She did know that about her sister. She was glad to hear that Chaz understood it, too.

"She's such a good mother, too. The kids are her world. Believe it or not, with all that showiness that she gives about wanting time away, she can hardly stand to be separated from them. I asked her if she wanted me to fly your mom and the kids out early, but she wanted this time alone as a couple as much as I did, no matter how much we miss the babies."

It hurt to watch Kaylie struggling just to make it through the day. "She wouldn't be any good with them the way she is now anyway. She's too sidetracked with Lacy. Do you think I should cancel the snorkeling? I know Kaylie was looking forward to it, but given the situation, maybe it's best?"

Lacy broke away from her parents and headed toward Kaylie.

"I think I'd better get over there." Danica headed in their direction before Chaz could answer.

Kaylie's eyes didn't waver from the purse she gripped in her hands. Lacy's lips moved quickly as she reached out to touch the purse with a hopeful smile. Kaylie turned abruptly out of her reach.

"Kaylie, wow, that's a gorgeous purse. Is it leather?" Danica planted herself between the two of them. She watched Lacy's contemplative eyes swim over Kaylie, like she was figuring out the best way to get close to her. Danica cringed when Lacy reached out to touch the purse again with a hopeful gaze. Sisters shared; they touched; they laughed. It was obvious that Lacy wanted that, and just as clear that Kaylie would just as soon kick her to the curb.

"I think it is." Lacy brushed the soft leather with her fingers. "That really goes well with your hair, Kaylie. What is that color? Tawny? Is that what you'd call it?"

Kaylie grasped the bag so tight her knuckles were white.

Danica put her hand on Kaylie's shoulder in an effort to calm her sister's nerves. "Kay, can I see it?"

Kaylie reluctantly released the bag. She seemed to pull from whatever state she'd succumbed to, and her feigned smile told Danica that she had enough control to avoid losing her cool.

"You know, this would go well with your hair, too, Lacy." Danica handed the bag to Lacy, feeling very much like a playground attendant. *Share nicely, girls.*

"Honey, if we're going to make the snorkeling class, shouldn't we get back to the hotel?"

Her father's use of the endearment surprised her. Unsure if he was talking to her or Lacy, she didn't answer. Then she realized he could only have been speaking to her—she'd scheduled the event.

"Uh, yeah, we should, actually. Geez, where did the time go?" Danica waited for Lacy and her father to head out of the store. "Kaylie, are you all right? Chaz and Blake are waiting up front."

"Yeah. Did you see the way he just handed his wallet over to her? What is she, a little princess or something?"

There was no mistaking the green-eyed monster that had hold of Kaylie's heart. "She is his daughter, too. He used to do the same thing for us."

Kaylie turned her determined blue eyes on Danica. "Did he? I don't remember." She stalked out of the store, hooking her arm possessively into Chaz's on the way out.

Chapter Seven

They stood at the water's edge, the sand warm and sensual beneath their bare feet. Danica listened intently to the safety procedures and precautions and memorized every word about breathing techniques. The snorkeling instructors were two of the most incredibly sculpted men Danica had ever set eyes on. They weren't thick and manly like Blake and Chaz, but as they stood confidently before the group in their matching swim trunks (sporting the hotel logo across the left leg) their sun-drenched skin glistened in the sun. They looked as if they'd just walked out of a fashion magazine. Lacy's eyes were glued to the dark-haired, older one, while Kaylie was doing her best to compete with Lacy's itsy-bitsy aqua-blue bikini. Kaylie's red and yellow two-piece rode low along her sleek hip bones. To anyone else, she looked like a twenty-something girl enjoying a carefree summer, but Danica saw the glint of competition in her eyes, the slight jut of her right hip, and the extra-deep curve of her spine as she cast her breasts higher, her shoulders pulled back in a proud, confident stance.

"We'll need a volunteer to show the others how this is done," the older instructor said.

Lacy's hand shot up, and Kaylie ran on her tiptoes to the

front of the group. "I'll do it!" she called out.

The instructors exchanged a glance and laughed, their shoulders lifting with matching shrugs, obviously used to gorgeous women fawning all over them.

"Okay, then," the sandy-haired one said. "You can both do it." His wide smile reached all the way up to his interested dark eyes.

The older instructor pushed his black hair back with a big, thick hand. A muscle in his biceps pulsated with the quick movement, and Danica thought Lacy might fall to the ground with weak knees. Kaylie caught Lacy's interest, and she sidled up to the sexy, dark-haired man.

"I'm Kaylie," she said in her best sultry voice.

Oh no. No, no, no.

The instructor's eyes were locked on Lacy, and Danica watched as he maneuvered his way to Lacy's side. Kaylie's eyes narrowed.

"I'm Justin," the fairer of the two said to Kaylie.

The darker man reached for Lacy's hand. "Dane," he said in a deep, husky voice.

Danica shot a glance at her father and Madeline, who appeared to be watching without much concern at all.

"Poor Chaz," Blake whispered, nodding at Chaz, who seemed to take his wife's flirting as some kind of joke.

Is that a laugh on his lips? "I'm going." Danica moved to Chaz's side, trying to figure out if Chaz was really okay with Kaylie's behavior. Lacy and Kaylie put on the masks and snorkels and slipped into waist-high water with their gorgeous instructors. "Hey, you okay with…this?"

This time she was certain Chaz laughed. "Are you kidding? This is Kaylie at her finest."

Danica didn't think before she reacted. "Um, yeah, it is. Isn't it?" She snapped around to find Chaz still smiling, his muscular arms crossed, his own hard muscles an easy match for the older, bigger of the two instructors. "Sorry, I didn't mean—"

"Danica, this is all fun and games to Kaylie. When we were in our hotel room, she said she'd be damned if she'd be outdone by"—he lowered his voice—"*that little trollop.*"

Danica couldn't stifle her laugh. *That's my sister, all right.* "Trollop? Really? Lacy is anything but that."

"I know. That's what makes it so funny. Kaylie is so wrapped up in some warped competition that she can't see Lacy for who she really is."

"Doesn't that worry you?" Danica watched her sister in action, holding on to the instructor's thick arm, flipping her hair as she threw her head back with a laugh when she removed the mask, and all the while, keeping one eye trained on Lacy, whose every move contradicted the term *trollop.* Lacy moved uneasily, with a naturally nervous and heartfelt smile. She used her hands to move her hair from her face when she breached the water. The instructor's hand moved swiftly and comfortably to the small of her back as she stumbled backward.

"Not in the least. I knew who Kaylie was in the first five seconds after we met. I adore her just as she is."

Danica swallowed the lump that was quickly forming in her throat. Was she going to cry her way through the weekend? That was all she needed. Between elation and worry, she just might run out of tears. Chaz loved Kaylie. He really, truly loved her for who she was, not for who he wanted her to be, or who she might one day become. He didn't love her for her looks or the party-girl attitude she still flaunted from time to time. He loved her for the spunky, somewhat unorthodox, competitive vixen that she was, and for that Danica was more than thankful.

They spent time getting used to breathing through the snorkels in shallow water, and Danica was surprised at how difficult she found it to inhale while her face was underwater. It was one of the most unnatural things she'd ever done. They'd been told to first practice with the snorkel on while their faces were out of the water and then, once comfortable with the apparatus, to try it with their faces submerged. That helped, though it still incited a little shock of fear with each submerged breath.

Once they all had mastered using the apparatus, they took a boat toward a nearby island they'd seen from the shore. A small plane flew in patterns across the cloudless sky, and Dane followed Lacy's gaze toward it.

"It's beautiful, isn't it? Weather changes here in an instant. Sometimes a storm hits so fast that it blindsides you. It doesn't happen often, but when it does, you'll think you've stepped into another world." Dane pointed far out into the middle of the clear blue bay. "But there's nothing more beautiful than the water."

Blake sat behind Danica, his arms wrapped around her, his chin resting on her shoulder. The wind whipped against their faces, causing Danica to blink, blink, blink.

"You okay?" Blake whispered.

"Yeah," she said.

"Do you know how much I love you?"

His voice sent a shiver of memory up her back. She closed her eyes, remembering the ache of the night before, the urgent, sexed-up look in his eyes when he'd whispered, *Tell me.* She shifted in between his legs and took a deep breath, reminding herself that they were in public, *with her father.*

"Tell me," she said, unable to stifle the urge to make him experience the same racing pulse as she was. She felt his understanding against the small of her back.

He leaned down, the stubble of his chin brushing against her cheek. "Oh, I'll tell you, all right."

Danica was sure everyone could feel the heat between them. Maybe she shouldn't play with fire after all. She breathed a sigh of relief when the boat slowed to a stop, and the instructors helped everyone put on their masks, snorkels, and fins. Kaylie held on to Chaz, and Danica studied the way she looked up at him. The love in her eyes when she looked up at her incredibly handsome fiancé was unmistakable. Danica knew that Chaz was right and that what she'd witnessed between Kaylie and the instructor had been nothing more than a competition. Lacy, however, stood shyly next to their father, while Dane helped her into her fins, his hands lingering on Lacy's slim calf.

"What's this scar from?" Dane asked, pointing to the outside of Lacy's right thigh, where thin white lines covered a long patch of discolored skin, as if someone had taken sandpaper to her leg.

Lacy blushed and covered her leg with her hand. "Just an accident from when I was younger." Her voice was thin and tethered.

Danica had an urge to go to her side, put a protective arm around her, and tell her how beautiful she was despite the scar, but she wouldn't dare hurt Kaylie that way when she was so obviously entrenched in staking claim as the prettiest of the Snow girls.

Dane finished helping her into her fins and then stood beside her. "Check this out." He turned and pulled the waistband of his swim trunks down an inch, revealing a long scar. "Only the best of us get to carry our scars forever." He winked and Lacy smiled.

Danica breathed a sigh of relief, thankful for Dane's tenderness.

Her father held Madeline's hand. "You're sure you're okay with this?" he asked thoughtfully.

"More than okay. This is what we always talked about, remember?"

Remember. There it was again, the acknowledgment that they had a life together. They had history, and Danica wondered how she and Kaylie fit into that history.

She felt Blake's presence beside her like a wall of sensuality. She moved to the edge of the boat and stepped off, landing in the cool water with a splash, taking her heated-up desire down a much-needed notch.

At first, the awkwardness of breathing underwater contradicted the vision of a peaceful undersea experience, and Danica wondered why on earth no one had explained how uncomfortable it would be. Once they'd spent a bit of time underwater, Danica's discomfort disappeared, and the beauty of the bay came to life.

Underwater, she reached for Blake's hand, surprised to realize that he was much farther away than he appeared. She saw a smile behind his mask and she gave him a thumbs-up, then kicked around in search of Kaylie. She spotted her a few feet away from Lacy. Kaylie watched Lacy like her life depended on it.

Spectacular purple and yellow plants danced from their

sandy base like a magical forest. Fish too plentiful to count, with stripes and other markings in reds and blues, yellows and silvers, shone brightly in the clear water.

Lacy kicked her feet gracefully, moving closer to shore, then dipped beneath the water. She broke through the surface with a large orangish starfish in her hands and wide eyes behind her mask. Dane's massive, muscular legs propelled him to Lacy's side.

Kaylie spotted Danica and dipped beneath the water, watching Lacy and Dane kick their feet to remain upright. Danica submerged and looked through Kaylie's mask. Her sister's eyes were filled with determination, competition, and something else Danica couldn't define, but one thing was clear. Kaylie had gone covert and was in full spy mode.

Dane turned toward them, and the outline of an impressive bulge in his shorts could not be ignored. Embarrassed, Danica looked away, catching Kaylie's startled eyes as she whipped her head around. They broke through the surface together and spat their snorkels from between their teeth.

"Oh my God!" Kaylie screamed.

Danica was laughing too hard to tell her to be quiet.

"Did you see that?"

"Yes!" Danica said as she came to her sister's side. "Shh."

They couldn't stifle their giggles, causing so much ruckus that Lacy looked over her shoulder and put her palm up toward the sky. *What?* she mouthed, causing Kaylie and Danica more fits of laughter.

They put their masks back on and swam underwater hand in hand. Danica pointed to their father and Madeline, just beneath the water's surface, both kicking to stay afloat. His hands rested on her ample hips as they gazed into each other's eyes. She felt Kaylie's hand slip through her fingers and followed her around to the other side of the boat, where she broke through the water's surface once again.

"You okay?" Danica asked, huffing for air.

"Yeah."

There was a softening to Kaylie's tone, and Danica waited to see if she'd say more. When she didn't, she moved closer and looked directly through her mask. Kaylie's eyes glistened.

"Kay?"

"I'm fine." Kaylie shoved her snorkel back into her mouth and swam away.

Chapter Eight

On the boat ride back toward shore, Dane recollected his last excursion in Belize, where he was tagging whale sharks. His brown eyes held Lacy's curious gaze, and it took all of Danica's will—and she expected Kaylie's as well—to keep her eyes above his waist. Blake's warm hand landed on her shoulder, turning off the underwater memory like a light switch.

Once back on shore, Dane continued. "I spend about half of my time fundraising. You know, it's easy to ask people to help save starving children, but getting them to contribute to the life of sharks? Not so much. Anyway, I'm just helping out today for fun. I like to teach when I have time, which isn't often."

Kaylie pulled Danica aside as they wrapped towels around themselves. "Do you think she noticed?" she whispered.

"How could she not?" Danica laughed.

"What're you two up to?" Chaz asked.

The girls laughed, and Blake tapped Chaz on the shoulder. "You get a look at that guy's junk?" he asked with a raised brow.

Waves of laughter burst from Danica and Kaylie.

"Apparently, they did," Chaz said, thrusting a thumb in their direction.

"You like that, huh?" Blake teased Danica.

"I didn't see any—" She couldn't even say the lie.

"What is so funny?" Madeline's voice came from behind, a sweet tenor to their roaring laughter.

Kaylie and Danica looked at each other and tried again to stifle their laughter. They looked back at Lacy, gently running her big toe across the sand. Dane said something, and Lacy's hand moved to cover her smile. He leaned in close and said something else that drew her eyes to his.

"I see you met my brother."

Danica turned toward the smooth, commanding voice, and the word *Adonis* sailed through her mind. With football-field-wide shoulders and hair as thick and lustrous as Blake's, the deep voice came from a man even taller than, and every bit as handsome as, Blake.

Blake shook the man's hand and gave him a brotherly embrace. "Treat." Blake winked, then nodded toward Dane. "I didn't think we'd see you."

"This is Treat? Treat Braden?" Blake had told Danica about his handsome, wealthy, and wickedly naughty cousins, but she'd never imagined any man rivaling her handsome prince. Treat had a kind smile and friendly, gentle eyes.

He took Danica's hand in his unbelievably large paws. "I cannot tell you what a pleasure it is to meet the woman who tamed the beast."

Danica blushed. Blake's history as a player was just that—history. She smiled back at him and then at Blake. "Someone had to do it," she joked. She introduced the others.

"I see you've met my younger brother Dane." He nodded toward Dane. "Just in from Madagascar, or Belize, or somewhere crazy like that. He insisted on taking you out today."

Danica shot an embarrassed look at Blake. The look on his face told her what was now obvious. He'd let them all think Dane was a stranger to see what would ensue. That talk about his junk must have been a family joke, and he'd played her like a tune. She narrowed her eyes. "You didn't say a word."

"Let me guess; he sat back and watched Dane in action?" Treat shook his head.

"Well." Blake splayed his hands.

"And?" Treat's eyes grew wide as an inside joke passed between them.

"How could they not?"

Treat threw his head back, and a deep, hearty laugh filled the air.

"Bro, how's it going?" Dane pulled Treat into a brotherly hug.

Seeing the two handsome men next to each other, the hereditary connection became clear. While Dane and Blake were evenly matched at just over six feet, Treat towered over both of them.

Danica must have been staring, because Dane said, "He's six foot six," with a shake of his head. He patted his brother on the back and whispered, "And not anywhere near my ten inches," just loud enough for Treat, and unfortunately Danica, to hear.

She clenched her jaw to keep her surprise at bay. She shot a look at Kaylie, who had been strangely silent since Treat arrived, looking away every time his eyes moved in her direction.

"Unfortunately, I'll miss the wedding, but I wanted to say hello. I'm leaving town tomorrow afternoon to check out another resort. Thailand," he said with a nod.

"Thank you for everything," Danica gushed. "The resort couldn't be more beautiful, and we really appreciate your invitation to use it for our wedding. Oh, and the island—"

Treat turned serious eyes to Blake. "They cleared it for you, right?"

"Yes, they reserved the whole island." Blake looked at his cousins with pride.

"I can't believe you own an island," Lacy said quietly.

"It's not much of an island. I mean, there's no resort, or even a house, for that matter." He must have noticed Kaylie lifting her brows at that. "Don't worry. We do have sufficient bathroom facilities for your event." He shook his head. "Even I can't spend time someplace without a proper bathroom." He turned his eyes to his brother. "Now, this guy. He can live without a house, a toilet, or even solid ground for months on end."

"Some of us are just more manly than others," Dane teased, throwing his shoulders back.

"And there are how many more of you?" Danica asked.

"Five brothers altogether, and Savannah, our sister." Dane put an arm around Blake. "And Blake, of course. He's just like one of the Bradens."

Not anymore, from what I've been told about you guys.

Blake cracked a smile.

"I wouldn't want to be the only sister in that testosterone-filled house," Danica said. She looked at Kaylie and wondered for a split second what it might have been like to grow up with a pack of brothers instead of a competitive sister.

Kaylie stuck her tongue out at Danica, and Danica knew that given the chance, she'd never change what she had.

Treat crossed his arms and rubbed his chin, watching Kaylie with a thoughtful eye. "Do I know you from somewhere?"

Kaylie's eyes connected with his, and Danica hoped she was

the only one who noticed the worry cleverly disguised as disinterest as Kaylie shook her head with a wide smile.

"I get that all the time." She flipped her hair with her hand. "It's the blond. You know, we all look alike."

"No, I feel like I've seen you before."

Kaylie fidgeted under his scrutiny.

What are you hiding?

"Look, I've gotta run, but if you need anything, just let my assistant, Scarlet, know." Treat shook the men's hands and hugged the women. "I'll try to stop in one more time before I take off."

Kaylie brushed him off, and Danica wondered what skeleton she was tucking into her closet now.

"I've gotta run, too. Blake, so great to see you, man." Dane hugged Blake and gave him a firm pat on the back.

"Are you still gonna make the wedding?" Blake asked.

Dane looked right at Lacy. "You can bet I'm gonna try. The rest of the family had to attend an award ceremony for Hugh and can't make it, so I'll be our emissary."

"Fantastic," Blake said, embracing him one last time.

"What kind of award?" Danica asked.

"Who knows? He's got a room full of them."

Before she could ask any more questions, he bade them farewell and headed down the beach.

The intrigue in Lacy's eyes was unmistakable as she practically salivated watching him walk away.

Kaylie elbowed Danica. "Oh yeah, she *definitely* noticed."

Chapter Nine

The mood around the dinner table was solemn as the exhaustion of the day settled in. Their sun-kissed faces glistened against the candlelight. Danica was surprised when Kaylie broke the silence.

"So, Lacy, do you work?" She must have felt Danica's eyes on her, because a second later Danica felt the side of Kaylie's shoe impale her calf.

Blake put his hand on Danica's thigh and squeezed. Between the kick and the squeeze, she realized that she hadn't been dreaming. Kaylie had really spoken to Lacy.

"Oh, me?" Lacy patted her mouth with a napkin. "I'm in advertising. I work for World Geographic as a senior advertising exec." She lowered her eyes, and Danica found herself warming toward Lacy's humble demeanor more and more.

"Wow, senior, huh? How old are you again?"

It was a loaded question, and Danica's body went stiff. Blake took his hand from her thigh and brought it up to her shoulder, pulling her closer. How could he possibly know she needed his strength?

"Twenty-six," Lacy said, her eyes darting to their father.

Madeline set down her fork and watched Kaylie's reaction,

as did Danica and Chaz; there was a quick nod, a clenching of her jaw.

"Your father and I have known each other since before you girls were born. We grew up together," Madeline said softly, while looking directly at Kaylie.

Danica dropped her hand beneath the table and took Kaylie's hand in her own, silently hoping the knowledge that she was there would center Kaylie the way Blake centered her.

Madeline continued. "We dated briefly when we were in high school, before he met your mother." She looked at their father, whose unwavering gaze remained on his half-empty wineglass. "When your grandfather died and your father came to settle his estate, we…reconnected."

Grandpa died when I was four. Kaylie was two. I don't even really remember him. Oh God. We were just babies. Dad, how could you?

"Maddy," their father pleaded.

"No, Don, they have a right to know, and if you can't communicate with your daughters, then I will."

"You don't have to, really—"

Madeline cut Danica off with a firm shake of her head. "Yes, yes, I do. Kaylie." It was a soft demand for attention, not a request. "I'm not going to pretend this isn't awkward, or that what we did was right. It wasn't."

"Mom," Lacy whispered a harsh warning.

"No, baby, it's okay. It has to be said."

Danica watched Kaylie eyeing their father as he took Lacy's hand, his gaze locking on Lacy with a silent apology. Kaylie's eyes narrowed.

Shit. We deserve that apology as much as she does.

Kaylie dug her nails in to the back of Danica's hand beneath the table.

"We hurt your family, and your mother—"

Kaylie cut Madeline off with a shaky, firm voice. "Don't you talk about my mother."

Madeline nodded. "I'm sorry. I don't mean anything bad. I just mean that I know there was a lot of hurt doled out, and it wasn't our intent—"

Danica squeezed Kaylie's hand as her sister began to rise from her seat. Kaylie settled back down, and Chaz put his arm around Kaylie and pulled her closer, just as Blake had done to Danica. *Thank God. What the hell is Madeline doing? Why now?*

No sooner had she asked herself the question than Madeline answered. "Okay, look." She sat up taller, laced her shaking hands together and set them on the table.

Please have the grace and tact of Blythe Danner. Please, please. Danica had a momentary vision of Kaylie jumping across the table with a wild scream, clawing at Madeline's eyes. She shook the image from her head and tried to hear past the rush of adrenaline coursing through her veins.

"What happened, happened. We can't change that. No matter how much we wish the circumstances could have been different, they weren't. Your father was married, and he and I broke his vows."

Kaylie's nostrils flared, and Danica held her hand even tighter, hoping to sway her attention toward her for just a second, but Kaylie had Madeline in her sights, and there'd be no distracting her from her prey.

"Lacy is *not*, and I repeat *not*, responsible for any of this," Madeline continued.

"I get that you're protecting your child. I'd do the same for my two children." Kaylie's voice was thick with self-control that

Danica did not recognize. "But whatever happened didn't just happen. You had a choice. He had a choice." Spears shot from her eyes to her father's. "Everyone had a frickin' choice in this matter except for me and Danica." She pushed her chair out from the table and threw her napkin down. "And Lacy," she added before storming out of the restaurant.

Chapter Ten

Danica caught up to Kaylie and Chaz out on the veranda. Kaylie's head rested on Chaz's chest, her hands clasped together beneath her chin as she nestled within his arms like a frightened child. Her sobs could be heard from the doorway, where Danica stood, contemplating her place in the intimate scene.

Chaz spotted her, and his worried eyes drew her closer.

"Kaylie," she said softly.

Kaylie turned her face away from Danica, and Danica felt a fissure form across her heart. She stepped closer and touched her sister's back. The rattle of her lungs as she sobbed vibrated beneath her fingertips. Danica rested her cheek against Kaylie's back and wrapped her arms around her. There were no words that needed to be said, no fixing of something that had been broken for far too long. Kaylie had a right to feel every emotion that tore at her soul, and Danica wondered why she wasn't feeling each one just as strongly. Had her years of being a therapist hardened her? Had she simply had more time to digest it all during the last year and a half of long phone calls and intimate letters passed between her and Lacy? Had she felt all those things when she first reached out to Lacy? Or was she repressing every nasty feeling she didn't want to deal with? That notion scared the daylights out of her and she pulled back. As she stood there watching the pain that her sister was dealing with, she couldn't deny that she'd brought this to Nassau with them. Danica had been the one to push for her father's invitation. The idea that she'd made an irreversible mistake burned in the pit of her stomach.

It was Kaylie's hand on her own that pulled her back into the embrace. Kaylie untangled herself from Chaz and looked up at him with sad eyes. She laid her palm gently on his chin and whispered through her tears, "Can you give us a second? Please?"

That one little touch from Kaylie unleashed a ripple of guilt and pain that Danica hadn't realized she'd been holding back. Kaylie wrapped her arms around her and held on tight. The lump that had formed in Danica's throat was quickly replaced with quick gasps of breaths as the pain and guilt combined into a rush of heartache. They were the sisters that had been left behind, and no matter how much Danica tried to forget it, Kaylie's pain brought it home.

Chaz leaned down and kissed her trembling lips. "I'll be right here." He pointed to a chair on the other end of the veranda. Blake came onto the porch and Chaz intercepted him.

Kaylie clung to Danica like a lifeline while they cried, their tears falling relentlessly, both powerless to stop the years of repressed hurt and anger from pouring out of their souls.

"It's okay," Danica soothed her, stroking the back of her hair. "We'll be okay." She felt Kaylie exhale; the tension she'd been holding on to since their father had arrived began to ease from her shoulders.

"I hate this," Kaylie sobbed.

"I know. I know, baby. It's okay." Each tear brought with it a painful memory. The phone call from her mother. *I shouldn't admit this, but I feel lost without him.* Kaylie's frantic, angry call later that night. *Dad's such a dick!* Danica's own repression of her feelings. *Who can I tell?* In the end, she hadn't told a soul. Kaylie had been graduating from college and Danica was embarking on her career as a therapist. The years between then and now seemed to have disappeared, and she relived the anguish anew.

Kaylie squeezed her tighter as she inhaled deeply and exhaled again.

"I know, Kay. Just let it out." *Let it out, Danica. Let it out.* Danica felt the lump in her throat expand and then burst into loud, pain-filled sobs, convoluting her thoughts and stealing her resolve to be strong for her sister. Knowing she was falling apart and unable to help Kaylie, she tightened her muscles, and slowly, as if pieces of a puzzle were sifting from space down into her body, she began to gather her determination piece by piece, layer by layer. Creating the strength to clear the tears that brought the unwanted emotions. The strength that guided her hand to Kaylie's chin and gave her the courage to look into her red-rimmed eyes.

"You're okay. We're okay," Danica assured her. They were the words she'd said to her so long ago, when Kaylie lashed out at everyone except her. When Kaylie began lashing out at herself, Danica realized. She searched her sister for the understanding of what Danica was only just then realizing and came back empty.

"Let it go, Kay. Let this go."

She wiped Kaylie's tears with the pad of her thumb. Kaylie drew away from her, her hands still clinging to Danica's upper arms. She sniffled and hiccupped as she tried to quell her tears and take control of her trembling body. Danica watched determination work its way back into her sister's eyes. She saw straight into her soul, and what she saw, she felt within the energy of her own body: a hurt so deep that nothing would ever take it away. Danica's years as a therapist had better prepared her for cataloging away the hurt and moving forward, but as she looked at Kaylie, she knew nothing would fill the void of knowing they were not the chosen ones. Nothing would fix the hurt they saw, felt, and tried to fix in their mother's heart. Nothing could take away the image of their mother holding herself together for their sake after their father had moved away to begin a new life with Madeline and Lacy, leaving her behind with nothing more than two grown daughters and an empty house. Danica also saw, as she stared into the well of Kaylie's eyes, a tenderness and strength that vied to come alive once again but was restrained by something Danica did not feel in her own body. Something Kaylie seemed to be contemplating as well, as she pulled her hands away from Danica, using her forearms to swipe angrily at her remaining tears. Contemplating as she pulled her shoulders back and grit her teeth, seething in such a way that Danica feared what Kaylie might do next.

She shot a worried look at Chaz and Blake, who stood from their seats, ready for flight or fight. Desire to protect their women's hearts was written in their flexing muscles and clenched jaws.

"She doesn't deserve this," Kaylie spat, then stomped from the room and marched right back into the restaurant—Danica, Blake, and Chaz on her heels.

"Kaylie, don't." Danica had no idea what Kaylie was intent on doing, but she knew her little sister well enough to know that if Kaylie wanted to take down the entire resort, she could do it with very few words, perfectly timed, with expert inflection.

Kaylie stalked across the restaurant and grabbed Lacy's arm, yanking her to her feet, ignoring the tears streaming down Lacy's cheeks. Kaylie hooked her arm through Lacy's, giving her no chance to escape.

"We're outta here," Kaylie said. She dragged Lacy out of the restaurant, leaving their stunned father and Madeline alone to wonder what the hell had just happened.

Chapter Eleven

The night sky was clear, but Danica felt the angst of the evening weighing her down like a wet, woolen shawl. She was torn between remaining with her sisters, Chaz, and Blake, sitting around a picnic-style table on the patio of a little bar down the street from the hotel, and returning to the hotel to make sure her father was okay. *The hell with it.* She downed another tropical drink.

An hour later, and three sheets to the wind, she looked across the table as the ocean breeze kicked up and blew both Lacy's and Kaylie's hair across their faces. They laughed at something Chaz said, and Kaylie reached up and moved the hair from Lacy's cheek. Danica realized that there was no place else she'd rather be, even if she wasn't really sure what was going on. Her sister had all but abducted Lacy.

She sighed as she took another sip of her drink. Even if she had invited him to the wedding, her father had made his own bed years ago. *Let him lie in it, swallowed by guilt and strangled by the knowledge that he hurt us. He didn't ruin us—not any of us.*

"I'm telling you, you didn't do it. He did," Kaylie said.

Uh-oh, maybe he did.

"No. No, no, no." Lacy swayed from too much alcohol. "I

was a mistake. If I hadn't come along, then who knows? Your parents might still be together."

Kaylie put her arm around Lacy's shoulder. "Honey, you were a product of what fucked up our life. You are not what fucked it up."

"Awww," Lacy said, resting her forehead against Kaylie's cheek.

"Even if you hadn't been born, they'd still have been to-gether." Kaylie gulped down the remainder of her drink. "Behind my mother's back." She threw her head back and took another swig, dribbling it down her chin. "And we were so stupid. We thought he was on business trips, 'cause he'd bring us chocolate and shit." She lifted her glass in Danica's direction. "Remember that? Ghirardelli? Oh yeah, like he'd been to San Francisco. Right. Fuckin' San Francisco." She didn't wait for Danica to answer. Kaylie slammed her glass down on the table. "They fucked us all up. Every one of us." Kaylie drew a circle in the air with her glass, spilling her drink on the table with a giggle.

"Fuckers," Lacy spat, then quickly covered her mouth with her hand. Her eyes grew wide. "Oh my gosh. I didn't mean to say that. I don't talk like that."

They didn't fuck us up. We're just fine, or at least we will be.

Blake and Chaz looked on with amusement, and Danica's attention turned to her man. She was compelled to drink more—to drink in every inch of him. His mouth moved slowly, sexily, as he said something to Chaz that Danica could not make out. She caught Blake's eye and licked her lips seductively. Or at least she thought she did. The right side of his mouth lifted into a playful smile. She dunked her finger in her drink and then sucked the sweet nectar from her skin.

Kaylie's voice broke through her drunken reverie. "It's them. They make you use that foul, disgusting language. They made me, too. Right, Danica?"

Danica blinked, coming back to the present. *Oh God, what did I just do? Why is Blake looking at me like a starved wolf? Did Kaylie just call me foul and disgusting?* She tried to shake the alcohol from her head.

"Right, Danica? It was them who made us use that foul, disgusting language. They fucked us up."

Oh, thank God. She lifted her glass. "Damn right, sis," she said, and eyed Blake, who still had that hungry look in his eyes. Danica put her drink down and felt a cool breeze across her wet finger. She closed her eyes. *Oh, Danica. You didn't.* She opened her eyes and looked at Blake. He licked his lips and his socked foot found her leg beneath the table. *Oh, yes, I did.*

They stumbled back to their rooms on the arms of their men, Lacy's arms linked between Danica's and Kaylie's. It was well past two o'clock in the morning, and Danica's head swam. She had to be up to meet her mother, Camille, and the rest of their guests at—she couldn't remember what time the next day.

Suddenly they stopped in middle of the hall. "This is me," Lacy said, dropping the girls' arms and pointing to a door.

"No, honey, you're not a door." Kaylie bent over, laughing, taking Lacy with her. "A door! You're not a door; you're my sister."

The hallway silenced, and all eyes focused on Kaylie as she chewed on her own words. Her jaw moving from side to side, her eyebrows drawing together, then relaxing again. She pulled herself upright and put one hand on Lacy's shoulder. Danica wanted to move to Lacy's side, but her legs would not obey. Thank God for Blake, who seemed to be the only thing holding her upright at the moment.

"You're not a door," Kaylie repeated. "You're my sister."

Tears streamed silently down Lacy's cheeks. She wiped them away and dropped her eyes. "You might not feel that way tomorrow," she said in what sounded to Danica to be a much-too-sober voice for having had as much to drink as they had.

Kaylie flung her hand around Lacy and tugged her against her chest. "I shall remember, sis." Her eyes connected with Danica's, passing a silent acknowledgment between them. "I shall remember."

Danica collapsed on the bed, staring up at the ceiling. "Please tell me I did not just dream that." Blake lay next to her, the liquor-sweet smell of his breath infiltrating her senses.

"Tell me I did not just dream *this*." He took her finger and put it in his mouth, then sucked it as he drew it out slowly.

"I kinda remember something along those lines," she admitted. "I think you're making me into a sex maniac."

"Maybe you dreamed that you want to be a sex maniac." Blake slid off the bed and pulled his shirt off over his head, flinging it across the room.

Danica licked her lips at the sight of his naked chest.

He removed her shoes, running his hands along her legs and up her inner thighs. "I seem to remember a certain someone falling off her too-high heels one night."

Danica smiled at the memory of one evening shortly after they'd first met. She was stone-cold drunk when they'd left Bar None, he with a girl on each arm, her alone. Danica had fallen off of her high heels and twisted her ankle. Blake appeared out of nowhere, without his two beautiful blondes, sweetly removed her heels and inspected her ankle, and they'd shared a steamy, flirtatious moment. She'd wanted it to be so much more.

"I see you remember that night, too," he said, kissing each of her toes and working his way up her left calf. "What do you say we play out what might have happened that night had we not been…"

Danica had closed her eyes when he was kissing her leg, and now she opened one eye and looked down at him. The hunger in his eyes pulled open her other eye. "What? Not been what?"

"Trying to restrain ourselves," he said innocently.

She looked up at the ceiling, remembering that evening and the pull that she felt toward him, which had grown ten times stronger in the weeks that followed. Now, as every fiber of her being ached with desire, that pull was even stronger. She patted the bed beside her, and Blake lay down, resting on his elbow, looking down into her eyes. She touched the bare flesh of his belly. A shiver ran through her and she mimicked his position, hoisting herself up on one elbow, the room spinning around them. She closed her eyes, and when she opened them, the room stilled, and Blake inched even closer. His black boxer briefs barely contained his desire.

"You were not wearing those that night. You had on clothes," she said.

"Indeed I did." He gathered her skirt in his hands and brought it up around her waist. "What have we here?" He ran a finger under the lacy string of her thong.

Danica fell on her back and pulled her arm over her eyes with a groan. "I wore those so I wouldn't feel unattractive sitting with my insanely beautiful sisters," she said, only half joking.

He moved her arm from her face so she had no choice but to look at him. "Do you seriously think they even compare to you?"

"*Pfft.* Yeah, right." She pulled her arm back, but he pushed it away again and turned her face toward his.

In his most serious voice, which to Danica sounded gruff and wildly sexy, he said, "I have yet to meet a woman who could hold a candle to not only your exquisite beauty, but your honesty." He kissed her cheek. "Your intelligence." He kissed her forehead. "Your laugh." Another warm kiss landed on her nose. "Your sense of responsibility." His lips met her other cheek. "Or your passion." He took her chin in his hand and turned her face toward his as she leaned up and met him in a long, deep, heart-thrilling kiss.

"Or my childlike need for compliments?" She laughed, pushing him onto his back and straddling his body. Blake was almost always the dominant one in their lovemaking, and this new position sent a rush of control through her. She whipped off her shirt and tossed it aside, then wrapped her hands in his hair and leaned forward, her hair curtaining their faces. "Tell me," she said in a throaty voice she did not recognize.

"Oh, you want to play, do you?" He grabbed her upper arms. Tight. And began to lift her off his body.

She felt so light in his arms, and her drunken state slowed her reactions.

"Uh-huh." Somehow she managed to wiggle free from his

grasp and trap his arms beneath her knees. "I do want to play." So this is what men like? Having control made her feel stronger, riskier. *Yes, I want to play! I do!*

"Careful now," he said as she dug her knees into his arms.

"Tell me," she repeated.

Blake closed his eyes. "Kiss me."

"Uh-uh." She gently pushed his eyelids up. "Look at me." Once she had his attention, she asked, "Where?"

He licked his lips, and it took all her restraint not to lean down and taste his wicked little tongue, which had brought her so much pleasure. But tonight was about control—or at least it seemed to be a good ride at the moment—and her inhibitions had yet to arrive, so she was taking full advantage of this loose, unrestrained Danica that had taken over.

He lowered his eyes toward his groin.

"I'm sorry, I can't hear you," she teased.

"Kiss my…lips."

Chicken. "Not so easy on the flip side, now, is it?" She leaned down and kissed him hard, taking his lower lip between her teeth on the way back up. Feeling him swell beneath her.

"Tell me." She took his finger in her mouth and ran her tongue in circles around it, then drew it out slowly. When he didn't answer, she repeated it again, only this time, she closed her eyes and moaned as she licked the salty taste from his skin.

"Touch me," he whispered. "There. Touch me there."

With one hand she unhooked her bra and tossed it aside, lowering her chest so her breasts were just out of reach of his mouth. He arched toward her, and she used her hand to caress his forehead, then locked his head down beneath her palm.

"Where?" she whispered.

"Touch yourself," he said.

Danica blinked. Then blinked again. Was that fair? Could he do that? She was in control, wasn't she? She never had him touch himself. *No, definitely not fair at all,* she decided.

"In your dreams." She held up one finger and then slid down his body and removed his briefs. He began to sit up, and she scrambled back on top of him, regaining control with a sly smile. With one hand, she held his shoulder down, while she used the other to remove her thong. Now wearing just her skirt, she took his hand in hers and ran her tongue along his palm, up, down, then up again, taking two of his fingers into her mouth and then drawing them out slowly.

"Touch yourself," she whispered, sliding sideways, allowing him access to do as she asked. Danica bit her lower lip in response to the shocked look in his eyes. The alcohol fueled her actions as she took his hand, which had stopped midair after she took it from between her lips, and she wrapped his fingers around his hard shaft.

"Danica," he pleaded.

She shook her head, feeling naughtier than she ever had before—and liking it. "Do it," she said.

His hand moved up and down, his head fell back, and his eyes fluttered closed. Danica kissed him until his strokes grew harder, faster, and he moaned into her mouth. She pulled away, watching him touch himself.

"Open your eyes." She watched him struggle to keep them open, his hand wrapped tight as he arched against his own friction. He reached for her breast and she pulled away, as if she were being driven by someone other than herself.

She heard herself say, "No. Watch me," as she touched herself.

His eyes dimmed with desire. "Danica," he called out,

reaching for her hot flesh. He covered her hand with his and rubbed her until she was ready to explode.

Damn you. He'd taken control and Danica was set to take it back. She grabbed his arms and pushed them against the mattress, sliding onto his shaft fast and hard.

He gasped a sharp breath, then groaned as she clenched and bucked atop of him, taking what she needed—what she wanted—and making him wait for his.

She slowed her pace as he grabbed her ass and worked her up and down to his own rhythm. She forced his hands off and trapped them again beneath her knees. He'd unleashed a seductress that she hadn't known existed.

"You're killing me," he said.

"This was your game. I'm just playing along." Feeling empowered and oh, so sexy, she ran her hand through her hair and was shocked that she so easily accepted the sexiness that she felt exuding from her body—a body that she never imagined could be taken to such heights.

"My game?" he asked through clenched teeth. Hunger and something dangerous mixed in his eyes, sparking a fire in her loins, and she slowed for a beat too long and processed the new, exhilarating emotions. In the space of a breath, he flipped her over onto her back and thrust into her.

She clawed at his shoulders, desperately wanting more of him. To hell with control.

He bent her legs at the knees and trapped them against his chest, driving deeper, harder. "I'm not a good loser," he teased.

"Win, baby, win," she coaxed as he took them both up and over the edge of ecstasy.

Chapter Twelve

No matter how much Danica tried to will it away, Saturday arrived. She rolled over, turning her back to the glorious sun streaming through the curtains. Her head pounded, and her mouth felt like she'd swallowed cotton. She covered her head with a pillow to drown out the constant hum of the air conditioner.

"Good morning, dirty girl."

Her heart skipped a beat as the night before came rushing back to her in foggy flashes. *Tell me. Touch yourself.* "Oh God," she groaned, pressing the pillow against her face. *Shit. Shit, shit, shit.*

She felt the bed sink as Blake sat beside her. What was he doing up already?

"You can come out now. I won't bite," he teased.

Danica lay perfectly still. She couldn't show her face, not after what she'd done with that beautiful man. Maybe she could hold her breath and die. Right here and now. *He must think I'm a tramp. A slut. A trollop!*

She felt his hand on her hip, and she was struck with another worry. She peeked beneath the sheet. *Yup. Buck naked. Ugh!* College memories of the walk of shame came to mind. Not that she'd have been caught dead taking that lonely walk out of the fraternity houses, but her friends had, and one friend in particular walked home with nothing more than two well-placed paper plates. *Please, God, kill me now.*

He lifted the pillow from her face, and she clenched her eyes shut.

The bed moved, and she knew Blake was shaking his head. She felt his face draw near, his freshly shaven cheek against her own. "Our love life never leaves this room. I adore you, babe. You have my word, and if you can't take my word, then you're with the wrong man."

His whisper was the warm coaxing, his promise the drive that she needed to open her eyes. She was met with the most adoring gaze. Blake stroked her hair with tenderness and love.

"My intent is to never hurt you, and that means respecting our privacy, your needs, and our love. And I will do everything within my power to make sure that I keep that promise."

"Thank you" were the only words that she could push past her swollen heart.

Blake tucked the sheet beneath her arms and said, "Sit up, babe. Now that you're covered, no need to be embarrassed."

"How do you know me so well?"

"Because I love you, and when you love someone, you notice them. Everything about them." He handed her a glass of water and two aspirin.

"You're a godsend." She swallowed the pills and relished in the icy cold water as it streamed down her throat. "I feel like such a different person around you, here, at night."

He shook his head. "You're the same beautiful almost-wife as you've always been. You're just beginning to trust me. To trust us, and it makes you even more beautiful." He took the glass and set it on the bedside table. "Danica, there is nothing you could do—short of sleeping with another man—that would make me think any less of you."

"Everyone says that." She fiddled with the edge of the sheet. "Look at my parents; look at yours. There are no guarantees in relationships. No one gets married thinking that they'll one day break up. Everyone dreams of the happily ever after."

"We're not everyone."

"That's so cliché."

Blake kissed her forehead. "What would you tell Kaylie right now?"

"Everything you just told me," she admitted. "Wipe that grin off your face."

He grabbed her ribs, and she rolled over in a fit of giggles.

"Ow, ow, my head."

"Okay." He sighed. "You have my empathy. Now, come on. Your mom will be here in half an hour."

Danica bolted out of bed, forgetting the sheet. She covered herself with her arms and frantically ran into the bathroom. "Half an hour? What time is it?" she called from the shower.

"Twelve thirty."

"Twelve thirty! Oh my God. I missed breakfast? What did my father say? How could you let me sleep?"

"Kaylie and Lacy didn't make it either."

She showered faster than she ever had before and came out of the bathroom with her hair wrapped in a towel and another towel wrapped around her body.

"Neither one? God, we must have really been hammered."

She picked through her clothes and quickly dressed in shorts and a tank top. On her way back to the bathroom, she noticed her thong hanging from the light on the wall.

Blake followed her eyes and laughed. "My sexy, hot girl-friend got a little carried away last night."

"Jesus!" she muttered. She snagged the thong and threw it into the pile of dirty laundry. "Please look for other articles of clothing that might out us as acrobatic sex freaks." Who knew that her walk of shame would cover only the span of her hotel bed to the bathroom?

Blake laughed heartily as she flipped her head upside down and dried her hair. Danica silently replayed every instance she could remember from the night before. She tucked the lusty love snippets away in the secret files in her brain where she kept dirty thoughts of things she'd never have, like sex toys and Hugh Jackman.

Kaylie, Lacy, and Danica sat together on a sofa in the lobby, each looking a little greener than the next, while Chaz, Blake, Don, and Madeline chatted just inside the doors.

"So, you don't hate me?" Lacy asked.

Kaylie shook her head. "Shh."

"I swear a monkey played the drums in my head last night," Danica said, rubbing her temple.

"I passed out cold when we got home." Kaylie leaned her head back.

"I stayed up all night thinking of Dane's junk."

Danica and Kaylie shot straight up. "What?" they asked in unison.

"Didn't you see it?" Lacy asked as if she were asking about baskets or berries. "I mean, my God, how could you miss it? It was like a…a python in his trunks."

Silence.

The three of them burst into giggles seconds later. Kaylie grabbed Lacy's arm as she bent over, gasping for breath between laughs, tears streaming from her eyes. Lacy threw her head back and howled, as they both reached for Danica to keep them upright.

"Ow, ow, ow," Danica complained.

"Shh." Kaylie laid her head back again.

"Damn that hurts." Lacy closed her eyes, folding her hands neatly in her lap.

Chapter Thirteen

Helen Snow arrived in a flurry of activity, with Lexi and Trevor chattering in their two- and three-word sentences about their trip, each trying to outshout the other.

"Mommy! Daddy!" they yelled.

Chaz intercepted them before they reached Kaylie and swept Trevor and Alexandra into his arms. "Trev, Lex, how are my beautiful babies?"

"We, we, we…" Trevor stuttered.

Lexi took over, as she almost always did. "We ride big plane!"

"You did!"

Kaylie mouthed, *Thank you*, to Chaz and kissed her toddler's soft cheeks. "I missed you so much!" She leaned in to kiss her mother's cheek.

It was hard for Danica to believe that Kaylie had spent so much time angry at their mother, thinking she was weak for staying with her father when she'd known he was cheating on her. But now that Kaylie had experienced motherhood, she knew Kaylie would do just about anything for her babies, and that experience had brought an understanding to their relationship.

"Thanks for taking such good care of them, Mom," Kaylie said.

When the twins were born, their mother had just begun dating again, and she'd joined a gym and dyed her hair red. Danica was happy to see the return of her mother's buttery blond shade. Helen looked around nervously, and Danica came to her side.

"He and Madeline went to grab some coffee."

"Oh, I wasn't—"

"Yes, you were. It's okay, Mom. You haven't seen him since he moved away either. It's been a long time."

Lacy stood by the sofa, her hands clasped before her, her conservative white shorts and button-down blouse perfectly pressed. Only her eyes held the remnant of the evening before and the fear of the moment.

Danica watched the connection take hold between her mother and Lacy. She took her mother's hand.

"Oh my goodness. She's gorgeous," her mother said.

"Do you want to meet Lacy, Mom?"

"Yes, I do. Very much."

The walk felt a million miles long, and Danica wanted to ask her mother what she was feeling, what she was thinking, but she wouldn't dare. Kaylie took her mother's other hand and joined them as they approached Lacy.

Lacy dropped her eyes, and Kaylie did something that stole Danica's heart right out of her chest. She went to Lacy's side and took Lacy's hand. The four of them stood with their hands interlaced and their lives intertwined. Linked by one man. A world of hurt and a world of wonder lay within the small circle of women.

"Mom, this is Lacy. Lacy Snow. Our sister." Kaylie looked

at Lacy and beamed.

Danica watched the strength pass from Kaylie to Lacy, and a heartbeat later, from Lacy to her mother.

"It is such a pleasure to meet you, Lacy. I have thought of you often."

The grace exuding from her mother gave Danica chills. Time stood still as Danica took in this new family of hers. At some point, Danica wasn't sure exactly when, Blake and Chaz joined them, and she became aware of Lexi and Trevor toddling around their legs. Lexi's thin blond curls bounced with each happy step, and Trevor's promise-blue eyes danced with delight. *Mommy! Daddy!*

Blake was the first to see their father and Madeline enter the lobby, and Danica followed his fading, then quickly righted, smile toward the man who was responsible for this new union and the woman who Danica knew from the longing in her eyes wanted to be there, too.

"Mom." Worry tethered Danica's voice as her mother turned toward the approaching couple, her brows drawn together, a hardening in her eyes. A sea of emotion swam through those little motions: sadness, longing, anger, shame. Finally, as the wrinkles in her brow faded and she dropped Danica's hand, the underlying strength that Danica always knew existed appeared, erasing the shame and anger. Kicking the sadness to the curb.

"Don." Her mother took a step forward. "Madeline," she said curtly with a brief nod.

Madeline managed a cordial smile. "Helen, you look lovely."

"Yes, I do. Thank you."

Wow, Mom.

Her father stood silently taking in the wife he'd tossed aside. There was no strength in the man who had torn their family apart. Madeline put her hand on the small of his back and gave him a little tap.

"How—how are you, Helen?" he asked.

Danica had seen a much humbler man in her father over the last few days, and it was a bit unsettling against the memory of the confident father who'd raised her.

"I'm well. Wonderful, actually. Thank you. And you?"

How on earth are you doing this? Danica shot a look at Kaylie; Lexi held on to her leg and Trevor wiggled in her arms, while Kaylie nursed a hate-filled look in her eyes. Her mother might be able to take this in stride, but Kaylie obviously could not. Danica was torn between staying between her mother and father—just in case—and dragging Kaylie's angry ass out of there before something happened that no toddler should ever witness. As Kaylie handed Trevor to Chaz, Danica sprang into action.

"Kaylie, Camille and the girls should be in any minute. Why don't you bring the kids to get a snack from the machines really quickly so they're not hungry." It was a mean tack to take, knowing the mention of a snack would start the pleas that would quickly become tears in an open forum such as the hotel lobby, but sometimes Auntie Danica had to do what was best for their mommy.

"Snack! Snack!" Trevor jumped up and down, and Lexi took her cue, yelling louder than Trevor.

"Snack, Mommy! Snack!"

Kaylie shot Danica a hateful look, then took Trevor's hand and headed toward the snack machines down the hall. Lexi and Chaz followed.

Danica turned her attention back to the tension that surrounded her mother and father, who were talking about Lexi and Trevor.

"Lexi is just like Kaylie. Do you remember when she used to try and answer for Danica?" Her mother's nostalgic smile was anything but feigned.

"And how Danica used to allow her to?" Her father shook his head.

"Lex does the same thing. When we sit down to eat, she says, Twevor wants peanut butter, and when I ask Trevor, he just nods."

"Kaylie said he stutters," her father said.

Danica didn't know why the genuine concern in her father's voice surprised her. Maybe because it was the first time since he'd arrived that he was vocalizing anything at all.

"Yes," her mother answered. "And I'm not sure that Lexi speaking for him is such a good solution."

"Dysfluency is quite prevalent in children between the ages of two and five. Most kids go through some sort of stuttering stage, whether it's pausing between words, repeating certain sounds and syllables, or starting and stopping altogether, but it usually resolves on its own. I wouldn't worry too much yet." Madeline spoke confidently, with practiced ease.

Her mother cocked her head in question or surprise; it was difficult for Danica to tell which.

"You know that I was a speech therapist by trade. Just retired two years ago, but you know how that goes. I'm not really retired. I still take on clients here and there, doing a little consulting," Madeline explained.

"I must have forgotten. Yes, you always said you would become a speech therapist. How's your brother?" Her mother's cold tone warmed by the second.

Brother? Always said? What is going on?

Madeline rubbed her hands together as if they suddenly caught a chill. "He's doing well. He uses a cane now, but his symptoms are manageable. He's enjoying a good life, and yes, he still stutters."

"He's a remarkable man," her mother said.

"Wait, you know her brother?" The question was out before Danica could think to stop it. She felt Blake's arm circle her waist.

Her mother held Madeline's gaze; then her eyes shifted to Don, and finally, settled on Danica. "Yes, we knew each other a very long time ago."

"I'm so confused. Madeline said they used to date, but I guess I never realized that you knew her, too. And her brother?"

"It's a long story, but yes. We went to the same schools, lived in the same areas, and as you know, Madeline and I loved the same man."

"Mom." Danica's heart ached for her mother.

Helen shook her head. "It's okay, Danica. This is all water under the bridge. Really, we're past this. You should be, too."

"But—"

"If it makes you feel any better, your mother stole him from me first," Madeline said.

Danica spun around and found Madeline smiling. *Smiling?*

"It's true," her mother said with a little laugh. "I did everything within my power to win his heart."

"And you did." Her father looked at her mother through eyes laden with love. He looked down shyly, then back up, and when he did, an appreciative smile formed on his thin lips.

Danica blinked several times. How could this be? Her

mother and father had been in some sort of strange love triangle? And now her mother's and father's eyes were locked in a way that should make Madeline uncomfortable, but she was still smiling. This was too much. Between the hangover headache that was thundering in her skull, Kaylie acting like a lion ready to pounce on her father at any moment, and her parents looking at each other like they'd like to do everything she and Blake had done last night—*Oh God! What I did with Blake! Shoot me now.*

Danica barely registered the warm breeze as the front doors of the lobby opened or the thunder of approaching footsteps.

"Let the party begin!"

Camille's voice startled Danica and instantly offered relief. She fell thankfully into her friend's arms. Camille's husband, Jeff, smiled from behind her, carrying an enormous suitcase in each hand.

"Who's getting married?" Camille teased. "Mrs. Snow! Wow! Blond again! You are beautiful!" Camille embraced Danica's mother as her other friends, Chelsea and Marie, squealed with delight and jumped up and down in the middle of the lobby.

"I can't believe we're here! Where's Kaylie?" Chelsea asked.

"And the kids!" Marie added.

"We fed them to the sharks," Danica teased.

Marie looked at Chelsea, and her eyes grew wide. "Sharks? I didn't know there were sharks here."

Danica kissed her cheek. "It's okay. I love you even if you don't get my jokes."

Blake hugged the girls, and they each greeted Don with careful words. Her friends knew about his affair—Kaylie had made sure that everyone around her knew not only about the affair, but how she felt about her father and Madeline, too. Danica wondered now, after meeting Madeline and Lacy, how she was going to change her friends' preconceived notions about the women. She had wanted to hate Madeline, but now that she'd met her, and found her to be pleasant, there was no way she could—even if Madeline had been *the other woman.*

"Auntie Camille!" Lexi ran across the lobby in her yellow dress and pink Circle Glitter Toms shoes. Kaylie was a Toms fanatic. Trevor was right behind Lexi in his ash-colored Cordones.

"Auntie Chel Chel…"

"Chelsea!" Lexi yelled, jumping into Chelsea's arms before Trevor had a chance to.

Marie swooped Trevor into her arms. "How's my handsome boy? You look so smart in your little polo shirt!"

The girls peppered her and Kaylie with questions.

"Are you nervous?"

"You look beautiful! Look how tan you are!"

"Look at that man of yours. God, you're lucky!"

When Lexi wiggled from Camille's arms, Camille pulled Kaylie aside. Danica eavesdropped in what she hoped was not an obvious manner. She leaned against the column behind which they were whispering and strained to hear every word.

"What do I need to know? Is the sister awful? Is she pretty? Do we hate her or love her?" Camille had been the leader of their girl group for long enough that Danica knew that the fate of Lacy lay in Kaylie's answers.

"She's gorgeous, sweet, and even kinda funny." Kaylie paused.

Danica held her breath and squeezed her eyes shut, praying that Kaylie wouldn't add, *But I hate her anyway.*

"I like her."

"No!" Camille gasped. "After all those years of inspired hatred?"

"Yes. I don't know what happened. Not that I like the evil mistress or the lying, cheating bastard, but Lacy, yeah, she's kinda cool."

Danica let out her breath. At least Lacy was in the clear. She still had work to do with Kaylie and her father—and Madeline. *Evil mistress?*

"Did you see how fat Danica has gotten?" Kaylie said.

Danica's jaw dropped. She touched her stomach, her sides. She'd lost ten pounds in the months after meeting Blake and she'd never put them back on. What was Kaylie talking about? She looked over her shoulder to inspect her backside, and Kaylie popped her head around the column.

"Gotcha!" She roared with laughter.

"You witch! I really thought you meant it!" Danica knitted her brows and laughed through her sneer.

"Well…" Camille tapped her chin.

Danica swatted her.

Camille laughed. "You're gorgeous, and you know it, little Miss I'm Getting Married To McDreamy."

"Yes, I am, aren't I?" She surveyed Blake from behind, standing between her mother and father. *My trusty mediator.*

"Oh my God!" Kaylie yelled.

The group silenced.

"Where's everyone else? Where are our dresses? Where's Sally and Max? Nancy, Rusty, Chase, and Michelle? They're coming, right? What about Gage?" Her eyes shot to Chaz. "Where's your family? I'm still waiting to meet your brother. Weren't they supposed to arrive around the same time?"

"There was so much confusion that I forgot to tell you. Mom and Weston are coming together. She was visiting him this week. Don't worry, but they had to switch to a later flight because of Weston's schedule. He had an emergency surgery." Chaz weathered Kaylie's moods like a sturdy ship in a storm. He picked up Lexi when she toddled by and kissed her on the cheek with a loud *mmwah!* "Abby and Astrid are coming in later tonight."

"He's having surgery and coming in the same day?" Chelsea asked.

Chaz laughed. "No. He's an orthopedic surgeon. He had to perform the surgery."

"Oh, you mean like Callie on *Grey's Anatomy!*" Marie said in an entirely too serious voice.

Chaz looked bewildered, so Danica chimed in before Marie got started on the characters and their backstories from *Greys*. "Sally, Gage, the kids, *and* our dresses should be here within the hour, depending on the immigration lines, and Blake's dad is arriving around the same time." Danica slid beneath Blake's arm, listening to her mother and Madeline talking about women they knew in high school and wondering why she felt like she was in an episode of *As the World Turns*.

The twins needed naps, and everyone was a bit harried from all of the excitement, so the group went their separate ways with a plan to meet in the lobby for a late lunch when the others arrived.

A gentle, warm breeze sifted through the large branches of

the palm trees that shaded the porch where Danica and Blake relaxed on a wooden swing built for two.

"I love how the water is so clear. Isn't it beautiful?" Danica rested her head on Blake's shoulder, finally feeling like the confusion was beginning to settle down.

"Gorgeous," Blake said. "What do you make of your mom and dad?"

Danica sat up. "It's weird, isn't it? I thought it was all in my head."

"There was definitely something going on. I know men, and I think I know women pretty well, and I definitely smelled smoke."

She groaned. "Me too. That's all I need. Kaylie won't even talk to my father, and she called Madeline the evil mistress."

"Hm. Evil mistress. I like that."

She punched his arm.

"Babe, I'm not sure what you think is going to happen over the next twenty-four hours, but you've gotta know that Kaylie may never come around, and that's gotta be okay."

He was right. She knew he was, but the last thing she wanted was for Kaylie's wedding day to be even more stressful. She could deal with stress at her own wedding. Hell, she expected it. It was a wedding. But Kaylie had come so far, and now, with her turnaround with Lacy, she had such high hopes that Kaylie would step up to the plate and find some cordial ground with their father.

"Whatever Kaylie does is okay. This is her life."

"Yeah, but it's yours, too." He kissed her forehead. "It's ours."

Chapter Fourteen

Kaylie's voice carried outside to the veranda. "Max!"

Another swarm of activity brought Danica and Blake back into the lobby. Sally and Rusty, Sally's teenage son, and Chase, Rusty's half brother, stood beside Nancy and her daughter, Michelle, while they checked in at the front desk. Max, Chaz's assistant, had her nose in her day planner. She looked up over her red eyeglasses and held up a finger to the woman behind the desk.

"It's all under control. I've got the dresses. They were delivered earlier today, and Treat's assistant has them safely put away. The bridesmaids gowns, too. The flowers—"

Danica cut Max short. "I'm sure you have it all under control." She embraced Chaz's assistant and sponsorship coordinator. In essence, Max kept Chaz organized and kept a constant stream of funding coming into the festival. Efficient and organized, Max was the perfect person to coordinate their wedding. "What's up with your new title? Work wife?"

"Kaylie calls me that. She's so weird." Max laughed.

"I'm anything but weird. You take care of him at work, and I take care of him at home. It all works out." Kaylie shrugged with a smile.

"See?" Max shook her head, and her long dark ponytail swung from side to side.

"How're you holding up?" Sally was glowing. Her flawless fair skin and her new chic layered bob gave her tall, slim figure an even more regal appearance. The linen shorts and top she wore only added to her aura of refined beauty. Sally had been working at No Limitz, the youth center that Danica owned, for almost three years, and her calm demeanor never failed to soothe Danica.

"I'm good. Really. It's been…a lot to deal with, with my parents and all, but we're managing." Danica embraced her, spotting Michelle, Rusty, and Chase looking out the enormous front windows. Michelle Parce had been Danica's Little Sister in the Big Sister program during a time when her mother, Nancy, had been in rehab for alcohol abuse. Nancy had been sober for almost three years, and though Michelle was no longer in the Big Sister program, she and Danica were still close. Before graduation, both she and Sally's son, Rusty, had also been working part-time at No Limitz.

"How was the trip? How's the gang?" Danica nodded toward the excited teens.

Sally smiled. "Moody, happy, horny. You know, everything you'd expect from recent high school grads. It's like they've been sprung from jail or something."

"And you and Gage? Where is he?"

"He was talking to some guy we met on the airplane. He'll be in soon."

"And?" Danica bit her lower lip with a mischievous smile.

"And…happy, horny, moody. Everything you'd expect from a guy who's too chicken to make a move on the girl who's just as scared." Sally turned and watched Gage come through the doors. "Here he comes."

Gage's eyes never left Sally. He also worked at No Limitz, and in recent months had increased his hours to full-time to manage their ever-growing sports programs.

"God, he's gorgeous," Sally whispered.

"Tell him, not me." Danica turned her back so Gage couldn't possibly hear what she had to say. "It's been almost three years since Dave died. You've known Gage more than two. Isn't it time to make a move?" Sally's husband had died in a skiing accident shortly before Sally started working for Danica, and Sally had yet to go on a single date. Danica spun around just in time to be pulled into Gage's strong arms.

"Hey, boss, how's it going so far?" He stepped back and surveyed Danica. "You're tan. That's a sign of relaxation."

"Not really," Danica said under her breath.

"Hey, I was thinking, if you girls are going to do dress and wedding stuff, how about if Blake and I take the big kids out somewhere? No sense in them hanging out at the hotel."

Danica wrapped her arms around his middle. "You're the best sports program manager ever! Can you check on Chaz, too? Room three ten. Oh, and don't forget Jeff." She hadn't noticed Blake's absence until just that second. She looked around and didn't see him anywhere.

The elevator doors opened, and Blake and Chaz stepped out, each with an armful of groggy toddler.

"Chelle!" Lexi yelled as soon as she spotted Michelle.

Michelle ran over with her arms spread wide and an enormous smile on her lips. "Lexi Lady! How's my girl?" Lexi climbed into her arms, and Trevor kicked himself free from Chaz's grip.

"Wusty!" Trevor said as Rusty lifted him into his arms.

"What's up Trevmeister?"

Trevor giggled.

"What's the plan?" Kaylie asked.

Max shut her planner with a loud clap. "If you're okay with it, and Chaz said you probably were, but if you're not, it's okay. I lined up a kids' day for Trev and Lex, so we can do a final fitting with the hotel's seamstress and go over the details. The rehearsal dinner is tonight at seven."

Kaylie put her arm around Max's shoulder. "Now you see why she's the work wife? This woman rocks my world."

"I'm gonna help Max get organized while you get the kids prepared for their big day," Danica said to Kaylie.

"And we'll get settled in," Sally said, gathering the teens.

"Chaz, we're going to go over wedding stuff, and Gage said you and Blake could hang with him and the teens. Is that okay?" Kaylie asked.

"Of course."

"Everyone was meeting for lunch first. I just remembered." Kaylie looked frantically at Danica.

"No worries," Chaz said. "I'll go let them know that you need to do wedding things. We'll feed the kids with them, snag Jeff, and then we'll take off."

"My future husband to the rescue," Kaylie said. She stood on her tiptoes and kissed him. "Be back in time for the rehearsal dinner and, Chaz, thank you."

Danica and Max inspected the bridal gowns and bridesmaid dresses with Treat's assistant, Scarlet, a pleasant, attractive woman with skin as dark as night and a sexy island accent.

"The dresses are so gorgeous. I can hardly believe we're getting married. Me and Kaylie. I never would have dreamed that we'd get married at the same time, much less in the same wedding," Danica said.

"Kaylie thinks the world of you. I think she's honored that you're sharing your special day." Max looked carefully through each dress.

"Really? Gosh, I'm not sure about that."

"Perfect. Every dress is perfect." Max smiled at Scarlet. "You are a lifesaver, Scarlet. Thank you."

"It is my pleasure. Danica and Kaylie's special day is special to us, too."

The door to the large office opened. "Hey there," Treat said as he stepped into the room. "Everything okay in here?"

Max's eyes were locked on Treat. She didn't just look. She didn't leer. She flat-out stared at the big, handsome man with the deep, soothing voice. It took Danica a minute to realize that she'd better step in.

"Treat, hi. This is Max, Chaz's wor—uh, assistant, and our friend. Max"—she turned her back to Treat and opened her eyes wide, mouthing, *Say hello*—"Max, this is Treat Braden, Blake's cousin."

Treat reached for Max's hand while his eyes consumed her from head to toe. "We've met, a few times over the telephone."

Max lifted her hand and managed, "Yes."

He kissed the back of her hand. "It's a pleasure to finally meet you in person, Max."

Max blinked several times, then pushed her glasses up onto their perch again. "Treat. Hi. I'm sorry. It was a long flight. I must have jet lag or something."

Something like you're hungry for a tasty Treat.

A second later, Max pulled herself together with finesse. It was no wonder Kaylie trusted her to be in charge. "Thank you for everything you've done. Scarlet has been a dream come true."

Scarlet stood demurely by the rack of dresses.

"Scarlet is a dream. I'd be lost without her."

Danica felt Max deflate beside her. *This ought to be interesting.*

Kaylie burst into the room, looking at the rack of dresses. "Sorry it took so long. Geez, you'd think—" She was so busy looking at the dresses that she bumped right into Treat. "Oh, sorry."

Their eyes locked.

Kaylie looked away.

What the hell is going on?

Treat pointed at Kaylie, and for the first time ever, Danica watched her sister shrink toward the wall, like she wished she could become a part of it and disappear altogether.

"I know where I've seen you before," he said.

"No, we've never met," Kaylie said quickly.

"You went to UC Davis, right?"

"Um…Yeah."

Oh shit. Please tell me you didn't fool around with him! Danica couldn't help but notice that Max was hanging on to every word that passed between the two, just as she was.

"There was a party, though I have no recollection whose party it was, and you were there."

Oh God.

"I went to a lot of parties," Kaylie said with a spec of arrogance.

"Didn't we all?" He laughed. "I was looking for my sister. Yes, I'm sure that's where I saw you."

Kaylie feigned a laugh. "I don't remember, but yeah, probably."

My ass, you don't remember.

Kaylie leafed through the dresses and changed the subject. "These are gorgeous, aren't they, Max?"

Max looked from Treat to Kaylie, clearly processing the odd interaction. "Yes. They're perfect," she said.

"Well, I just wanted to make sure you had everything you needed. I'll be off, then. Max, it has been a pleasure working with you, and I hope we find more occasions to get together."

Kaylie stilled.

Max blushed.

Danica cursed under her breath.

Chapter Fifteen

"Do you mind telling me what the hell that was all about?" Danica and Kaylie were in the ladies' room washing their hands. Max and the other girls were waiting for them with the seamstress.

"What?"

"Kaylie? All that tension between you and Blake's cousin? Treat?"

"Nothing. I saw him at a party at college; that's all there is to it." Kaylie fluffed her hair in the mirror. She straightened her white tank top and looked at herself from the side. "I can't believe I was as big as a house two years ago."

"You were pregnant with twins," Danica said with a sigh. "Did you sleep with him?"

"Who?"

"Kaylie!"

"Are we still on Treat? Geez, Danica." She leaned against the sink and looked dreamily up toward the ceiling. "I saw him at a party and we had…a moment. We never even spoke to each other." She looked down her nose at Danica. "We didn't kiss; we didn't touch; we didn't do a-ny-thing."

"Thank God for little favors. Then why were you so uncomfortable?"

"I didn't say I never wanted to do anything."

"Kaylie!"

"Not now! Then! I crushed on him for a few weeks. So what? I was in college. I was supposed to be crushing on guys, and you have to admit, he's pretty crushworthy."

"So, why are you uncomfortable around him *now*? Please tell me you're not still attracted to him. You're about to get married to an incredible man. The father of your children."

"Don't you know me better than that by now? A few years ago? Maybe. Before Chaz, not after. Now? No way. I was just shocked, that's all. I had no idea if he felt the same *moment* as I did, and I still don't. But he did remember me."

"Why do you sound so proud of that?"

"I don't know. Maybe because I've been wondering ever since Marie mentioned his brother two years ago." She touched Danica's arm. "Come on, Danica. You know the feeling. You see a hot guy across the room, and he's looking at you; then he leaves, and you're left with only a mental image to play with and manipulate as much as your horny little mind desires."

"You're going to be the death of me."

"I doubt it. If anything, it will be that crazy wild sex you're having with your man."

Danica glared at her. "What?"

"I happened to pass by your room the other night, getting ice or something, I can't remember. Anyway, there were some loud moans coming from behind that door."

Danica felt her cheeks flush. She turned her back to Kaylie and crossed her arms, wishing she could shrivel up into a tiny ball and roll away.

"You don't have to be so embarrassed. Sex is good. It's

healthy. Besides, it's about time you had some fun."

Danica spun around. "But you heard us? I mean, really, did you hear us?"

Kaylie smiled. "No. But now I know you are having wild, crazy sex."

Danica groaned and covered her face.

"Are you really that repressed, sis? Come on. It's me you're talking to. I mean, Chaz and I have great sex. There's nothing I wouldn't do with him." She looked up at the lights. "To him. For him. Mm-mm."

"Kaylie!"

"It's sex, Danica, not drugs, for God's sake. You're telling me that there are do's and don'ts in your bedroom?"

Danica swallowed hard and remained silent.

Kaylie gasped. "Oh, no, sister sister. Come talk to Mama Kaylie." She put her arm around Danica as Danica shrank away.

Shut up. Shut up. Shut up.

"Listen, the way I see it, we've got one chance to have a little fun, and after tomorrow, we'll have one man to have that fun with. For the rest of our lives!"

"So?"

"So, you know. Spice it up. Have some fun. Role play. Get some toys. Do all the dirty things you read about in *Fifty Shades of Grey* and all the things the porny girls do in movies."

"You watch those?"

Kaylie shrugged. "Only sometimes. With Chaz."

Danica pulled away. "Well, I have no interest in watching porny girl movies."

"So get porny boy movies."

"You're sick."

"I'm liberated. I own my sexuality."

"Whatever."

"All I know is that you have a fine specimen of a man who is soon going to be your husband. He chose you out of all of the other women who you know paw at him all the time. He loves you. He desires you—and God knows he's always flirting with you, touching you, kissing you. I mean, it's like, *Get a room already!* The man oozes sensuality. And so do you."

Danica screwed up her face in protest. "I do not."

"Oh baby, yes, you do." She spun Danica around in the mirror.

"Look at yourself." She dug her fingers under Danica's mass of curls and clenched fistfuls of her hair, then pulled. "Your hair is the perfect, *Oh baby, yes, more*, hair." She released her hair and stood behind her, grinding her hips into her sister's behind. "Look at that ass. Perfect. And your hips." She splayed her hands on Danica's hips and pressed her breasts against her back, then moved her hands up toward Danica's breasts. "Oh baby, yes, more, more, touch me, lick me, fuck me."

Danica shook out of her sister's grasp. Embarrassed to admit that the idea of Blake seeing her that way turned her on.

Kaylie laughed. "Really, Dan? I say, go for it. Live out your every fantasy with that man."

"And what if he leaves me after I've done all those dirty things? He'll say I'm a tramp. He'll know I'm a slut. He'll—"

Kaylie's face stopped her cold. Her sister's jaw hung open. Kaylie pointed at her, then covered her mouth with her hand.

"What?"

"You're afraid, too. It's not just me. You. The ex-therapist. Little Miss Get Over It Already."

Danica lowered her eyes in shame.

"Oh, you poor girl." Kaylie's sweet tone drew Danica's eyes

to Kaylie's image in the mirror. She was shaking her head, her eyes filled with love and compassion. "That's the worst feeling in the world, isn't it? I hate it. I hate Dad."

"Kaylie, what are we gonna do?"

"I don't know about you, but I'm gonna get married to the man I love; then I'm gonna have crazy, wild, animalistic sex while Mom watches the kids."

Danica laughed through a groan. "What are you gonna do about Dad? I mean, you can't go your whole life hating him."

"Why not? It's worked well for me so far."

"Three reasons. Trevor. Lexi. Lacy."

"I do love Lacy. She's so quiet and so not me, but she's so frisky and funny in her own little demure way."

"Welcome to life with a little sister."

"Dan, I'd worry more about your sex life than my issues with Dad. If you're hung up on Blake leaving, how's your marriage ever going to work?" Kaylie asked.

How is *my marriage ever going to work if I'm hung up on the possibility of his leaving? How did Kaylie get so wise?*

Kaylie took Danica's hand and laid it on her own forearm. "Shall we? We have dresses to try on. You taught me well, Yoda."

Chapter Sixteen

The hostess led them to an enormous private room in the back of the restaurant, decked out in gold, pink, and white, the colors of the wedding. The long cherry table had a glorious floral centerpiece, and every chair boasted ringlets of the same colorful ribbons.

Danica hugged Blake's father again. "I'm so pleased that you were able to come. I know it was a really far trip."

Harry Carter looked just like the old movie star Clint Walker: thick and wide chested, with leathery skin from too much sun, thick hair that must have once been as dark as Blake's and was now more salt than pepper. His voice was as gravelly as Clint Eastwood's. Danica had instantly liked him when they'd met last year, and watching the way he looked at Blake, like he was the proudest father in the world, endeared him to Danica even more.

"I wouldn't have missed this for the world. He's a good man, Blake is."

"He sure is."

Kaylie walked in arm in arm with Weston, Chaz's older brother. He was every bit as handsome as Chaz, though he wore his thick, dirty-blond hair shorn close to his head, and his face had begun to show the effects of his high-stress life as a surgeon, with fine lines across his forehead and at the corners of his eyes.

"I still can't get over my baby brother getting married before me," Weston said.

"We'll find you a wife, Weston. Leave it to me," Kaylie assured him.

Great. Kaylie's matchmaking service. Danica turned to thank the hostess. On the wall behind them were life-size photographs of Kaylie and Chaz and Blake and Danica kissing, in various stages of laughter, and gazing into each other's eyes, obviously taken since they'd been at the resort.

"When did Treat do all of this?" Danica gaped, in awe of the vibrant, sharp images and the blatant elation that gleamed in their eyes.

"That's Treat for you. He never holds anything back," Blake answered, as he took in the photographs. "He and his brothers have always been competitive, but I guess Treat brings his best to everything in his life."

"Wow, that's just amazing!" Kaylie gushed.

"You look stunning," Abby, Chaz's younger sister, said to Kaylie. Abby was in her mid-twenties, like Lacy, but she had idolized everything about Kaylie since the day they'd met.

"Aw, you're too sweet," Kaylie said, pulling her into a hug.

"Oh my God! Look, Kaylie, that's you!" Marie said.

Kaylie raised her brows and opened her eyes wide. "Really? Is it?" she mocked.

Everyone laughed, except Chaz's mother, Elise. She scowled and surveyed the room in her prim, chenille suit. Her stiff white shirt covered her wrinkly neck like a religious collar.

"It's a little strange, having a rehearsal dinner without so much as a wedding rehearsal," Elise said with her chin tilted up, her eyes looking away, and a wave of her hand, pinky pointed at the ceiling, like she was part of the royal family.

Danica watched her mother swallow a retort, her eyes narrowing in a stalking-her-prey manner, reminding her of Kaylie on more than one occasion.

"It is kinda weird that you're not rehearsing anything. I mean, she's right. It is a rehearsal dinner," Astrid, Chaz's older sister, said innocently. Astrid was practical, and beautiful in an old-fashioned way, with straight blond hair and a slightly rounded, though not heavy, figure, and each time Danica had seen her, she'd been dressed primly, with neatly pressed lines and perfectly polished shoes. Even so, she didn't exude an ounce of privilege. She was a kind and warm woman.

Kaylie glared at Chaz, and Danica snickered silently as he shrugged, clearly unable to control tonight's outcome where his mother was concerned.

"Kaylie didn't want to rehearse the wedding, so we figured we'd make the best of the gathering and still celebrate the night before the wedding with a nice family dinner," Max said confidently, leaving no room for if, ands, or buts.

The rehearsal had been the only bone of contention between Danica and Kaylie. Kaylie felt that the wedding should be spontaneous. She didn't care if the kids froze as they walked down the aisle, or if the bridesmaids came down in the wrong order. She believed that whatever was going to happen, happened for a reason, while the ever-practical Danica had wanted to know what to expect. Danica had known the lack of a rehearsal would cause conflict with Kaylie's very traditional future mother-in-law, who already alluded to Kaylie having "trapped" her son. Danica secretly wondered if perhaps Kaylie refused the rehearsal to goad Elise, staking her claim to their life as husband and wife. Silently telling Elise to butt out. So Danica backed off, and the compromise they made had worked out well. Max created a full outline of every aspect of the wedding, which Danica had spent the previous two months memorizing.

Now, as everyone moved to find a seat, Danica's pulse raced again. She watched the teens settle in at the far end of the table. Chaz's family sat to Chaz's right and Sally, Nancy, and Max sat across from them, followed by Lacy and Madeline. Chaz and Kaylie sat with two high chairs in between them, and Danica sat on Kaylie's other side.

Her sister was nestled far enough away from the remaining chairs that being near her father shouldn't be an issue. Danica watched Blake's father pull the chair out at the head of the table for her mother; then he sat down beside Blake. Her father settled into the only seat left in the room, beside Madeline and to the immediate left of her mother.

Danica hoped her interpretation of what she'd witnessed between her mother and father earlier in the day had been misconstrued. She breathed a sigh of relief once everyone was seated and the meal was served.

"Dane didn't make it?" Lacy asked.

"He wasn't expected to come to the dinner," Blake explained. "He had a business meeting most of the afternoon and evening. He's still hoping to make it to the wedding, though. Treat may stop in at some point, but he's so busy, I wouldn't count on it."

Danica was pretty sure Blake didn't pick up on Lacy's disappointment in his answer, but she could not ignore the lackluster way that Lacy now picked at her food.

Chaz's mother looked at Chaz, though she was addressing

Blake. "What kind of family doesn't make it to a rehearsal dinner?"

"Mother," Chaz said sharply.

"That's okay," Blake said with a seemingly sincere smile. "Dane does a lot of international work and fundraising. He has to take his meetings and calls when his clients allow. He's a remarkable person, really, with the work he's doing."

Lacy listened with wide eyes and bated breath. "He's been on a humanitarian project in Belize, tagging sharks and raising money to help save them."

"Sharks?" Elise made a *harrumph* sound.

"Mom, did you know that Blake's cousin Treat, Dane's brother, owns this resort?" Astrid winked at Blake as she engaged her mother in a conversation about the elegance of the hotel.

Danica's father and Madeline had been murmuring quietly all night in between his conversations with her mother. Now Danica's father looked at her uncomfortably, like he had a mouth full of rocks that he couldn't quite spit out.

"Excuse me," her mother said as she stood. "I'm just going to run to the ladies' room."

Blake's father stood as she left the table, then settled back in beside Blake and went right back to their conversation about Blake's business.

Danica was beginning to see where Blake learned how to charm the ladies. Everything his father did was natural and sincere, just like Blake.

"Do you want me to go with you, Mom?" Danica offered.

"I think I can find it by myself. I'll just be a few minutes." Her mother hurried out before Danica could respond.

Jeff came around the table and took her seat while she was

gone, diving right into the conversation with Blake and his father. Weston joined the conversation from the other end of the table, and the group of them eventually moved to the middle of the room.

Lexi began to whine, and Trevor was not far behind. Kaylie and Chaz picked them up and tried unsuccessfully to soothe them.

"It's getting late. Maybe we should put them down," Chaz said.

Kaylie agreed, and Abby and Max were right behind them. Abby offered to help with the kids, which Danica knew was just an excuse to get closer to Kaylie, and Max offered to arrange for one of the staff to stay with the children for the evening, as suggested by Treat earlier in the day.

"Danica, do you mind if we go down to the beach for a while?" Michelle asked.

"You're a high school graduate now. Do you even have to ask? If your mom says it's okay, I don't mind at all," Danica answered.

Rusty had grown to be almost six feet tall, but remained lean and lanky. He'd matured a lot since his father had passed away, leaving behind the angry boy and coming into his own as a confident young man. Standing next to each other, Rusty and Chase looked and acted like brothers. They were half brothers by blood, and she remembered a time when Rusty wouldn't even acknowledge Chase's existence. Now he'd almost never leave him behind.

Chase swung an arm around Michelle's shoulder, and though she knew Michelle and Chase had been an item for months, she still thought she saw a twinkle of jealousy in Rusty's eye.

She watched the trio walk out of the restaurant and felt the stirrings of nostalgia tickling the recesses of her mind.

"It wasn't that long ago that you were that age," her father said.

She laughed. "Maybe not for you. To me it feels like a lifetime ago."

"If you'll excuse me," her father said. "I just want to make a phone call."

Astrid, Sally, and Madeline were chatting about how beautiful Nassau was, and Danica took the opportunity to pop outside for a second and get a breath of fresh air.

She crossed the hotel lobby on her way to the veranda, and a laugh caught her attention. She followed the familiar sound down a corridor and was about to round a corner when the laugh grew louder, followed by a male voice that stopped her cold. *Dad? Mom?*

She stood with her back against the wall and peeked around the corner. Her mother and father stood much too close for Danica's comfort, and why was she looking at him that way? Laughter filled the corridor. Her mother touched her father's chest in a flirty manner. *Mom!* Danica popped back around the corner and covered her mouth to hold in her surprise.

"What are you—"

"Shh!" Danica took Lacy by the hand and dragged her out to the veranda.

"What were you doing?" Lacy asked with a laugh.

"Nothing." *What the hell is going on?*

"That's not the look of nothing." Lacy crossed her arms and tapped her foot.

Danica watched the lobby like a hawk.

Why are they still there? Together? Laughing?

"Danica, if you don't tell me, I'll go take a peek myself."

"No, you won't." Danica dragged her to the side of the veranda, out of the line of sight from the lobby.

"We have to go back inside." Danica paced, chewing on the image of her mother flirting with the man who had ruined several years of her life.

"Okay, let's go." Lacy headed for the lobby. "I'm going to take a peek—"

Danica didn't realize she'd said it aloud. She caught up to Lacy and grabbed her arm. "My mother and your father are…talking."

"Talking?"

"Talking."

Lacy shrugged. "So?"

Danica knew better than to raise a red flag to anyone until she knew what was really going on. Maybe they were just happy to see each other. Maybe her mother was just pretending to be nice. *She was flirting. I know flirting when I see it. Damn it, Mom.*

"Oh, there's my mom." Lacy crossed the lobby and called out, "Mom."

Danica's eyes jetted between Madeline and the hallway where her mother and father were. She hurried over and took Madeline's arm, taking quick glimpses behind her. "Let's talk a bit," she said nervously.

"Okay, that would be nice." Madeline smiled.

"I'll come along," Lacy said, narrowing her eyes at Danica.

"Um, so, what are you wearing to the wedding tomorrow?" *Now what?* She had to place herself so she could watch the lobby but Madeline couldn't. She guided them to a little conversation pit with a sofa that faced away from the lobby and two comfortable wing chairs facing the sofa. *Perfect.*

"I hope you don't mind that I'm wearing blue. I know your colors are silver and pink, but I didn't want to step on Helen's toes, and I wanted to go with a safe choice, so it was either blue or gray, and gray seemed too dingy." Madeline sat on the sofa. "Oh, this is nice."

"Lacy, why don't you sit next to her?"

Lacy sat in a wing chair with a smirk on her lips. "I'm fine here. This way I can look at my beautiful mother."

Great. Lacy sees right through my ruse.

"What a lovely dinner that was, Danica. How are you and Kaylie holding up? We haven't had much time to talk. Are you nervous? Having cold feet at all?"

Why did Madeline have to be so damned nice? It made Danica want to protect her from whatever was going on between her mother and father.

Danica shifted her eyes between Madeline and the corridor. "Cold feet? No, nothing like that. We're doing great. The dresses are here and they fit. Our families are here. Everything should be just fine."

Her mother entered the lobby and looked around nervously, then quickly walked back into the restaurant. Danica glanced at Lacy, who was also watching the corridor. In the next second, her father followed the same guilty track.

Lacy's hands clenched the arms of the chair.

"We should get back inside." Danica stood and headed to the restaurant with Madeline and Lacy in tow.

Danica spent the rest of the evening with one eye on her parents.

"You okay, babe?" Blake asked.

"Fine, why?" *This is not my problem.* She needed to stay out of whatever was going on and focus on the wedding.

"You seem distracted. You're not having second thoughts, are you?" He nuzzled against her neck.

"Get a room," Max said as she and Abby returned.

"Sounds good to me," Blake teased.

"Did the kids go down okay?" Danica saw her mother take a quick glance at her father. Her stomach was tied in such tight knots that she thought she might be sick.

"Yeah, fine. Lexi is such a little bossy girl," Abby said. "Cute as a button, but no man will have a chance with her around."

"She's Kaylie, version two." Danica flashed a smile, then pretended to cough as she turned to look at her parents again. Her father was looking right at her, and she was compelled to go speak to him. "Is Kaylie coming down?"

"She said she might, at least to touch base," Max answered.

"I'm gonna talk to my dad for a minute." *Don't say anything. I didn't see anything.* "Hi, Dad."

"Danica."

"You look like you wanted to say something to me."

He put his hands in his pockets, then took them out and nervously rubbed them together.

"Dad?" *Please don't tell me that you and Mom are cheating on Madeline, because I'd have to die. Right here and now before I ever have a chance to marry Blake.*

He shoved his hands in his pockets again and took a deep breath, then lifted his chin. "Danica, I know it's been a very long time since we've spent any time together."

"We sent letters and we talked on the phone." *I'm so lame.*

"Yes, you're right. We did. But we haven't. Well, I don't really know you and Kaylie very well anymore."

The truth hurt. The knot in her stomach tightened a notch.

"And, well, ever since you girls were little, I dreamed about giving you away at your weddings."

Oh my God. How could I not have anticipated this? There had never been a question in their minds about walking down the aisle. Neither Danica nor Kaylie had brought up their father giving them away. One afternoon when their mother was playing with the babies, their mother had asked them who was walking them down the aisle, and Danica remembered looking at Kaylie and thinking that if anyone had the right to give them away, it was their mother. She'd taken Kaylie into the nursery and asked her how she felt. Kaylie said she preferred her mother, but felt even more strongly that she and Danica walk down the aisle together. The choice was an easy one. Until now.

"Dad."

Kaylie sailed into the restaurant and grabbed Danica by the arm. "Excuse us," she said as she dragged her across the room.

"What? Is one of the twins sick?"

"No." Kaylie shook her head, then threw her hands up in the air. "We can't sleep in our rooms tonight."

"What? Why?"

"The grooms aren't supposed to see the brides on their wedding day until the ceremony!"

"Do you really believe in that?" Danica needed a change of rooms like she needed a hole in her head.

"Danica, turn around."

She turned and faced their guests.

"What do you see?"

Danica scanned the room. "Mom, Dad, Blake—"

"Not who! What?"

"I don't know. People talking."

"God, Danica. Broken marriages—everyone in here is broken in some way. Chaz's father cheated on his mother. Granted she's a bitch, but still. Dad cheated on Mom."

Mom and Dad are cheating on Madeline.

"Don't you see it? We can't take any chances. We need a plan. Where's Max?" Kaylie looked around the room. "There she is. Thank God." She headed for the table, where Max sat next to Chaz's brother, Weston.

"The weather is supposed to be beautiful and the boat to the island will leave at one p.m. sharp." Treat's deep voice cast a positive spin on a room that felt to Danica like it was quickly spinning out of control.

The smiles on everyone's faces told her that she was the only one looking around with a skeptical eye. She cast a smile in Treat's direction, noticing how distinguished he looked in his dark suit and white shirt. He'd worn equally attractive attire earlier in the day, and she wondered if he always dressed that nicely.

"Fantastic," Blake said with a wide smile. "We'll be ready."

"It looks like I might be here to sail with you and stay for the ceremony after all, but I won't know until tomorrow morning." He looked around the room, then said, "I'll be right back." Treat headed toward the table.

Max stood as he approached, and Danica noticed for the first time that Max's hair was no longer in a ponytail, but billowing over her shoulders. She'd traded in her shorts and T-shirt for a cute little navy shift, and she was actually wearing makeup. How had she missed that? Wow, she looked cute!

Kaylie took a step away when Treat arrived. He touched Max's arm, and Danica moved in closer to eavesdrop on the conversation.

"Sure. We can arrange that," Treat said.

Arrange what? What's she doing now?

"Max, do you want to come with me? We can work out the details." He took Max's arm in a formal manner and guided her out of the restaurant.

"What was that all about?" Danica asked.

"I'm getting us a room. You and me. We're bunking together tonight."

"You're leaving Chaz with the babies the night before the wedding? And what about Blake?" She missed him already.

"Relax. Chaz said he'd switch rooms with Mom, and you know she won't care if she sleeps in the room with the kids. She adores them. But we have to get upstairs before midnight. I don't want to take a chance that Chaz sees me after midnight."

Kaylie had it all figured out, and Danica should have been thankful. Instead, her stomach hurt, and all she wanted to do was curl up in Blake's arms and fall asleep listening to the familiar rhythm of his heart beating against her.

She looked across the room, and her father was watching her with sad puppy eyes. She groaned.

"What's wrong?" Kaylie asked. "You don't have your period, do you? Because—"

"God, no. What is wrong with you? Dad wants to walk us down the aisle." She waited for the scream, the stomping foot, the angry stare that could melt ice.

"He does?" Kaylie's eyes grew wide, like she was surprised, but her voice softened, as if she were actually considering the possibility. "I don't know, Dan. I mean…"

Danica had to do a double take to make sure she really was talking to Kaylie. "I know…Let's not worry about it…" Her voice trailed off as she looked across the room again. Madeline and Elise were deep in conversation, with a glass of wine in their hands and smiles on their lips.

Her father was nowhere in sight.

Neither was her mother.

Where the hell is Lacy?

Chapter Seventeen

With the room situation sorted out, Kaylie was relaxed and ready for a good night's sleep. She lay on the bed reading, while Danica paced the room.

"What on earth is wrong with you?" Kaylie looked over the edge of her magazine at Danica.

"Oh, it can't be that I'm getting married tomorrow, could it?" She hated to lie to Kaylie, but what was she supposed to say? *I think Mom and Dad are sneaking around together?*

"Take an Ambien." Kaylie reached over to the nightstand and rifled through her makeup bag. "Here." She held out a prescription bottle.

"You're still taking those? I thought those were just to get you through that rough period you had when you were too high-strung to sleep."

"No, I'm not still taking them. I mean, yeah, I took one tonight so I would be fresh faced tomorrow, but I don't usually." She thrust her hand out. "You should too." She yawned. "You don't want to be all puffy eyed tomorrow, do you?"

Danica went back to trolling the floor. Puffy eyes were the least of her worries. She'd never answered her father about walking them down the aisle, and she wanted to tell Blake what she'd seen, but Kaylie had been in too big of a rush to get to the room before midnight. Blake would have calmed her down and said just the right thing to center her around what was important. What was important? *The wedding. Sleep. Mom and Dad. Shit.* She knew what she had to do.

"I'm gonna go down to the lobby and find a book or a magazine or something. I'll be right back."

"Take the key." Kaylie said. "I'll be asleep in ten minutes."

Danica pocketed the room key and headed down the hall to Lacy's room.

She knocked once. Twice. Three times.

Danica headed for the elevators in search of Lacy.

She tried to concentrate on the glow of the moon on the water to calm her nerves, but her mother's laugh ran through her mind as she headed out to the veranda, cursing beneath her breath. Danica wondered what she was doing, the night before her wedding, searching for the half sister she'd only just met and worried about her divorced parents making out behind her father's wife's back. She leaned on the railing and banged her head against the iron.

"You know, you could hurt yourself doing that."

Danica came to attention. "Treat. Hey, sorry. I lost my mind for a minute."

"Most people do before they get married."

"You're serious." She watched him lift a glass of liquor to his mouth and wondered how he'd made it to his late thirties without being nailed down by a woman. He was handsome, incredibly wealthy, and as kind as the day was long. "Have you ever been married?" she asked.

He shook his head. "Not yet."

"Why?" She remembered what Blake had said about the brothers being players, and she was suddenly embarrassed.

"Not because of the reasons Blake may have told you." His smile didn't reach his eyes, which were still dead serious.

"How could you know what Blake said?"

"Because we Braden boys are known for being ladies' men. Just about all of us. Except my father, that is."

She looked out over the water, thinking about his admission. As a therapist, she'd have asked him why he'd chose that lifestyle, what appealed to him about it. That was the old Danica. As a woman, she wanted to know this: "Is it really that great, sleeping with different women all the time?"

For a long time, he said nothing. He looked out over the water, sipping his drink and seemingly not doing much else. Just when Danica was about to apologize for asking, he said, "It has its moments of pleasure, but that's not why I'm not married."

Danica heard her mother laugh and she stopped breathing, listening intently for where they were. The wind carried noises from all around, and she looked frantically from side to side.

Treat leaned down next to her and pointed to a palm tree to her right. Below the tree stood her mother and father. Together. Alone.

Treat tapped her shoulder and pointed across the lawn to a table beneath another palm tree. If he hadn't pointed it out, Danica wouldn't have noticed it. Lacy stood beside the table watching her father; her arms hung limply by her sides.

"Oh no."

Treat turned his back to the railing and finished his drink.

"How did you know I was looking for them?"

"I saw you earlier this evening in the lobby, and I put two and two together. Lacy came out about an hour ago and looked like she was searching for something." He shrugged. "I just wanted to be sure everyone was okay. Blake's family. You're going to be family, too, and if there's one thing the Bradens do, it's look out for family." He shrugged again, like that should explain his innate ability to see when things were amiss.

"I should go to Lacy." Danica watched Lacy, still as a statue. "You didn't see Madeline, my father's wife, did you?"

He pointed up toward the hotel rooms above them.

"Oh, that can't be good." *Dad left Madeline alone to be with Mom?*

"If you need anything, just let me know. I'm going to head in and do a bit of paperwork." Treat took a step forward, then turned back around. "One question. Max? Is she…spoken for?"

Danica smiled. "No, she's not. But I'm not sure she's one for one-night stands."

He nodded. "Understood. Good night, Danica."

Danica caught up to Lacy in her spot under the tree. "Hey," she said softly.

"Hey." Lacy kept her eyes trained on her father and Danica's mother. "This is what you were looking at before. Them, right?"

She desperately wanted to lie to her, to tell her anything but the truth. She didn't want to hurt sweet Lacy, but she wouldn't lie to cover her father's tracks.

"Yes."

Lacy nodded. "I've been watching them for a long time. I can see how they must have been together. They're so easy with each other. I think I'd be angry, or at least, if I were your mom, I'd be angry at my mom, even if your mom did steal him away first."

"I'm not sure what that means, *steal him away first*."

Lacy lowered herself into a chair. "My mom was married to him. Only for a year or so, when they were in high school."

"What? No way. I'd have known that." *Married?*

"Would you?" Lacy asked. "My mom was pregnant. They married. She lost the baby. Your dad—*our* dad—and your mother got together. End of story. Or so I thought."

Danica's lungs stopped functioning. She was going to pass out. Throw up. Both. *Oh God.* She sank into the empty chair, feeling as though shards of glass had shattered her heart.

"I guess paybacks really are hell," Lacy said as she tore her damp eyes from their parents and looked stoically at Danica.

Chapter Eighteen

Danica paced the floor of the women's bathroom, where she'd escaped with Lacy on her heels. Her pulse raced, her head hurt, her stomach ached. "How can this be? This is wrong on so many levels."

Lacy leaned silently against the sink with a stricken look on her face.

"Why didn't your mom say something when we had dinner that first night? She took all of the blame." None of this made any sense. Danica couldn't even think straight.

"Who knows? I can't think of any reason she'd want to protect your mother, but…" Lacy shrugged.

Maybe she wasn't protecting Mom. Maybe she was protecting me and Kaylie. Kaylie. Oh God. "What am I gonna tell Kaylie? How can I get married with this shit going on?"

"It's not your life."

Danica looked at her incredulously.

"I mean, it's their lives they're messing up. We're adults. We're not little kids anymore." Lacy shrugged. Her eyes were cold, her face, a blank slate.

Lacy was so matter-of-fact about the situation that Danica had to wonder if her father had done this other times, with other women. *My God, what has Madeline been through?*

"Do you think it is what we think it is? I mean, it could be innocent."

Lacy shrugged. "How would I know?"

"How can you be so blasé about this?"

"Blasé? Am I blasé?" Lacy furrowed her brow. Anger or hurt—Danica couldn't tell which—filled her eyes as her chest lifted and fell with each breath, each one a little harder than the one before. "Look at my life, Danica. I grew up knowing you guys were out there, and every breath I took brought with it a wonder. *Will they hate me? Will they ever accept me?*" Tears filled her eyes. "My mother was his mistress. Do you know how embarrassing that is? Do you have the tiniest idea what that feels like? What it feels like when kids at school ask you why your father isn't at Father-Daughter Day? Why your father doesn't pick you up at birthday parties or why you talk about imaginary sisters that no one believes exist?"

"Lacy, I had—"

Lacy pushed away from the sink and wiped her tears. "You had no idea. No shit. You think I blame you? I don't. And I don't blame Kaylie either. I blame my friggin' mother and my lame-ass father, who put us all in this situation. And your mother?"

Danica felt the protective armor slipping into place.

"Your mother? How can anyone blame her? Was she the first one who stole him away, or was my mother the first one in high school, or middle school? God, how can anyone know what to believe? It's all shit. Shit, shit, shit." She sank to the floor and sobbed.

There were no words to fix what she was feeling. Danica couldn't therapy this hurt away in the bathroom of the hotel, mere hours before her wedding. This would take years, ages of therapy. Lacy was just as broken as all of them were. And here Danica thought they had the perfect little family, the ideal father-daughter relationship.

She sank to the floor beside Lacy and took her hand. Lacy's head met her shoulder, and together they sat, tears streaming down their cheeks, hands interlaced. Two sisters, two broken hearts, and a world of hurt lying just outside the bathroom door.

Chapter Nineteen

Danica paced the hotel room she shared with Kaylie. Her heart told her that Kaylie needed to know what was possibly, maybe, going on. But her head told her not to thrust that stress on her sister. It was their wedding day. Why ruin it for her? *Because I can't get married.* How can I get married knowing how messed up everyone is?

A knock at the door pulled her from the turmoil in her head. Danica hadn't slept all night, and as she passed the mirror on the way to the door, she paused. Her eyes were puffy and bloodshot. Even her face looked like it was retaining water. Forget the way her shoulders drooped, because there was no way she could find the energy to stand up straight, much less walk down the aisle.

It was six o'clock in the morning. It had to be Lacy. Who else would be up at that ungodly hour? She pulled the door open.

"Good morning!" Scarlet smiled brightly.

"Scarlet? Oh no. Has something gone wrong? It's so early."

"Oh no, quite the opposite. Mr. Braden has scheduled a spa treatment for the brides this morning."

"Spa treatment?" *I'm too tired to even think of a spa treat-*

ment. This can't be happening.

"Yes." The word came out as on long syllable, a purr of sweetness. Scarlet walked into the room, as if barging in on guests at six o'clock in the morning was something she did every day. "I suggest that we wake Miss Kaylie to join us. Mr. Braden was very specific about treating the brides like queens. He's got the entire spa staff ready and waiting."

Danica was so tired that she couldn't think straight.

"Really? Thank you," was all she could manage.

The idea of being pampered didn't appeal to her at all. All she really wanted to do was burst into her mother's room and ask if what Lacy said was true. Then she wanted to go to her father's room and punch him in the nose. And then…then…she didn't even know what she wanted to do next, but she wanted to do something. Run as fast as she could, as far as she was able. Yes, running would be good. *Blake. Oh, Blake.* She didn't even want to be in his arms at that moment. He couldn't fix this hurt. He couldn't make it all disappear or convince her that the last twenty-four hours hadn't really happened.

But he can soothe me.

He can help heal me.

He can hold me.

He can—

"A spa treatment? Incredible! I love Treat already!" Kaylie popped out of bed like she'd been up for hours.

"Were you only pretending to be asleep, or did the words *spa treatment* filter through your rem state and spur your energy?"

Kaylie waved a dismissive hand at Danica. "Wow, Danica, you look like shit," she said on her way to the bathroom.

Everything about the spa was sumptuous. From the glass doors with gold filament to the black marble floors and the staff of six of the most gorgeous people Danica had ever seen, dressed in perfectly pressed white and gold outfits—the women in silk dresses that ended just above the knees, the men in white linen slacks and shirts. *Where does he hire from? Victoria's Secret and GQ?*

"I will leave you in the capable hands of Olivia and Kaleb." Scarlet unfolded her hands as if she were Vanna White presenting a gift.

"Thank you, Scarlet. This is simply amazing." Kaylie looked around with stars in her eyes.

"Thank you. I'd like to thank Treat in person." *When I'm human again.* Danica couldn't even imagine when that might be.

"Yes. He's leaving sometime today, but I will advise him of your wish to see him."

The perfectly coiffed blond bun on Olivia's head must have taken an hour to create, and not a hair was out of place on Kaleb's gorgeous head, either. His skin was the color of honey, his eyes as dark as the night sky. Their pearly whites gleamed through smiles that hadn't changed since Danica and Kaylie arrived, which Danica found a bit unsettling. *Stepford Wives* came to mind, then *I, Robot.* Exhaustion had sucked her brain cells dry, and it took all of her energy not to continue running through movies and books that might fit the situation. *It's Complicated* starring Alec Baldwin and Meryl Streep. *Stop. Stop.*

Stop!

"Shall we get you changed?" Olivia had one arm around Kaylie and one around Danica, though she barely touched their backs.

"Isn't this amazing?" Kaylie gushed. "What are we having done?"

Kaleb stood silently by, his hands still neatly folded in front of him as they walked past. What on earth was he even there for? His looks? Well, it worked. Danica's mind had officially been off her troubles for the past five minutes. And now, with the eye candy gone, she was right back where she'd started. Only now Kaylie was talking up a storm and she was being told to undress. Everything. Take it all off. *We don't want to get our lotions and creams on your delicates.* Danica groaned as she pulled off her clothes and wrapped the thick, insanely soft white robe around herself and tied the belt.

Couldn't she just lie down on the pretty little white settee in her private, ample dressing area and close her eyes? Forget the whole night before and maybe sleep through the day and wake up after everyone had gone home?

"Are you coming?" Kaylie called from beyond the dressing room door.

Kaylie's smile was too bright and too cheerful for Danica's thumping head. She looked like she'd already been pampered. Her hair was sexily mussed and her skin tan and smooth without the unsavory sights having sucked the life out of them from the night before, like Danica's.

Despite her resolve to pretend that all was well, despite the smile Danica forced for Kaylie's sake, an exhausted sigh escaped her lips.

"What on earth is wrong with you? I told you to take the

Ambien last night."

"This way, ladies." Kaleb's voice was every bit as scrumptious as his looks. "We'll be soothing our way from the top down today." He looked from one woman to the other. "I promise you, you'll never feel better than when you leave our hands." His eyes lingered on Kaylie, whose eyes were so round she looked like a kid in a candy store.

I bet.

"And don't worry," he added, turning toward Danica, "there are no blemishes we cannot take care of."

Blemishes! It's fatigue, you evil handsome man.

Danica lay on a cushioned table, strong hands rubbing, kneading, caressing, and generally making love to, her face. Her skin stretched and pulled in ways she'd never even tried to achieve. The tension in her jaw and beneath her eyes magically dissipated. She could lie there all day. Yes, that was a good plan. Soothing music drifted around her in the room she shared with Kaylie, who lay on the table next to hers.

"This is too delicious," Kaylie moaned.

The thought of talking was too much. Danica lay silent, hoping she'd fade into sleep.

"I can't believe Treat did this for us. I wonder if Chaz and Blake knew. What about Mom? Oh my God, Camille and the girls will be so jealous."

Please shut up. I just want to have this person massage me until I no longer exist.

"What did you do last night? At some point I woke up to

pee and you weren't there. Where were you?"

Sleep. Precious sleep.

"Danica!"

Danica startled. "Yeah?"

"Are you even listening to me?"

"I'm tired, sorry. I must have been getting a drink or a magazine or something when you got up."

"Huh." Kaylie paused.

Thank you.

"I didn't see any new magazines or any dirty cups or anything. Where did you go? Did you go to the café or restaurant and eat there?"

"Mm-hm."

"Which one?"

Oh my God! Stop! Why do you care?

"Dan, where did you go? Was anyone else up? I didn't see Michelle or the boys anywhere when we went upstairs. Did they have fun?"

Danica was about to lose her mind, when one of the masseurs cleared his throat and said, "The tension will fall away much easier if we're quiet. Respecting our minds and our body's need for peace." He made a *tsk* sound and waved his hand.

"Sorry," Kaylie said in a pouty voice.

Danica reminded herself to tip the man well as she drifted off to sleep.

An hour later they were being led down another wide hallway.

"Next, we'll move on to our body ceremony." Olivia spoke of the *body ceremony* like they understood what she meant.

Danica couldn't help but envision men bowing down to her and Kaylie as they donned some sort of Egyptian attire while standing on an altar.

Instead, they were led into another room with cushioned tables. A fireplace threw wavy shadows in the dim light, and some sort of chant played through wall-mounted speakers. Another beautiful Stepford Wife stood beside each table, their hands folded before them. Their updos left no hair out of place. They, too, boasted the somewhat eerie and still smile.

Danica lay on the table on her stomach with nothing but a towel covering her butt and her face settled in the comfortable face cradle. She watched the reflection of the fire dancing across the marble floor. She missed Blake. How could one night feel like a year? She wondered if he missed her, too, or if he was thinking about their wedding. *God, I'm getting married today. Married!* She reveled in the happiness that brought until she was unable to push the image of Lacy from the night before from her mind.

She couldn't stop thinking of Lacy's admission. She'd come apart right in front of Danica, and Danica hadn't known what to do. How could she have practiced therapy and helped so many people when she couldn't even help her sister? Half sister or not, Lacy's pain was Danica's pain. Maybe not as painful as it would have been if it were Kaylie falling apart on the bathroom floor, but it was awfully close.

Kaylie.

Tell her.

I'll ruin her wedding day.

I can't tell her.

Keep it to yourself, then.

Okay. I will.

There.

There.

Settled.

Danica closed her eyes and allowed herself to fade into the foggy darkness of her mind as the hands of one of the Stepford Wives traveled across her shoulders and down her back, easing the ache with every intense rub. One of them explained that after their massage, they'd be given a detoxing Mayan herbal wrap, which was just too complicated for Danica's mind to even process. Sleep, blissful sleep, swept her away.

Danica didn't know how much time had passed, but she groggily followed Kaylie and another *GQ* model to yet another room. A pungent, sweet and spicy smell intertwined with an aroma akin to hot oil. The combination alit her senses.

"Are you nervous?" Kaylie asked.

"Are you kidding? They can do whatever they want to me. My muscles are in heaven already, my head doesn't hurt as much, and we're not even done yet."

"I mean about the wedding," Kaylie snipped.

"Oh." *Yes. Scared shitless that I'll run from the altar, or that Mom and Dad will do something that will make the whole thing fall apart.* "Nah. It'll be wonderful."

"On the way through the lobby, I heard someone say something about a storm front heading this way."

"Not today. Treat said yesterday that the weather was expected to be beautiful."

"Right."

Danica looked at her sister then. Really looked at her, and what she saw surprised her. Kaylie didn't look any more relaxed than she had when they arrived. In fact, she looked a little worse. "Are you okay, Kay? You look a little peaked."

"I'm sure I do. I just keep thinking, maybe we should have had the rehearsal. What if the kids freak out? What if no one does what they're supposed to?"

"What happened to, *Whatever happens, happens?* I thought you were all about a spontaneous, memorable wedding." *And you have no idea how memorable this trip already is.* "Stop worrying," she assured her. "It's gonna be fine." *I hope.*

Kaylie let out a breath as Mr. GQ left the room and two more beautiful women explained that they were going to wrap them in heated sheets infused with Mayan herbs to detoxify their bodies and draw the toxins to their surface.

"Sounds lovely," Kaylie said.

What do they do after the toxins rise to the surface?

Their robes were removed and Danica moved to cover herself.

"How are they going to wrap you in Mayan-herb-infused sheets if you're all covered up?" Kaylie asked.

"I don't look like you," Danica hissed, glad the women were busy with the sheets.

"Who are you kidding? You are stunning. Just look at yourself."

"No, thank you." Danica reluctantly dropped her hands and was surprised when the women guided them into yet another room, where enormous sheets covered low tables that were triple the size of the ones in the previous room. She shivered, not from the cold, but from the embarrassment of standing naked in a room.

Kaylie must have noticed her discomfort. "You're so repressed, Danica."

"No, I'm not."

Kaylie rolled her eyes.

"Okay, maybe a little. I'm modest; that's all."

The Stepfords began exfoliating their skin, explaining what they were doing as they moved swiftly across every inch of their bodies. At first Danica braced herself against the abrasive touch, but then she began to enjoy the strange roughness against her skin. To her surprise—and embarrassment—her body responded in ways that it shouldn't have. Her nipples peaked, and as the woman worked her way up her inner thighs, she felt herself clench down below. *Please don't let her notice.* The woman moved from her upper thighs up her pelvis and along her hips. Danica glanced at Kaylie out of the corner of her eye. Her sister's eyes were closed, and her body didn't seem to be reacting in any way. Heat rushed up Danica's chest and cheeks. *What have I become?*

Ten embarrassingly painful minutes later, they were eased down to a lying position on the warm sheets, and the women began wrapping them in the infused sheets.

Even the touch of the warm sheets against her skin sent sensual shivers through Danica. *What on earth is wrong with me?* She clenched her jaw against the reactions and told herself to think about something bad. Painful. Ugly.

Spanking.

Oh God, no!

A punch in the gut.

Yes, that's good.

She hung on to that awful thought as they completed the process. The women left the room, and Danica listened for Kaylie. Why wasn't she going on and on about something nonsensical?

"Kay?"

"Shh."

"But I want to talk."

"Honor your body's need for relaxation," she parroted.

Danica thought about her mother and what she'd say to her when she saw her. It had to be a mistake. Surely her mother wasn't dumb enough to go back to a relationship that had hurt her so deeply. They were probably just waxing nostalgic. Yes, that must be it. Danica had to let this go. That was all there was to it. She was marrying Blake, and she couldn't let anything stand in her way, especially something that she wasn't sure really existed.

"Hey, Dan," Kaylie said.

"Yeah."

"We're gonna be okay, right? We're not gonna end up like Mom, are we?"

I sure hope not. "We're gonna be just fine. Don't you worry, Kaylie. You're gonna have your happily ever after and live a long, happy life with the man who adores you and your babies."

The words didn't taste as confident as they sounded.

Chapter Twenty

Rejuvenated and refreshed, with impeccable skin, hair, and nails, Danica and Kaylie crossed the lobby toward the elevator. Danica promised herself she'd leave the parental stress behind and *respect her mind's and body's need for peace.*

They ran into Max at the elevator.

"Max?" Danica noticed that she was wearing the same cute shift that she'd had on the evening before.

"Wow. You two look stunning."

"Thanks. So do you," Kaylie said, obviously oblivious to Max's rumpled outfit.

"Where are you coming from?" Danica asked with a coy smile.

"I, um." Max pointed toward the corridor that led to Treat's office. "I had to go over the details for today."

I bet you did.

The elevator doors opened, and Lacy stepped out, looking every bit as beat up as Danica had just hours earlier.

"You okay?" Danica whispered.

Lacy shrugged.

"Go to the spa. Tell them you're with me. You deserve it."

"I can't do that. I'm fine."

Danica took Lacy's hand and looked into her sad eyes. "Lacy, honey, you need to let this go." She walked her toward the spa. "They'll massage it out of you, and I promise you, you'll feel loads better."

Lacy looked at her watch.

"It's not even ten. You have plenty of time. Go. An hour or two will do wonders for you."

"Are you sure?"

"Yes, go." She lowered her voice. "Oh, and I didn't tell Kaylie. I think it's best if we keep this between us. They're adults. Let them figure out their own mess."

As Lacy headed in the direction of the spa, Danica headed for the elevators.

Treat suddenly appeared beside her. "How was the spa?"

Danica was beginning to think that he was some sort of wizard who could appear out of thin air. "Incredible. Extravagant. Sinfully delicious. Thank you." She smiled at him, but he wasn't looking at her. He was staring right at Max.

In the elevator, Danica noticed Max's leg bouncing nervously in her heels. She nibbled on her lower lip as Kaylie spouted on and on about their spa treatment. Danica tried to tune out Kaylie and figure out what Max was so nervous about. Could it be just the wedding? She was so organized, Danica knew the wedding would be perfectly coordinated.

Just when the elevator doors opened and Max looked as though she might sprint away, Kaylie stepped into the hallway and said, "Are you even going to tell us why you're wearing the same clothes as last night, or are we all going to pretend that Max didn't just have a tropical tryst?"

The blood drained from Max's face.

"Kaylie!" Danica moved toward Max. "It's okay, Max. She's just teasing."

"I didn't have a tryst." Between the folding and unfolding of her arms and the way Max looked away, she was looking more and more like a guilty teenager.

"Then what's with the walk-of-shame clothes?" Kaylie teased.

"Okay, so I was out all night, but I didn't…you know," Max admitted.

They started down the hall.

"Well, why the hell not?" Kaylie asked.

Max stopped walking.

Kaylie turned around. "What?"

"That's private, don't you think?" Danica chided Kaylie. *Treat. She had to be with Treat. How could she have resisted him?*

"Please don't say anything to Chaz. I like to keep my personal and professional life separate."

"Don't worry," Danica assured her. "Kaylie and I won't say a word."

Kaylie rolled her eyes. "Max. Max! This is me you're talking to. Kaylie! I won't tell Chaz, but Danica and I are getting married. Taken off the market for good. All we'll have are stories from our single girlfriends to live vicariously through. Come on. Share a little tiny bit?"

Max's cheeks turned an even deeper shade of red. "Well."

"You don't have to do this," Danica said.

"It's okay. It's not like I'll ever see him again."

Oh no! Treat? I'll kill him. I told him you weren't a one-night-

stand girl!

"Late yesterday afternoon I took a walk down by the beach and I met this guy. I guess he teaches snorkeling here."

Dane?

"Anyway," Max continued, "Justin asked me to go out for a drink, so I met him after the rehearsal dinner and we had a few drinks."

"All night?" Kaylie asked with an arched brow.

"No. After drinks we went for a walk."

"Okay, now we're getting to the good stuff." Kaylie rubbed her hands together.

"Not that kind of good stuff," Max said. "We walked and talked, and then we just sat and watched the water. That's it, until the sun came up."

"And?" Kaylie pushed.

"And then we went to a little café down the road and had breakfast. We walked and talked some more, and…" She shrugged.

"That's it?" Disappointment weighed down Kaylie's words.

"That sounds like a perfect romantic evening," Danica said, hugging Max.

"It was. He was kind and easy to talk to. I really enjoyed it." Max looked away as she spoke, as if she didn't quite believe that she enjoyed it.

"Then why won't you see him again? Are you a glutton for punishment?" Kaylie didn't notice the back-off glare Danica cast in her direction.

Max shrugged. She fidgeted with her hands, and her eyes filled with sadness. "I just…I'm not that into him…Oh, never mind. I'm just tired."

If you were with Justin, why was Treat leering at you? "You know what I think? Enjoy it while you're here. Don't overthink what might or might not be, and see where you are when you leave tomorrow."

"Perfect advice," Kaylie said. "Leave the door wide open for a good romp."

Before opening her hotel room door, Max said, "I almost forgot to tell you. Chaz and Blake will meet you at the island. Chaz said they can't ride over with you because Kaylie insisted that you guys not see each other before the actual ceremony."

"I can't believe he remembered," Kaylie said.

"The man adores you. What can I say? Oh, and your mom has the kids, and Camille and the rest of your entourage said they'll meet you in your room at eleven thirty." Max stepped into her room and Kaylie and Danica continued toward theirs.

"Look at her go. She's here a few hours and hooks up with one of the hottest guys at the resort. Good for her." Kaylie fiddled with her keys.

Danica was so much more relaxed than she'd been earlier. As the memory of their parents under the tree floated into her mind, she was able to force it away. Today was their day, and she wasn't going to let anyone ruin it. Including herself.

Chapter Twenty-One

The spa had done wonders for Lacy, who was helping Kaylie into her wedding dress while Camille took photographs and Chelsea and Marie assisted Danica with her bridal gown. Lacy's hair was shiny, each curl in place, and while her skin had looked tired that morning, it was now lustrous and revived. Each of the girls wore a gold strapless bridesmaid gown that shimmered against the light and accentuated their slim figures. Danica, Blake, Chaz, and Kaylie had given them each a pair of pearl earrings to commemorate the day and to thank them for the generosity of their time and energy.

The girls chatted about how beautiful Kaylie looked in her sleek sleeveless satin gown, which matched the style of the bridesmaids' except for the length. Her straight hair framed her face, and Danica thought she'd never seen Kaylie look so beautiful.

Chelsea zipped Danica's dress and said, "Voilà!"

There was a collective gasp in the room.

"What?" Danica frantically looked down at her gown, expecting to see a big stain or tear, something to cause such a reaction.

"Danica," Kaylie said in a breathy voice, "you are the most

beautiful bride I have ever seen."

Danica turned to look in the mirror as Chelsea and Marie came up behind her, gazing over her shoulder.

"Without a doubt," Marie said.

"Gorgeous," Camille agreed.

While Kaylie's dress hugged her body, sweeping into a glamorous flare just below her knees, Danica wore an elegant David Tutera strapless gown with a basque waistline. It was made of reembroidered lace and three-dimensional organza, and it flared into a structured accordion pleated skirt with a chapel-length train. The hairdressers had lifted the sides of her hair and secured it with sequined combs, leaving tendrils of curls dangling sexily to her chin. She touched the slim waist she saw in the mirror, ran her fingers gently up her neck. She could hardly believe that the gorgeous woman looking back at her was, in fact, her. She touched her cheek, her flat stomach, the pleats in the skirt. Danica was mesmerized by her own image, her heart fluttering in her chest. *I am a beautiful bride.*

Someone answered a knock at the door, and a minute later, her mother walked in. Helen covered her mouth in awe. Tears welled and fell without warning. "Danica," she whispered. Then she turned to Kaylie. "Oh my goodness. You're positively beautiful." She turned back to Danica, whose face had heated and flushed. "Both of you."

Kaylie broke the trance of the gowns. "Mom? Where are Trev and Lexi?"

"Oh, they're with Michelle and the others."

"Did they eat? Are they ready?"

"Yes, Kaylie. Bathed, fed, dressed, and being perfect little angels. I just had to see my two beautiful girls."

"Thank you, Mom." Danica hugged and kissed her mother,

then wiped away the light red lipstick print she'd left on her cheek. "Did you see Blake and Chaz?"

"Oh yes," she said. "They're nervous as the day is long, but ready. And *so* handsome."

"When are they going over? When can we go downstairs?" Kaylie asked.

"You girls are going to go first. They said they wanted you to be prepared and all that. So, are you almost ready?"

"Yes," Max said. She picked up her day planner and began leafing through it.

"Max, look at you. I don't think I've ever seen you look so beautiful."

Danica heard the sincerity in her mother's voice and took in the figure-hugging gold dress and Max's long, lean legs. Her hair, like the evening before, billowed around her shoulders. The dark of her hair and the shimmer of her dress highlighted her hazel eyes.

"She's right, Max. You are gorgeous." Danica's eyes swept the room. "Good Lord, look around. This room has the hottest women in the entire hotel."

That started a din of compliments as they headed toward the elevators, Camille, Marie, and Lacy holding the brides' trains off the floor.

"Mom, do you need to go down and tell them we're coming? We don't want them to see us," Kaylie said.

"They're waiting in the restaurant. Don't worry. They have strict orders not to enter the lobby."

Suddenly the image of her mother and father under the palm tree rushed back at Danica, almost knocking her off her feet. Panic rose in her chest. "Wait! I have to go to my room for a minute." Danica grabbed her purse from Max and ran down the hall. Her train pulled from the girls' hands and bounced along behind her.

"Danica!" Kaylie yelled.

Danica opened the door to her and Blake's room and yanked her train inside, then slammed the door, leaning against it. Her heart thundered in her chest. She breathed fast and hard as she stumbled to the bed, telling herself to calm down.

She picked up the pillow and brought it to her nose, inhaling deeply. The smell of Blake filled her senses. She lowered it to her lap and ran her fingers over the pillow. *I love you so much.*

She didn't know why she'd run away. Shutting herself in the room wouldn't solve anything. What the hell was she thinking? She was getting married, damn it, and all this other shit needed to go away.

Someone knocked on the door.

"Be right out. I just need a minute," Danica called.

"It's me."

Lacy.

Danica stared at the door, picturing Lacy crying beside her in the ladies' room, feeling her fingertips in her own.

"Danica? Can I come in?"

Danica crossed the room and, with a shaking hand, opened the door for the only other person in the world who knew what was racing around inside her and shattering her heart.

Lacy came into the room and closed the door. They stood facing each other.

Lacy tried to force a smile, but only the right side of her mouth lifted.

Danica nodded, understanding Lacy's failure to feign a smile, which mirrored Danica's inability to figure out how to handle the worry, fear, and sadness of the thoughts that secretly led them through the day.

"It's okay," Lacy said.

"Yeah. I know."

"We're not them. Blake's not him." Lacy reached for Danica's hand.

Danica turned her face away so Lacy wouldn't see the dampness in her eyes. She spotted a light blue envelope on the counter in the bathroom. She dropped Lacy's hand and retrieved the envelope, recognizing Blake's handwriting in her name on the front. Danica ran her finger under the seal and withdrew a card. On the front was a picture of a dark-haired couple embracing, set against the backdrop of winter. They both wore jeans, and the woman had on red boots and a red hat. The man's back was arched with the weight of the woman, and her legs kicked happily off the ground. Blake had written "You" and drawn an arrow to the woman and "Me" with an arrow pointing toward the man. She smiled as she opened the card and read Blake's handwritten note.

My beautiful Danica,

The second I saw you in the café, everything in my life changed. Oxygen wasn't enough, food tasted bad, my heart felt empty, and each breath no longer felt complete. The night we kissed for the very first time, my lungs began to function, and my heart realized what it had been missing. When we first made love, you became my only lover and my best friend. You became my oxygen and my breath itself. When we moved in together, I knew I'd never long for another person in my life the way I longed to be with you. Every second we're apart, every breath that's not comingled in our kisses, every minute we disagree, it's like all those moments are part of something bigger that draws me closer to you, making me want you as my wife, my lover, my friend. And today, if you do me the honor of loving me and being my wife, I can promise you that I'll be your oxygen when you need it. I'll be your strength when your heart hurts, and I'll be your friend, sharing in your laughter, your sadness, your joy, and your worry. I can't promise you that we'll never argue or that I'll never say the wrong thing, but I can promise you that I'll forever be the man that you hope I'll be. The man that you deserve.

Beautiful Danica Joy Snow, don't let the worries of others keep us from having what we both want and deserve. I'm not him. You're not her. We're not them.

Join me in making us.

I love you with every piece of my soul.

To the island—
Blake

Danica wiped her tears and held the letter against her heart. Never before had she felt so cherished. She ached from the comfort of his words and from the fear that if she allowed her parents' nightmare of a divorce to take over her mind, she might run away from the one man she adored.

"Are you okay?" Lacy asked.

Danica had forgotten she was there. She tucked the letter back into the envelope and set it on the counter. She used a tissue to dab the wetness from her eyes, then turned to Lacy with a lump blocking her words. She did the only thing her mind and body could agree on. She reached for Lacy's hand.

Chapter Twenty-Two

The elevator doors opened and Max stepped off. "Wait here while I make sure the guys aren't in the lobby."

"They wouldn't dare," Helen said.

Danica was still thinking about the card. Blake had swept her off her feet again. He was her knight on the white horse, except he had arrived in a little blue envelope. She looked at her mother, smiling behind Kaylie, positively glowing, and she wondered if her father had ever made the same promises to her. Had he written her a letter? Had he said such intimate, loving things to her?

She looked at Lacy and thought of Madeline. Her stomach clenched, and she knew she should push the painful thoughts from her mind like she would a rabid animal from her leg, but she was powerless against them. Had her father spent those years when he was hiding his second family telling Madeline the same things he told her mother? The same promises in the dark? Did he sneak away from Madeline and Lacy to call her mother? Was he even there when Lacy was born?

She dropped her eyes, trying her damnedest to keep the hateful thoughts away, but images and memories swirled like a hurricane in her mind.

Her mother and father beneath the palm tree.

Lacy standing alone in the dark, watching them.

Her mother's shattered voice on the phone. *Daddy and I have separated.*

The girls' voices seemed far away.

Kaylie's anger at her mother for those painful years after the separation and subsequent divorce filled her ears like a balloon. *She's weak. She's pathetic. She should have left.*

Danica reached for the wall to brace herself against her failing legs.

She pictured Blake's face looking down at her while they made love, his eyes never leaving hers. Love so thick between them she could taste it in the air.

Had her father looked at her mother that way?

Had her mother believed him?

Blake was a player.

Was she missing something? Was it all a farce? Did she have blinders on?

She gasped a breath.

No. No, that's not right.

Her head spun in circles.

The elevator was moving beneath her feet. She heard voices calling her name. She clawed at the wall, but she was falling. Falling. Falling. Into the darkness, until everything fell away.

Chapter Twenty-Three

The harsh smell of ammonia shocked Danica's brain into submission. Her eyes fluttered open, but the lights were too bright, and they slammed closed once again. *Just let me sleep.*

"Danica? Babe? Open your eyes, baby. It's me. Open your eyes."

Blake's voice hovered somewhere above her. She reached for him, but her arms were too heavy. Her arms weren't moving, were they? Sleep. She needed to sleep.

"Danica?"

Who is that? Where's Blake?

"Danica?"

A man's voice. *Where am I?* She needed Blake. *Blake?* She opened her eyes, blinking away the haze and the heaviness that threatened to close them again.

Blake.

There he was, right above her. His beautiful green eyes were looking right at her. *He looks so sad.* She wanted to touch his face. She couldn't move her hand. This wasn't real. She must be dreaming. Her eyes fluttered closed again.

"Danica!"

There's that voice again. Who the hell is that? Leave me alone.

Someone squeezed her hand. She felt it. She wasn't sleeping. *What is wrong with me?* She opened her eyes again and blinked. *Stay awake!*

"That's my girl."

Blake? Where are you? His head came into view. *There. Right there. There you are.*

Blake's head moved out of view and someone else's came into focus. *Chaz? No, that's not Chaz.*

"Danica? It's Weston. Dr. Crew, Chaz's brother."

Weston. Weston? Oh, right, Weston. She nodded. She was sure she did because a pain pinched in the back of her head.

"You passed out in the elevator and hit your head. Can you hear me?" he asked.

Danica blinked. *I need to speak.* She forced her mouth to work. "Yes."

"Okay, good."

She tried to push herself up.

He gently held her down. "Not just yet. You need to rest a bit. You hit your head pretty hard. Can you tell me where you are?"

Danica squinted, thinking. "Hotel," she said.

"Yes, good. Do you know what year it is?"

"Two thousand thirteen. My wedding day."

"I think she's okay," he said, obviously not to her.

Blake's face came into view again. He took her hand and held it against his cheek as he leaned over her. "Sweet girl. You scared me to death. You're okay?"

Danica nodded, wincing at the pain.

"Don't move. Just rest."

"Our wedding?" she managed.

"It's fine. The wedding can wait."

Everything came rushing back—her mother and father, Lacy, the elevator. "Where's Kaylie?"

"She's in Scarlet's office. She's fine. Don't worry. Lacy's with her."

Lacy? Lacy! Oh God, I have to get her away from Kaylie. "No, no. I have to get up. It's her wedding too." She blinked the last of the confusion away and pushed herself up, wincing again but pushing through it. The room spun and she closed her eyes until the sensation passed.

"You really need to rest for a bit," Weston said.

"I have plenty of time to rest. I need to talk to Kaylie. And Lacy," she added.

"I'll get them," Blake said.

Weston held her shoulders as she wobbled from side to side. She sat on what felt like a massage table, but it couldn't be. The office was lined with bookshelves, and there was a big wooden desk. Something was off. She was in an office with a massage table?

"Danica, no sudden movements. You might have a concussion. You really knocked your noggin pretty hard."

She looked around again. "Where are we?"

"Treat's office."

"With a massage table?" she asked. She touched her dress, gathered and bunched around her middle.

"I guess when you own the place, the masseuse comes to you." He smiled, warm and friendly.

"Danica?"

Kaylie.

There she was, her little Wedding Barbie sister. Kaylie took a step forward, and Lacy came into view. A push of adrenaline soared through Danica. She gripped the edges of the table, searching Kaylie's eyes for some sort of indication that Lacy had revealed their parents' infidelity.

Kaylie hugged her tight. "I was so worried. What happened? Why did you pass out?"

Because of all the crazy shit in our family. "Lacy didn't tell you?"

"Tell me what?" Kaylie turned to Lacy, who shook her head.

Thank goodness. "I…I'm just exhausted, that's all. I didn't sleep last night, and I guess sleeping during our spa visit wasn't enough. I'm so sorry."

"No, no, don't apologize," Kaylie said. "I was afraid something was really wrong. I was so scared."

Danica took her hand, feeling more like herself but with the added benefit of a raging headache. "Everything's fine, and I'm sorry I ruined…How long have I been out?"

"Not long—less than a minute or something like that," Kaylie answered.

"Wow, I'm sorry."

"It's okay. Maybe we should delay the wedding. Those reports of a storm are still coming in."

She remembered Blake's letter. "No. I'm doing this today. We're doing this today. I'm fine."

Weston stepped forward. "Danica, I don't think—"

"I'm fine, really. I have a killer headache, but other than that, I'm really fine. Can't you just give me Tylenol or something?"

"Yes, of course. Blake, can you watch her closely for the next few hours? As long as she's awake and functioning, not having areas of weakness or numbness, she should be okay," Weston said.

"It's our wedding night. I'll be sure to keep her up," Blake teased.

The door opened and her mother flew into the room. Danica's heart stalled.

"You're okay. Thank goodness. What happened? Are you pregnant?" her mother asked.

"What did I hear about pregnant?" Blake asked.

"I'm not pregnant. At least not that I know of. I'm on the pill. I'm sure it's not that, Mom. I'm just exhausted." Danica's eyes drifted from Blake to Lacy and held a silent plea for her to keep the parental issues out of the room.

"Since you've already seen me, can we go over on the boat together?" Danica managed a smile.

"You can bet I'm not leaving your side. But are you sure you're okay to go on a boat? All that movement might make you sick. I'm sure Treat can arrange to hold the ceremony here on the beach."

Blake held her hand so tight that it gave her strength. "No. This is Kaylie's dream, and we're gonna make it come true. I'll be fine. I just need a minute to pull myself together. My hair must be a mess."

"Not a hair out of place," Blake said. He touched her dress. "And your dress looks gorgeous."

"You're lying, but I love you for it."

A half hour later, the Tylenol had taken the edge off the headache, and Danica felt much better. They crossed the lobby again toward the entrance, a pack of formally dressed people all watching Danica like she was a porcelain doll.

"Something blue!" Chelsea yelled. She turned frantically to Camille. "Where are the garters? Did anyone bring them? Oh God, they'll have nothing blue!"

"The garters?" Max asked; then her eyes grew wide. "Oh! I know where they are! I'll go get them."

"Need me to come along?" Chelsea asked.

"No, they're just in Treat's office. I'll grab them." Max hurried toward his office.

"I completely forgot. Let's see," Kaylie said, looking down at her dress. "Something borrowed?" She held up her wrist and then grabbed Danica's and held it up, too. "Camille's bracelets. Check. Something new?"

"Wedding gowns!" Danica said, mimicking Chelsea's excitement. "And we look awesome, I might add."

"Prettiest brides around!" Kaylie said with a grin.

"Something old?" Chelsea asked.

They both lifted their gowns, showing the heels they'd owned for years.

Max came around the corner waving the garters above her head. "I've got them," she called out.

Danica caught sight of Treat heading down another corridor toward them. Dressed in another handsome suit, his white shirt contrasted sharply against his olive skin. His eyes scanned the group as he approached, landing on Max.

Max lowered her hand and stopped in her tracks.

"What's that all about?" Kaylie whispered.

Danica shook her head, although her instincts told her that they were witnessing chemistry too hot to touch.

"Well, come on now," Chelsea said, taking the garters from Max's hand.

"Max." Treat's voice was husky, with a cool edge that confused Danica. Maybe she'd misinterpreted their attraction.

Max fumbled with her day planner. Her fingers moved up and down the page. "I think we're all set. Thank you for everything," she said in a nervous voice.

He nodded, holding her gaze a breath too long. Throwing Danica off once again.

Danica broke the odd interaction that held all of the wedding parties' eyes captive. "So, we're off to the island."

"There have never been two more beautiful brides. I never believed that brides really passed out before the wedding," Treat teased. "You've proven me wrong."

He threw an arm over Blake's shoulder. "I have to catch a plane. I'm really sorry to miss the ceremony, but you know I love you."

He spoke so openly about his feelings, it took Danica by surprise.

"We appreciate everything you've done, Treat," Blake said.

"Family, man. Listen, there are murmurs of rain heading our way by nightfall. You should have a few hours before it hits." He checked his watch. "You should be fine. I have to run, but Blake"—Treat put a hand on his cousin's shoulder—"let's make sure we see each other more often. Family should never go this long without connecting."

Family.

Connecting.

Mom and Dad. Oh no.

"Dane had to leave early this morning, but he wanted me to give you his best and…" He scanned the group, then walked over to Lacy. "Lacy, he asked that I tell you he's sorry that he missed you."

Lacy cringed with embarrassment. "That's okay. We didn't

have any plans or anything."

The right side of Treat's lips lifted into a coy smile. "He wanted you to know."

"Thank you," she said.

If one more person blushed, Danica thought she might just scream. There were enough hormones circling that she worried they'd all get pregnant by osmosis. Thinking of hormones brought her mind to Michelle and the other teenagers, whom she hadn't seen since dinner the evening before.

"Does anyone know where Michelle and the others are?" she asked.

"Yeah, they took the kids to the beach to run around," Chaz said.

"The beach? They'll get all sandy and wet in their nice clothes," Kaylie said with a glare.

"They were getting antsy."

Danica put a hand on her sister's arm. "Whatever happens, happens, remember? It's all okay."

Kaylie drew in a deep breath, pushing her hands out in front of her as she blew it out. "Right. It's fine."

Danica and Kaylie stood on the ramp, in awe of the two awaiting yachts. Pink, white, and gold streamers blew from their tethers at the rear of each one.

"Wow," Kaylie said.

"Wow is right. Treat must be überrich." Danica reached for Kaylie's hand. "Can you believe this didn't cost us a penny?"

"No. I still can't believe he's the same guy I saw at that

party."

"We don't need two boats," Danica said.

"He said he arranged for the smaller one last night so we and our grooms could go over separately and a little while apart. He totally understood about us not seeing the grooms before the wedding. Why don't we still use it, just the four of us?"

Hand in hand, they took one last, long look at each other, smiled until their cheeks ached, and then looked over their shoulders at their family and friends. Then they each cupped their hands, held them in the air, and twisted them at the wrist like the Queen of England.

The people on the beach turned to watch. Danica watched them clap and whistle. She swallowed past a lump in her throat. *They're doing that for us.* She reached for Kaylie's hand as children they didn't know ran toward the two beautiful brides in their long white gowns and parents struggled to catch up across the warm, deep sand.

The wind picked up and blew their trains around their feet. Danica and Kaylie scrambled to bundle their dresses. Chaz and Blake came to their aid as the onlookers hooted and hollered, cheering them on when the dresses were finally under control.

"I feel like a princess," Kaylie said.

"Forget princess. I feel like a queen."

"Queen? Wait, I want to be the queen," Kaylie complained.

Danica rolled her eyes. "Fine, we'll both be queens!"

Chapter Twenty-Four

The wind picked up halfway to the private island. The boat rocked as it cut through the increasing swells.

"Should we worry?" Danica asked.

"No. They wouldn't take us if they were worried," Kaylie answered.

They went belowdecks to preserve their carefully coiffed hairstyles.

"Ladies, I'm Bradford, and I'll be your host this afternoon. What may I offer you on your beautiful wedding day?" Complete with a white napkin layered over his arm, black slacks, and a traditional white button-down shirt, the mild-mannered fortysomething attendant was every bit the gentleman.

"Thank you," Kaylie said, bringing her hand to her heart.

Danica could tell she wanted to jump up and down and yell, *Oh my God! We have an attendant!*

"Might I interest you and your fine men in champagne?" he asked.

"Oh yes, thank you." Kaylie arched a brow and mouthed, *Wow!*

Danica grinned at her excited sister. Her passing out episode completely forgotten, she went to the steps to retrieve Blake and Chaz.

"Oh no, madam. I will request them." Bradford opened a cabinet, picked up something that resembled a large telephone receiver, and spoke into it. Two minutes later Blake and Chaz descended the stairs.

Kaylie grabbed Danica's hand and dragged her behind the cover of the men. "OhmyGodohmyGodohmyGod!" she said, and before Danica knew what was happening, she was doing a little dance alongside her sister, like two foolish teenagers. They emerged a minute later, completely composed, and Danica couldn't remember a time when she'd felt so carefree. *Thank you, Kaylie.*

"A toast," Blake said, holding up his champagne. "To a world of happiness."

They clinked glasses and drank their champagne.

"This really is a dream come true, Blake. I feel badly that neither Treat nor Dane was able to stay." Danica kissed him, then closed her eyes to soak in the moment.

"I don't remember seeing Max. Did you see Max?" Kaylie asked.

Danica's eyes flew open. "Didn't she get on the other boat?" She remembered seeing Max when Treat approached, but after that she'd been swept into the excitement of getting to the island. She hadn't looked for Max, or anyone else for that matter.

"Please tell me that you didn't lose my assistant," Chaz teased. "I'll call her." He took out his cell phone and tried to call, but he had no service.

"Excuse me, Bradford? Do you have a way to contact the other boat?" Kaylie asked in her sweetest voice.

"Yes, ma'am. We should be docking in about two minutes. Would you like me to call?"

"Two minutes? We can wait, thank you."

True to his word, two minutes later they reached the long dock that led to the most glorious island Danica had ever seen.

"This is like walking into a photograph," Danica said as they stepped from the boat to the dock. She gathered her dress to combat the wind and surveyed the island as she waited for the others to join her. The sand was almost as white as snow, and the deep sandy beach receded into a mass of palm trees. There were lines of tables and two groupings of chairs, set in orderly lines, and just beyond, she spotted what must be the altar, though from so far away she couldn't make out the design of the structure.

As the other boat docked and their family and friends joined them, Danica's heart soared. Her hair whipped in the wind. Kaylie struggled with her own dress, her hair flying in the wind, too. Danica tried to keep from appearing as frustrated as she felt with yards of material whipping around her, ruining the lovely updo she'd been so proud of.

A mischievous smile crossed Kaylie's lips. She took long, determined strides across the dock to Danica's side, and with a spark in her eyes, she said, "Take it down."

"What?"

"Your hair. Take it down," Kaylie answered.

"But they went to all the trouble of making it beautiful and we haven't even had pictures taken!"

Kaylie shrugged. "Whatever happens, happens, right?"

"Right." Danica laughed.

"Chaz, honey, come here." Kaylie asked him to take a picture with his cell phone.

They stood arm in arm, trains in hand, their hair whipping across their cheeks and the happiness of the day displayed in their beaming smiles while Chaz snapped picture after picture. Blake joined in, sweeping Danica off her feet. Chaz clicked away, catching the surprise on her face. The next thing they knew, Camille and Sally were taking pictures, then Marie, and even their father was clicking away like they were all mad, laughing and joking as the wind whipped their dresses and carried their laughter into the afternoon.

Chaz caught every frame of Kaylie pulling the combs from Danica's hair and her mass of curls springing wild and free.

Even after all the stress of her parents, and Kaylie and Lacy, and the fall in the elevator, she couldn't have imagined a more perfect day. All of that stuff went along with family, she supposed, but the rest, dancing with Kaylie, the boats, the spa treatment—even though she hated the idea of it—the letter from Blake, it all made for the best wedding day she could imagine.

As the others made their way to the beach, Danica and Kaylie stayed back to thank Bradford and the crew of the other boat.

"Mr. Braden asked us to return for you in three hours. Is that still acceptable?" Bradford asked.

They glanced up. Clouds crawled across the sky, threatening to steal their sunny afternoon.

"The weather reports are calling for rain this evening, but not before seven." He consulted his watch. "I can remain if you'd like."

"Oh, no, that's all right," Kaylie said. "We'll be fine. Can we call you if it starts to rain?"

"Yes, ma'am. The staff has a radio. There's no cell reception on the island."

Swept away in the excitement of their pending nuptials, Danica and Kaylie hugged the surprised man. They waved as the captains pulled the yachts away from the dock, and then they headed, hand in hand, toward the beach.

At the end of the dock, a thick path had been covered with tiny stones. Kaylie and Danica took one look at each other, then kicked off their heels and left them behind as they walked barefoot through the sand, their trains trailing behind, leaving smooth traces in their wake.

The island was even more beautiful up close than it had first appeared. Palm trees sprouted where the sandy beach met the woods, growing at different angles and measures. A few thick trunks stretched inches above the ground like thick fingers crawling toward the water, with heavy fronds arching above, creating pockets of shade. Other palms grew straight up from the ground, as if they were reaching for the sun, some with roots above the ground, reaching like tentacles around the base of the trees and beyond.

There were long tables with white and gold tablecloths set up and manned by dark-skinned, smiling men, each dressed identically to Bradford.

"This is incredible," Kaylie said.

They made their way down the beach. The beautiful altar boasted thick, artfully carved wooden pillars with intricate designs whittled from top to bottom. White and pink flowers wrapped around the pillars like vines. A canopy of white gauzy material stretched across the top and hung down the sides, blowing in the wind.

"Kaylie."

"I know."

Danica could not remember a time when something had taken her breath away as what lay before her—except, perhaps, for the witnessing the birth of Lexi and Trevor.

Camille was hurrying down the beach toward them.

Danica spotted Lexi and Trevor rolling a green and yellow coconut along the sand, her father and mother standing guard over them. *Mom and Dad. No, I can't think about them.*

"You guys okay?" Camille asked.

"Perfect," Kaylie said with a dreamy look in her eye.

"Good, because I gotta tell you something, and I don't want you to freak out."

Danica and Kaylie exchanged a worried look.

Camille took their hands. "We can't find Max."

"I told you!" Kaylie said to Danica. "I knew she was missing."

"That's ridiculous. She was at the hotel. She brought the garters, remember?" Danica looked down the beach, but even as she scanned the group, she knew that there was no way Camille had simply overlooked Max. "They have a radio. We'll call the hotel."

Kaylie was already headed toward the attendants. "She's the one who planned this whole thing. We can't have the wedding without her."

"Don't worry. I'm sure they can bring her over. Treat seems to have unlimited resources." The words were true, but she had a sinking feeling in her gut about Max. She'd seen her face lose color when she saw Treat, and now Danica wondered if the story about Justin hadn't been true. If she'd made it up to cover her tracks with Treat.

"Kaylie, does Max date a lot?" she asked.

"Max? No. I told you, I've never even heard her talk about a man. To be honest, I wondered if maybe she was gay."

"She's definitely not gay. I saw her out on the beach with some hottie last night," Camille said.

"You did?" Kaylie and Danica asked at the same time. Danica wondered if it was really Treat that she'd been with.

"Yeah, some young hot guy. He had sort of light brownish hair, I think. Why? Is something wrong? Are you worried someone did something to her?" Camille asked.

Definitely not Treat.

"No, no. It's just that Max never misses anything. Not a phone call, not a meeting, and she'd never miss the wedding that she spent so much time facilitating. She was on the phone day and night getting things organized," Kaylie said.

They asked one of the attendants to call the hotel and have them page Max.

"Where could she have gone?" Kaylie asked.

"It's not like she'd forget—or she wouldn't have seen us. We were like a herd of elephants we were so loud." Danica had a thought. "Maybe she was in the bathroom when we left, and she couldn't find us when she came out?"

"Max? You know she'd be on the radio herself putting a stop to the boat." Kaylie stared out past the water, and Danica could see the gears of her mind working overtime.

"It'll be fine, Kaylie. She must have a good reason for not being here." A gust of wind blew one of the tablecloths up over the food, and the attendants were quick to right the presentation.

"Fifteen minutes later they had news. Scarlet had seen Max talking to Treat an hour earlier.

"Where were we an hour ago? How long did it take to get here?" Danica asked.

"Forty minutes or so," the attendant said.

"And we've been hanging out for another half hour," Kaylie said. "I thought Treat was leaving."

"He was. Excuse me, sir, would you mind asking Scarlet to try and reach Mr. Braden to see if Max is with him? And if she's not, could you have her ask Mr. Braden if he knows where Max might have gone?"

Kaylie paced the beach with Camille by her side, holding her train so it didn't get snagged on a twig.

"I'm fine, Camille. I don't really care if it gets dirty."

Danica looked down the beach again, wondering how they would explain to everyone that Max was missing. She spotted Blake and Chaz talking with Weston and Jeff and Michelle and the other teens playing with Lexi and Trevor. Madeline and Elise were seated under an umbrella, along with Abby and Astrid.

Sally and Gage were talking with Blake's father by the water's edge.

Danica took a few steps down the beach.

"Where are you going?" Kaylie asked.

"I'm not. Nowhere."

Where the hell are Mom and Dad? And Lacy?

Chapter Twenty-Five

The attendant carried the radio in his hand as he approached.

"Yes?" Kaylie and Danica answered in unison.

"Miss Scarlet couldn't reach Mr. Braden, but she was able to confirm that he'd missed his flight."

"Oh no," Kaylie said as she sank into one of the chairs. "What does this mean? You saw Max with him. She was nervous, or embarrassed. It's not like they stayed back for a tryst. Danica—"

"Kaylie, don't overreact. So what, he missed his flight. He probably misses flights once a week. It doesn't mean it has anything to do with Max." Danica bit her lower lip. She had no idea what could have happened or where they could be, and she was having the damnedest time trying not to focus on whatever her parents were doing. Not to mention the nagging guilt of knowing that wherever they were, Lacy was certainly not far behind—alone in her anguish.

"Don't overreact? We can't get married if she's not here. I'd never forgive myself."

Camille put her arm around Kaylie. "Okay, then we'll wait. What should I tell everyone? Want me to tell them to eat, so they don't worry?"

"Good idea. Yes, please." Kaylie gave her a quick hug. "Thank you, Camille."

"Do you think we have to worry? I mean, girls turn up missing and then they find their bodies. It happens all the time at resorts. Remember that girl in—"

Danica held up her hand. "Enough. We're not even going to entertain those kinds of thoughts. It's a little extreme, don't you think?"

"Extreme? Max is the most efficient, organized, well-mannered person I know. She'd never, ever miss something this important. She'd at least call or text."

"The phones don't work. Maybe she did," Danica said with a nod.

"Yeah, maybe." Kaylie sighed. "She must be with Treat. At least if she is, we know she's okay. The kids are probably driving everyone crazy by now." She looked down the beach. "Here comes Chaz. I have to tell him. He'll know what to do."

No, he won't.

When Chaz caught up to them, he looked from one sister to the other. "Are we still getting married today, or did I miss a memo?"

Kaylie touched his belt. "Yeah, we are." She smiled playfully up at him.

Really? Just tell him.

He took her hands in his. "Then…what's the holdup? Trev's getting a little cranky."

"Ask Mom to walk him a little. She's got the golden touch with that boy."

Danica jumped in. "I think Mom went for a walk."

"A walk?" Kaylie asked.

"Yeah, I saw her go through the woods. Maybe she just

went to use the bathroom or something." *Please don't be "or something."*

"They have fruit. Just give him some and that'll keep him busy for a little bit. We have to take care of a few little things."

He kissed her. "Okay, sounds good."

When he was far enough away not to hear her, Danica asked, "Why didn't you tell him?"

"Listen, Max is his work wife, so he'll just worry."

"Yeah, yeah, you keep saying that."

"She is. She takes care of all his stuff. I'm so thankful she does, too. He seriously worries about her like she's a sister. I'm surprised he didn't notice she was missing. I don't want to worry him until we have to."

Danica wiped wetness from her forehead, too sidetracked to notice what it was from. "I thought you said he'd know what to do. I knew he wouldn't, but you should still tell him."

"I will," Kaylie said.

Danica walked out to the water's edge, wiping droplets of water from her arms and forehead. She looked out at the water as rain sprinkled her skin. She swiped at it, then realized what it was. "Oh no."

She turned and ran for Kaylie just as the sky darkened.

"It's raining," Kaylie yelled.

The attendants quickly covered the food and took up the tablecloths. "Excuse me, Miss Kaylie, would you like me to radio the captain?"

"Danica!" Kaylie yelled. Just as Danica came into earshot, the rain picked up its pace.

"What should we do?" Danica asked.

"Is there a building here?" Kaylie asked, even though they'd been told there was none.

"Only four small facilities," he answered.

"Danica?"

Down the beach, their family and friends ran for the cover of the trees. Blake sprinted up the beach toward them in his tuxedo vest, the legs of his pants rolled up. By the time he reached them, his clothing was drenched and his hair lay matted against his forehead.

Kaylie had tears in her eyes, and Danica knew that she, too, looked like a drowned rat. The pleats in her dress were soaked right through to the material beneath.

"Hey, babe," Blake said, out of breath. A smile crept across his lips as he looked at her through wet lashes.

"Hey." She couldn't help but return the smile. Even soaked, he was devastatingly handsome, and his positivity hadn't been dampened one bit.

"Hey?" Kaylie shouted. "Hey! It's raining! Do you see what's happening here? Do you feel the rain? Do you hear my children crying? Do you see what I look like? My hair? My ruined dress?" Her face was beet red; her hair dripped from the ends down her chest.

Danica took a step closer to Blake, her eyes never leaving his. "Whatever happens, happens." She wrapped her hands around the back of his neck and pulled him into a passionate kiss.

"You guys. You guys! Danica!" Kaylie's panic heightened.

Danica ignored her sister's rant. She wanted to remain in his arms for the foreseeable future—forgetting that Max was missing, forgetting that her parents were God only knew where, and forgetting that Lacy was probably tailing them and falling apart as Danica pretended that none of them existed. She knew better. She knew those issues wouldn't resolve themselves. As much as she wanted to, she couldn't pretend they didn't exist.

She reluctantly pulled away from Blake. Kaylie's makeup had streaked with the rain and her tears. Her dress was ruined, and she looked as though she just might punch Danica in the jaw.

"I think we should call the captain," Danica said calmly.

Chapter Twenty-Six

It was obvious that the attendants were used to sudden storms like the one that had arrived in the blink of an eye and was currently wreaking havoc on the island. They had wrapped the food and carried the tables into the center of the woods, where they constructed a wall of tables against the wind. Danica, Kaylie, and their guests hovered beneath the palm trees, within the confines of the makeshift walls, as winds whipped and whirled around them. Angry waves slammed the sandy beach.

"Michelle and the boys took Lexi and Trevor into the bathrooms," Danica hollered over the winds to Kaylie. "Blake said they're fine, and the bathrooms aren't like outhouses, so they're safe."

"Our wedding is ruined, Max is missing, and…and…look at our dresses!" Kaylie sobbed.

"Miss Danica?" One of the attendants was handing her the radio. "If you please? It's Scarlet."

Danica snagged the receiver. "Scarlet?"

She listened as static on the line scraped at her nerves. "Captain can't come…too harsh…Max…No justice of the peace. Mr. Braden…officiate…on his way…boat with Ma…" The line went dead.

Danica handed the receiver to the attendant but knew her face would betray any attempt to hide the fear or the worry that gripped her gut. *Max and Treat were out there somewhere. In the storm.*

"What?" Kaylie yelled.

She felt Blake's arm around her, turning her to face him. She stared into his dark eyes and opened her mouth to speak, but nothing came out.

"Babe, it's okay. Tell me what she said."

Danica nodded, gathering her thoughts and her courage. Had she heard what she thought she heard? She must be misconstruing something.

"Kaylie," she yelled over the wind. "Where's the justice of the peace?"

Kaylie looked around. Elise and Madeline shivered with their arms around each other. Weston, Abby, and Astrid huddled around them. Camille and Jeff somehow had smiles on their faces, their hands tightly clasped together as they laughed—*laughed*—with Chelsea. Marie huddled down low, as if she might blow away with the wind, her beautiful dress now covered in wet, mucky sand.

"I don't see him!" She grabbed Danica's arm. "He's not here."

Danica grasped Chaz's arm in one hand, Kaylie's in the other. "There was too much static to hear for sure, but it sounded like Max must have realized that he wasn't here and she stayed back to find him. I don't know for sure, but it sounded like Max and Treat were on their way here."

Chaz broke free from her grasp. "They're on the water? In this storm?" He ran to the edge of the woods, searching the raging sea. "Max!" he yelled against the wind.

"Oh no! What about the boat? They can't come to get us?" Kaylie cried.

"They can't. I think she said the storm's too harsh." Danica turned to look at Chaz, standing in the pounding rain, his tux whipping in the wind. "Treat will know what to do. He must pilot boats all the time." She turned to the attendant, "Right? He can do this, right?"

"Mr. Braden is an excellent seaman," the attendant confirmed, but the way his eyes flitted up toward the blackening clouds told of his silent concerns.

Kaylie ran to Chaz. Her wedding gown dropped from her body, the bottom thick with wet sand, torn in several places.

"Blake." Danica tried to keep her voice quiet, but she had to talk loud enough so he could hear her. "Mom and Dad? Where are Mom and Dad?"

He surveyed the group, then brought his hand to his mouth, readying to shout.

Danica jumped up and grabbed his arm. "No! No!"

She dragged him out of the enclosure. "I saw them alone last night, outside." She held his gaze until understanding dawned in his widening eyes. "Lacy saw them, too. They left the party before the rain. I don't know where they went, but they went together—and I think Lacy must have trailed them."

"Danica, we have to get the men to help find them. What if they're lost?"

Blake was right. Why else wouldn't they have come back when the rain started? As she looked at Madeline huddled with not just Elise, but also Blake's father, she couldn't imagine bringing a world of hurt down upon her shoulders, either.

"Take Weston and Jeff. No one else. Please."

Blake took off in the direction of the facilities, and Danica stood motionless. Everything was falling apart.

She watched Kaylie clinging to Chaz out on the sand. She knew Kaylie was nearing a complete meltdown, and she didn't know what to do. She couldn't fix this. She couldn't swim out and find Max, or make sure she was safe. If anything happened to Max—

"Miss Danica?" the attendant asked.

"Yes."

"There!" He pointed to bright spotlights coming in and out of focus, indicating a large boat in the distance.

"Is it Treat and Max?"

"No way to know, but it's definitely one of ours."

Danica watched the boat careen first to one side, then the other as it broke through the treacherous waves. The nose of the boat lifted so high she was sure it would tumble over backward. She grabbed the attendant's arm with a gasp. The front of the boat slammed down against the water, sending sprays higher than the boat itself as it was swept to the side, keeling hard to the right.

"Make them go back. They'll never make it!" Danica yelled.

"Nothing I can do. The captain will know what to do."

The boat seemed to make no forward progress, and it was tossed like a toy in the hammering waves.

Kaylie appeared beside her. "I'm going to the kids. I can't do anything here, and between Max and the ruined wedding, I need to know they're okay."

"I'm coming with you."

The fronds of the trees cut most of the wind and rain, but gusts still found their way through. Carrying her bundled, soaked gown in her arms was like carrying dead weight—too much dead weight—while slogging through wet sand and mud.

"This is so messed up," Kaylie complained.

"More than you know," Danica muttered.

"Worst wedding ever!" Kaylie said. "Ow! These things kill my feet."

Danica ignored the prickling pains in the bottoms of her bare feet as they hurried across the spiny roots and fallen leaves.

"At least it'll be the most memorable wedding day ever." Danica tried to see a bright side in their epic failure of a wedding.

"What if something really bad does happen to Max?"

What if something happened to Mom and Dad? "She's with Treat. He'll take care of her." *Even if it's not how he prefers to be taking care of her.*

"There!" Kaylie ran toward four small buildings in a clearing near the edge of the forest.

If Danica didn't know better, she'd think they were secured to the ground with thick foundations and running water. They looked more substantial than temporary outhouses. Then again, this was all Treat's doing, and from what Danica had seen so far, everything Treat did looked expensive and well put together.

Kaylie pulled open the first door. In the small enclosure, no bigger than eight by eight, there was a toilet, a cute little counter with elegant hand towels and bottles of hand sanitizer, and a small supply cabinet. Sitting in the middle of the clean floor, save for the wet footprints near the entrance, were Rusty, Chase, and Trevor.

"Mommy!" Trevor's eyes lit up as he pushed from the floor and flew into her arms.

Kaylie melted into tears. "Baby, baby. It's okay." She rocked him from side to side, holding him so tight that Trevor tried to wiggle free just to breathe. Kaylie buried her face in his neck.

"We…we…we…" Trevor was too excited to speak.

Rusty stood with a halfhearted shrug. "We're playing make-believe army. There's a storm outside of our camp and we have to come up with plans to save the day."

"You're a godsend," Danica said to him. "Are you guys okay? Has he been scared?"

"Nah." Chase rose to his feet. "Trev's so cool. He's got the best plans of all of us."

"Plans!" Trevor said with a beaming smile.

"Okay, honey." Kaylie set him down and he ran between the teens. "The boat will be here soon to get us. There's no need to be scared."

Danica knew that Kaylie's trembling could spark fear in Trevor faster than the rain pummeling the roof. She grabbed Kaylie's hand and guided her back out into the rain. "You guys figure out the plans. We'll go rally the troops."

Once out in the rain, Danica dragged Kaylie to the next building. "Try not to scare Lexi. Don't let her see your fear or she'll feed off of it."

"Right. Okay." Kaylie took a deep breath and ran her hand along her matted hair.

They opened the next door, expecting Lexi to jump into Kaylie's arms. They were met with an empty bathroom. Kaylie ran to the next building and opened the door. Another empty bathroom.

"Damn it! Where are they?" Kaylie yelled, holding her heavy dress up while she ran to the fourth and final facility. She sobbed as she tugged the heavy door against the wind and looked inside.

Kaylie stumbled backward into Danica's arms at the sight of the empty room.

Chapter Twenty-Seven

"Where is she? What's happened to her?" Kaylie cried.

Danica knew that Michelle was too responsible to go wandering away or to take Lexi anywhere dangerous. Danica realized that she and Kaylie had been the ones to take Lexi someplace dangerous—by bringing the children to the island—but she couldn't thrash herself for that now. They had to find Lexi.

"Kaylie, look at me." She pushed Kaylie back and made her look her in the eye. She shook her shoulders to be sure she had her attention. "Michelle probably took Lexi back to the group. Let's go back and we'll find her. I'm sure we'll find her."

Kaylie grabbed for the bathroom door one more time and stared into the empty room.

"Kaylie! We're going back to the group." Danica took her hand and slogged forward a few steps, then stopped. She lifted her bridal gown and tore away the bustle from beneath, instantly feeling fifty pounds lighter. Kaylie's satin dress had no bustle to remove, but she knew the weight of the soaked gown must be too much for her sister.

She knelt and grabbed the edges of a wide gash in the fabric. She tore with all her might until it found a path and opened along Kaylie's leg, clear up to her thigh. Then she grabbed a sharp rock and used the edge to cut the fabric horizontally, until she was able to tear away the bottom half of the dress; it bunched at Kaylie's feet like a forgotten mound of treasure.

"There!" Danica said triumphantly.

Kaylie looked down at her shivering legs and savagely ripped gown. "Great. How could I have ever thought this was a good idea? My daughter is lost, and the wedding is ruined."

Danica then took the rock to her own gown and did the same island surgery, tearing away pieces of her gown until her legs were free, too. She ripped four shreds of materials and tied them on their feet.

"She's not lost; she's with Michelle. This may not do much, but it'll help. It'll be easier to walk without the dress dragging."

Then she tossed the rock and took Kaylie's hand. Without a word, she nodded at her sister and they pushed through the thick mass of palms, through the dense, wet sand and dirt. Danica held the fronds open for Kaylie to pass through, then ran ahead and cleared the way every few feet.

A few minutes later, Kaylie yelled, "I don't remember seeing that!" as they passed a fallen palm tree.

"Me either. We must have been too focused on reaching the kids." They weaved through trees and traipsed forward, but the beach that had seemed so close when they first took the trek was now nowhere in sight.

"This isn't right! Danica, we're lost." Kaylie dropped her hand and looked frantically around the woods. "I don't remember any of this, and look at that hill." She pointed to a slight increase in the terrain.

Danica didn't remember it either, but she couldn't be sure that they hadn't been too focused on finding Trevor and Lexi to see it. She remembered seeing higher trees in the middle of the island from the view from the boat.

"Okay, let's think. We can't be that lost." The rain picked up, coming down in sheets between the palms. Danica shielded her eyes with her hand and yelled over the noise of the rain breaking through the thick fronds. "Which way did we come from?"

Kaylie looked to the left, then the right. "Everything looks the same," she yelled. Her body trembled and shook.

"Hold on," Danica hollered as she scanned the woods. She shook her head. "I can't find the path, but it must be here." She took a few steps forward, wiping the rain from her face with her arm. Each time she dried her eyes, new rain streaked her face again.

"We're lost, Danica." Kaylie sank to a crouch and buried her face in her hands. "I need Chaz. Where is he? Why isn't he looking for me? This was the dumbest idea ever! Why did you let me plan an island wedding?"

"I...we..." *Damn it.* "Kaylie, we have to get to Lexi. Get up."

Kaylie remained in her broken-down state, crouched and soaking wet as the rain pelted her.

Danica took her hand and pulled her to her feet. "Get up. Now. Your daughter needs you, and you cannot fall apart right now." She looked from side to side and realized that if they were at the center of the island, walking one direction or the other would have to take them back toward the beach on either side of the island, and they could just follow the beach around until they found the others.

"It's the rain," Danica proclaimed. "It just has us turned around. Come on." She marched forward, in the direction where she believed they'd find the group.

Their feet sank into the mud as they trudged through the forest, weaving through thick groups of palm trees and bushes. Minutes passed in silence, broken only by Kaylie's emotional outbursts of sobs.

"Why did this happen?" Kaylie cried. "If only we'd had the wedding in Colorado."

"You didn't want a Colorado wedding. Lexi will be fine, Kay. You'll see." Danica hoped she was right.

Kaylie stopped walking. She hiccupped as she sucked in deep breaths to control her sobs; then she turned to Danica with serious eyes and asked, "Don't you wonder if this is a sign?"

Her voice startled Danica more than her words. She was serious. This wasn't a frantic question, but a real concern.

"Not at all. Storms happen." Danica stopped walking and searched Kaylie's eyes. "A sign? Kaylie, is there something you want to talk about? I mean about you and Chaz? Are you unsure about getting married?" *Go ahead; pile one more load of shit onto my day.*

Kaylie shook her head. "No. I want to marry him, but between Max and Lexi and the storm, it seems like someone's trying to give us a sign."

Thank God. Danica put her arm around her sister's trembling shoulders. Her skin was covered with goose bumps. "You know what I think? I think this is just a test of our strength, if it's anything at all, and that we are gonna come out of it, along with Max and Lexi, just fine."

As quickly as the storm had reared its ugly head, it began to taper off. The winds subsided and the rain now trickled from the fronds that sheltered them. They both lifted their eyes toward the sky.

"Another sign?" Danica joked.

Kaylie smiled; then her brows drew together. "Listen!"

Dripping rain tinkled against the palms, and beyond that, a voice. No, a laugh. *A laugh!*

Kaylie dashed toward the sound with Danica on her heels. "Michelle?" Kaylie yelled. "Lexi?"

They followed the laugh around the trees and up a slight incline. "Michelle? Lexi?" The laughter silenced with Kaylie's shouts.

"Kaylie?" they heard.

"Mom?" Kaylie ran around the last group of trees and found her mother and father huddled against a small hillside. She fell into her mother's arms. "Mom! Did you see Lexi and Michelle? I can't find them. Lexi's missing, Mom. She's gone."

"Oh no. We'll find her, baby. Don't you worry. Michelle's very responsible. I'm sure she's got her safely tucked away somewhere. Don't you worry."

Danica scanned the immediate area. She knew Lacy would be nearby. She walked a few feet in the other direction and listened as her mother explained to Kaylie why she was out in the woods.

"Your father and I were looking for the bathrooms and we got lost," she said.

It was then, in that moment, that Danica spotted Lacy crouched behind two dense groupings of palm trees, and at that very same moment, she recognized the lie in her mother's voice, the faltering confidence that she'd learned to pick up on during her years as a therapist.

Chapter Twenty-Eight

Danica ignored the way Lacy flinched as she approached. Had she not been looking for her hiding among the trees, Danica would have missed her, huddled between two large groups of palm trees.

She knelt beside Lacy. "You okay?" she asked.

Lacy didn't respond.

"I know you followed them. They said they got lost."

Lacy's eyes narrowed, and Danica knew in an instant that her instincts were right. She took Lacy's hand. "Come on. Let's get back to the group. We have to find Lexi and Michelle."

Still staring at her father, Lacy said, "They're with the group. I saw them pass behind me about fifteen minutes ago."

"You know where we are? You're not lost?"

Lacy pointed behind her and to the right with her thumb.

Danica followed the line of her thumb toward the noises of the group that she only now recognized.

"Blake?"

Lacy pointed toward the group.

"Jesus. What a mess."

"Danica?" Kaylie was headed in their direction.

Danica popped around the trees, leaving Lacy to decide her

own path. "I'm here. Lexi and Michelle are with the group. I heard them." She purposefully walked Kaylie away from Lacy and pointed in the direction of the group.

"Oh, thank goodness. We should get Trevor now that the rain has let up."

"No, you go back, see Lexi. I know the girls are probably frantic by now, wondering where we are. I'll have Blake get Trevor and the boys."

As her parents approached, Danica broke away. "I'll be there in a minute." She caught her mother's eye and held it, hoping she'd read the disappointment Danica made no effort to mask.

Her father said something to her mother, and they followed Kaylie back toward the others.

When they were all out of sight, Danica went back to Lacy. "So, what now? Are you just going to hide out here?"

Lacy stood, wiping her dress and making no progress in looking presentable. Her hair was drenched and her legs were covered in mud and scratches. "Nope. I'm gonna ignore whatever it was that I just saw and go on with my life as if it were normal." She headed toward the group.

What you saw? Danica held her tongue. Lacy was an adult, and the last thing she needed to do was start a long discussion about something that neither of them had answers to.

Blake ran across the wet sand. "I was so worried," he said. He pulled her in close, his heart thundering against her chest. He took a step back and looked at her dress, then carefully moved a soggy curl from her cheek. "You okay, babe?"

She nodded, knowing he'd see the weight of the afternoon in her eyes.

He pulled her close again as Lacy walked past.

"I love you." He held her cold cheeks in his warm hands. "I love you so much."

"I love you, too." She watched Lacy making a beeline for Madeline and pulled away from Blake. "Has there been any word about Max yet?"

"No word on Max yet. The boat we saw coming in turned back, but they're sending a boat for us. We should be back at the hotel soon."

"Oh, good. Blake, would you mind getting Chase and Rusty? They're with Trevor in the restrooms."

"Sure. Sorry about our wedding."

"What? We're still getting married. Today. No matter what else happens. Once we know Max is okay, we are tying the knot."

Blake's smile was all the assurance she needed to know she was doing the right thing. As he headed for the restrooms, Danica saw Sally down the beach.

"Rusty! Chase!" Sally hollered, waving her arms above her head.

Danica turned to find Rusty, with Trevor on his shoulders and Chase by his side. Blake changed his path and met them, taking Trevor from Rusty and tickling his belly. For the first time ever, Danica heard the whisper of a thought in her mind. *Children?* She'd spent so many years building her career, and before Blake, she'd never had a partner that she wanted to have children with. No. She rolled the thought around in her mind for a moment or two. She wasn't ready for children yet. She was enjoying her time with Blake too much to want it to change just yet. She was just discovering a side of herself that she *wanted* to explore even more. *Maybe one day*, she thought, and pushed the thought away.

She headed for Lacy, still hoping to stall any ideas of outing her mother and father. The way Lacy stalked toward her mother, hands clenched in fists, each determined step a little harder, faster, told her that Lacy might not be thinking rationally enough to hold her tongue.

"Danica!" Camille and Chelsea ran toward her. "They found her! They found Max!"

"Oh, thank goodness!"

"Apparently she got a call as we were boarding the ship that the justice of the peace came down with something and he couldn't officiate. She was trying to figure out what to do when Treat came to the rescue." Camille tried to catch her breath.

"Treat? Did he know someone else?" Danica asked.

"No. Apparently, when he opened the resort, he got ordained. He can hold the service. They were heading here in one of Treat's private boats—or yachts, or whatever it is that he owns—before the storm hit. The storm was too strong, so they detoured back to the mainland. That must have been the boat you saw earlier."

Danica shot another glance toward Lacy. Short of sprinting down the beach, there was no way she'd reach her in time to thwart whatever she intended to do.

"Good. Then they're okay?" Danica asked.

"We think so."

Chelsea touched Danica's dress. "Oh, honey, look at you. You're a mess."

"Really? I thought I looked island chic." Danica smiled.

"Aw, I'm sorry!" Chelsea said. "What are we gonna do about the wedding?"

With one eye on Lacy, who was sitting beside Madeline and her father, and the other on Kaylie, standing beside Chaz with her little girl in her arms and an enormous, relieved grin on her lips, Danica said, "We're having a wedding."

Blake and the boys joined the group as they left the woods and congregated on the hard, drenched sand. Sun parted the clouds in slanted streaks, warming the chilly air. Danica searched for her mother, hating herself for feeling the need to make sure she was okay after what Lacy had implied. She found her sitting beside Nancy and Sally on the chairs that the attendants had set up.

Her mother's eyes darted toward her father and Madeline one too many times. Danica's pulse sped up, and it took all of her energy to restrain from saying something right there and then. She could not fathom what her mother was thinking.

A horn from a boat in the distance called her attention. Danica turned toward the sound and took in the surreal scene; the treacherous waves had morphed into less threatening swells. Far off shore, she made out a large boat cutting swiftly through the swells toward the island. Danica breathed a sigh of relief.

"Let's get everyone to the dock," she said to one of the attendants.

With their clothing drenched, their hair matted to their heads like they'd walked out of showers, the group moved toward the dock.

"What a day," Madeline said.

"Nothing like a little excitement," Blake's father said as he wiped his hand down his face.

Even with her dress ruined and the craziness of Lexi and Max missing, Kaylie bounced Lexi in her arms. "That was a crazy afternoon, huh, Lex?" she said, then planted a kiss on Lexi's forehead.

"Lexi was so brave!" Michelle raved to Kaylie.

"Well, she is my daughter," Kaylie said with a grin.

Right. Danica trudged through the wet sand behind Chaz's mother and sister.

"This was not a typical wedding day."

Elise. Danica froze. She had almost forgotten how unpleasant the woman could be. She feigned a smile and turned to face Kaylie's soon-to-be mother-in-law.

"No, not typical at all," Danica admitted.

Elise leaned closer to Danica and arched a perfectly plucked brow. "It was actually a little exciting."

Danica blinked away her surprise. She didn't know if she should take the prim woman seriously or if she was making a cruel, sarcastic comment. She chose the safest assumption.

"I'm so sorry for the hassle and the rain—"

"You couldn't have helped it. This is nature at its best." Elise looked at Chaz, with one arm around Kaylie, the other wrestling to keep hold of Trevor's wiggling body. "It's created a most memorable day."

Maybe there was hope for their wedding day yet. If Elise could find good in such a horrible afternoon, she couldn't be all that bad.

"That, it has," Danica agreed.

Chapter Twenty-Nine

The ship had been stocked with warm, dry towels, and clean sweat suits were supplied in various sizes by the hotel. They'd been waited on hand and foot and provided with warm beverages and a full meal to hold them over on the forty-minute ride.

As they headed back into the hotel, Kaylie said, "Treat must be behind our royal treatment."

Treat. Max.

Scarlet met them in the lobby, quick to apologize for the afternoon's less-than-ideal circumstances.

"It's okay," Danica assured her. "No one can control Mother Nature."

"Mr. Braden would like to offer the executive balcony as an alternative location for your wedding."

Scarlet's poise made Danica remember how awful she must look. She felt horrible that the hard work the spa employees had lavished on them was all for naught, and she wondered if Scarlet was thinking the same thing.

"Let me talk to Kaylie and see what she'd like to do. Do you know where Treat and Max are?"

Scarlet nodded toward the main entrance of the hotel. "I do

believe they have just arrived."

Max walked through the doors looking every bit as uncomfortable as she had earlier in the day, when Treat had joined them in the lobby. Her hair was tussled and her face was flushed. Treat, walking a few feet behind Max, no longer wore a suit, but donned a pair of pressed blue jeans and a black polo shirt.

Does the man ever look bad?

Blake and Kaylie were the first to reach them, with Chaz on their heels.

"You're okay?" Kaylie wrapped her arms around Max. "I'm so sorry. I was so scared that something happened to you!"

Max was silent in Kaylie's arms.

"We hit a rough patch," Treat explained, "so we docked a few miles down the beach. We didn't mean to worry you."

"You missed your flight?" Danica asked.

"When I heard what had happened, I told Max I could officiate the service." He looked at Max, who was now in Chaz's arms, and something changed in his voice. Danica saw sadness sweep through his eyes, then disappear quickly, as if he realized he shouldn't reveal his inner thoughts. "I didn't mind missing my flight."

When Chaz released Max, Danica noticed that she did everything she could to keep from looking at Treat.

"Well, thank you, for everything. The staff on the boats were incredibly kind, and all these clothes. We'll pay for it all, of course," Danica offered.

"Of course we will," Blake said, wrapping an arm around Danica's waist.

"No need. Remember what I said about family?" Treat took one last look at the back of Max's head, then nodded and excused himself.

"Max, everything okay?" Danica held back her real question. *What the hell happened out there?*

"Yeah. I'm so sorry. I know you really counted on me to do everything right, and I'm sorry. I should have had a backup plan for the justice of the peace."

"Don't be silly," Chaz said. "You did everything perfectly. It was the perfect day, and we're not going to let a little storm ruin our attitudes. Right, Kaylie?"

Kaylie broke into a wide grin. "Nope. Whatever happens, happens. Right, Danica?"

Danica was too tired to think about why she kept repeating her mother's words.

"What now? Should we just table the wedding and go to the justice of the peace in a day or two?" Kaylie asked.

"You're kidding, right?" Danica knew she wasn't. Danica looked at Blake and knew he'd be fine either way. They could wait to get married or they could get married right that very second, with wet hair and matching sweat suits. She looked at her mother, and in her mind she heard, *There are no happily ever afters.* Danica steeled herself against the words as she drank in Blake's loving gaze and the way Kaylie leaned her head against Chaz's arm, a sleepy baby girl in her arms. *Oh, yes, there are.*

"No way. I wanna get married. I don't care if it's midnight and we're the only two on the balcony. Blake, I want today to be our wedding day." Danica took his hand and said, "Just say okay. Please. Let's do this."

Blake took her in his arms again and kissed her. "You don't have to ask me twice," he said with a satisfied grin.

The kids were almost asleep by the time they decided to take Treat up on his offer for an evening ceremony on the balcony. Scarlet and Max agreed to work together to firm up the details, and Kaylie agreed to have two of the hotel staff members watch the kids rather than try to hold a ceremony with two overtired children and worn-out parents.

Blake and Danica collapsed into sleep minutes after taking hot showers and lying on the bed to rest. Danica awoke an hour later. Unable to go back to sleep, she left Blake a note and snuck into the hall in search of Lacy. Again.

She knocked on Lacy's door.

No answer.

She knocked again, tapping her foot as she waited for Lacy to answer.

She stared at the door, afraid to move. Afraid of a repeat episode of the night before, or worse, after whatever she said she'd chosen to ignore seeing out on the island. Danica took a deep breath and knew she had to face things with Lacy head-on or she'd spend the rest of the evening worrying herself to death.

Downstairs, she went out to the veranda and searched beneath every palm tree she could see. She was on her way to the pool when she heard her voice.

"Danica."

She spun around and found her mother, freshly showered, hair styled, makeup in place. "Mom?"

"Let's take a walk," she said.

Danica followed her mother out the front doors and down toward the beach.

"How are you holding up?" her mother asked.

"It's been a crazy day," Danica replied.

"It's been a crazy few days," her mother corrected her. "Who were you looking for on the veranda?"

"Oh, no one."

"Not Lacy?" Her mother lifted her chin toward the outside bar, where Lacy sat in the sweat suit she'd been wearing when she left the boat.

"How long's she been there?" Danica asked.

Her mother shrugged. "I came down about a half hour ago and she was there. Come, let's sit with her."

Danica stopped walking. "Let's give her some space. I think she wants to be alone."

"I think we should go sit with her."

"Mom?"

Her mother looked at Lacy, then back at her. "Danica, I make my own beds and I sleep in them. Even when they're full of rocks." She nodded toward Lacy and began walking in her direction.

Can today get any worse?

Lacy lifted her eyes as they approached, then turned her chair away from them.

"Lacy, my mom wanted to sit with you." She hoped Lacy would read her message in the inflection of her voice. *Let's not talk about it.* "I think she thought you could use the company. I tried to tell her that you wanted time alone." Danica watched Lacy's stoic face and her mother's determined eyes as she made herself comfortable in the chair beside Lacy.

"Danica, sit, please," her mother said.

Danica sat across from her, feeling like the earlier storm was simply a prelude to the hurricane that was about to hit.

They sat without talking for a few minutes. A waitress took their drink orders and brought a round of iced teas. It was already almost seven o'clock and they were meeting at nine for the ceremony. That gave them two hours to either address the elephant in the room or accept that it was too big to deal with. Danica hoped for the latter.

"Lacy, we haven't had much time to get to know each other." Her mother sipped her tea.

Lacy didn't respond, but Danica didn't miss the clenching of her fingers around the arms of the chair.

"Mom, maybe we should do this another time. I still have to do my hair." Danica reached up and touched her springy curls. She'd noticed that they were out of control when she walked by the mirror in her room, but was too focused on finding Lacy to care. Now it wasn't her hair she was worried about; it was Lacy, whose lips were pressed so tightly together they were turning as white as her knuckles.

Her mother was not persuaded. "I think we need to talk. A lot has been revealed to you girls, and—"

Lacy kept her eyes trained on the beach as she spoke in a hard, flat tone. "Revealed? I don't think that's the right word."

"Lacy." Danica reached toward her.

Lacy turned hate-filled eyes toward Helen. "Revealed doesn't begin to cover it. To reveal means to make something known to others, to cause or allow something to be seen. What you are doing is covert. It's hidden."

"Is it?" her mother asked.

Danica had never seen this combative side of her mother,

and it momentarily stilled her thoughts. Was she saying what Danica thought she was saying? Did she want to get caught with her father? Was this some sort of ugly revenge aimed at Madeline, who didn't even seem any wiser to the whole sordid affair?

"Mom?"

Again her mother ignored her.

"So you were trying to get caught? Because I can think of better ways to do it than hiding beneath the trees." Lacy dropped her eyes to her drink and ran her finger around the edge of the cup. "Was that your master plan?"

"There was no master plan. I'm not out to hurt anyone."

What on earth are you doing?

"You're not out to hurt anyone? Is that what you're telling yourself? You and my mother, you're both so messed up. No wonder everything around me keeps blowing into smithereens."

"Nothing is blowing to smithereens, and I don't have to tell myself anything. What happens, happens."

Whatever happens, happens. Kaylie. Danica shot a look at her mother. She'd heard Kaylie repeat her mother's words so often she could hear her voice ringing in her ears. Hearing those words come from her mother's mouth struck a chord with her. *How is Kaylie involved? Oh God, does Kaylie know?*

Lacy was persistent. "How can you say that? If you and my father are fooling around, then you two are forcing this to happen. It's not just happening." Lacy was calm. Too calm.

Danica worried she'd lose her calm facade any second, and she didn't know Lacy well enough to know what that might mean.

"Lacy, your father and I are friends. We always have been and we always will be. Your mother knows this. She knows we talk."

"Does she know you kiss?" Lacy asked.

Kiss?

Danica watched the color drain from her mother's face and felt it drain from her own.

"That's right. I saw you today on the island. And don't try to deny it. I was there. I saw it with my own two eyes."

"Mom?"

Her mother looked at her. "Yes, there was a kiss. *A kiss*, not many kisses, not passionate kisses. A kiss."

"Mom, how could you?" Danica mouth went dry. She took a drink and closed her eyes, trying to escape her mother's admission.

"It was a mistake."

"It didn't look like a mistake," Lacy accused.

"No, I suppose to you it wouldn't. Your father and I go back a long way, Lacy. Seeing him again didn't just bring back the hurt he caused me, but it also brought back the friendship that we once enjoyed, and I got carried away."

Lacy didn't respond, and Danica couldn't have if she wanted to. The idea that her mother had kissed someone else's husband sickened her. Not to mention that Danica genuinely liked Madeline. She was a nice woman, despite the fact that she stole her mother's husband in the first place.

Danica forced herself to speak, though it came out as a whisper. "Mom, how could you?"

The pain in her mother's eyes told her that whatever transpired had been a mistake—one she wasn't sure she'd ever get past.

"I don't know, and I plan to tell Madeline, regardless of what your father thinks."

"No," Lacy said adamantly. "You can't tell her. You'll only hurt her."

"It'll hurt, but it'll hurt more if she finds out in a month, or a year, or five years. Lacy." She reached for Lacy's hand, but Lacy stepped back. "I don't want him back. I don't love him. I don't want to hurt your mother, but I do need to tell her what happened, and if she hates me for it, then she does. She deserves to know."

Danica felt like she'd been punched in the stomach. Her mother kissed her father. The man who hurt her so deeply that it took years for her to find her footing again. Anger stewed within her and came out in hurtful words. "He hurt you. He threw you away like trash without ever looking back. What were you thinking? You deserve every hurtful thing she gives you."

"You're right, I do."

Her mother made no move to hide her face or hide behind any false pretense. She was ready to take her due, and that knowledge rivaled the need in Danica's head for her mother to be the woman who hadn't done the wrong thing. The woman who would never have done anything but the right thing. The woman who raised her.

"Can't you just not tell her at all? Ever? Why hurt her?" Lacy's swiped at her damp eyes.

Danica couldn't tell if they were tears of anger or tears of hurt for her mother's impending pain.

"Because if she finds out later, which she will, it will hurt ten times as much."

"She's right," Danica said, thinking of Kaylie's reaction to her parents' divorce. "The one thing that we all learned from Dad's affair was that covering it up only makes it a whole lot worse when it finally comes out."

"So now you're on her side?" Lacy spat.

"No." She looked into her mother's eyes. "I hate what she did." She turned back to Lacy. "But I would hate it more if everyone lied to your mother and pretended that there wasn't something going on right under her nose."

"I have been looking all over for you guys." Kaylie's voice caught them all by surprise. "What?" Kaylie's eyes danced from her mother to Lacy and finally to Danica.

"Nothing. We were just shooting the breeze." Danica stood. "What did you need?"

"Oh, Treat arranged for wedding dresses and bridesmaid gowns! I swear someone is going to be lucky when they marry that man. He holds nothing back."

Danica thought of Max again and made a mental note to get her alone and make sure Treat hadn't done anything that upset her while they were out. Although she'd place her money on the fact that if he tried anything at all, the only emotion it would evoke would be pleasure—hot, steamy, toe-curling pleasure.

Chapter Thirty

Treat's office looked like a bridal gown shop. Exact replicas of Kaylie's and Danica's gowns hung from steel dressing rods, along with bridesmaid gowns almost identical to the ones the girls had worn earlier in the day.

"Mr. Braden apologized for the bridesmaid gowns. The supplier didn't have the exact dress your ladies were wearing in stock. These were the closest match." Scarlet's smile was strained until Kaylie said they were perfect. "The men's tuxedos will be sent to their rooms."

"I really don't know how we can ever repay him for everything," Danica said to Scarlet.

"Mr. Braden doesn't expect you to. You're family, and family knows no limits."

An hour later, Danica's head was upside down as she dried her hair with the diffuser, thinking of her mother. They hadn't had any sort of closure on their conversation after Kaylie arrived, and now Danica worried about the timing of her mother's admission to Madeline. Would it ruin the evening for everyone? Surely she'd have more tact than that.

"I smell burning hair," Blake said as he entered the bathroom.

"Oh gosh." Danica turned off the dryer and fluffed her hair.

"Gorgeous," Blake said, looking at her lasciviously. "Is that what you're wearing?" He ran his index finger under the lace strap of her thong.

She wiggled out of reach. "Do you mind, Mr. Carter? We're not even married yet." Her heartbeat raced from the two-second touch, and beneath her camisole, her nipples became erect.

Blake touched the side of her breast. "*They* don't seem to mind if we're not yet married." He lifted her camisole and took her breast in his mouth.

"Blake," she whispered. His tongue sent shivers down her back and heat between her thighs. "Blake," she said louder.

He lifted his eyes.

She took his chin in her hands and drew his lips away from her chest. "You will have to wait. I have to go get ready, and I really don't want to take another cold shower."

He looked down at his erection and feigned a little frown.

Blake looked so cute with his smoldering dark eyes pleading for a quickie that she opened her mouth to give in, but the words that came out were words of reason. "You're on your own, sweetheart." She planted a kiss on his cheek before passing by him and putting on her jeans and T-shirt. "See you soon, future husband." She slipped out the door, wishing she could have stayed and satisfied his every desire. Who was she kidding? *Her* every desire.

Danica and Kaylie stood before each other, surveying their wedding dresses for the second time that day.

"Are we ready to try again?" Danica asked.

"Whatever happens, happens."

There they were. Mom's words. "What?"

Kaylie arched an eyebrow, and Danica knew that Kaylie had no idea what she was referring to. She was obviously parroting her mother's words from something else altogether.

"Nothing." Danica sighed.

"What's up with you? After everything we went through today, are you still nervous?"

Just about when everyone will find out about Mom and Dad.

Kaylie shook her head. "I guess it is your wedding day, so you have a right to be nervous."

Danica reached for her sister's hand. "It's your wedding day, too."

"Whatever happens, happens," Kaylie said again as she answered the door.

Danica was about to seal her worry away when Lacy came into the room and flopped onto the bed.

"Your mother kissed my father," she said to Kaylie.

"What?" Kaylie asked.

Lacy looked at Danica, and Danica shook her head. *Don't you dare.* "Lacy means before, when they were married. She's just having a hard time putting it all together." Danica glared a silent threat at Lacy.

There was another, more urgent knock at the door. Danica

opened the door and Max stomped into the room, flopping onto the bed beside Lacy.

"Hey," Max said.

"Hey," Lacy said.

"I think I'm losing my mind." Max covered her face and fell back on the bed.

Kaylie and Danica exchanged a confused look.

Madeline walked into the room. "It was open. Sorry for barging in. Have you seen La—Oh, there you are." Madeline sat next to Lacy. "I've been looking all over for you. Your father had this crazy notion that you thought we might be getting divorced."

"You're divorcing?" Max asked. "See? This whole relationship thing is so complicated. And here I thought you two were happy."

"Are you girls ready?" Their mother swept into the room and stopped in her tracks, taking in Madeline and Lacy on the bed, sitting next to Max, who looked completely bewildered. "Oh, sorry. Did I interrupt something?"

Before things could get any more complicated, Danica said, "I think we'd better go. Shoes? Where are our—Oh my God! We left our shoes at the island."

"No, you didn't," Max said. "The attendants got them, but they're ruined. Scarlet has others for you. I'll get them." She jumped to her feet and ran for the door.

"Wait. We'll all come with you," Danica said, dragging Kaylie with her into the hall.

"There you are!" Abby ran up and hugged Kaylie. "We were wondering where you girls were getting ready. Mom has something for you."

Elise was in another traditional skirt and jacket. She must

have gone to the hairdresser in the hotel, because not a hair was out of place. She held a small jewelry box toward Kaylie.

"This is for you. It was my grandmother's, and each of the Crew women have worn them on their wedding day."

Kaylie covered her heart with her hand. "Elise? You don't have to do this."

Elise handed the open box to Kaylie. "I know. And, in fact, I didn't, earlier, but then I watched you with Chaz, and with your sister, and your babies. My grandbabies. Kaylie, I'm sorry I ever doubted your intentions toward my son."

Kaylie hugged her future mother-in-law. "Thank you. They're gorgeous," she whispered. She slipped the blue sapphire earrings on and said, "Something blue!"

Camille ran down the hall. "Danica!"

"You're always running." Danica laughed.

"Put this on. Something blue. You need it." She slid a child's bracelet on her wrist.

"Isn't that Lexi's?" Kaylie asked.

"Yeah," Chelsea said, coming up behind Camille. "Elise said she had earrings for you, but we had nothing for Danica. I hope you don't mind. Now you both have something borrowed and something blue."

"Oh, I forgot," Kaylie said. "We had your bracelets before. I think we left them in the room."

"We talked about it, and we were afraid if you wore the same ones, you might jinx the wedding." Camille shrugged. "You never know. Okay, now, go!"

Patrons turned to stare at the two beautiful brides crossing the lobby toward their future husbands, trailed by pretty bridesmaids with bright smiles. Danica had never felt as beautiful as she did at that very moment. The hunger in Blake's eyes was second only to the pride as she approached him.

"Wow," Blake said, taking her hand.

"You're pretty *wow* yourself," she said.

Her mother tapped her on the shoulder. "You look beautiful."

"Thanks, Mom." Danica didn't mean for her words to sound as clipped as they did, but she was not yet over her mother's indiscretion.

"I'm sorry," her mother said with sincerity.

"Great, Mom." Danica craned her neck, looking for Max to return with her shoes, wishing for a reason to disengage from her mother.

"Danica, look at me."

She reluctantly looked at her mother and was surprised by the tug in her heart—the longing for the woman she thought her mother had been. She wanted that woman to return, the woman who would never kiss another woman's husband. The woman who had finally found her footing after wading through oceans of pain and loneliness.

"I know what I did was wrong, and I'm sorry. I told you I'd sleep in my own mess, and I meant it. I'll come clean to those who need to know, but there's no reason for you to be snappy with me."

Danica pulled her mother away from the crowd. "Really, Mom? You kissed the man who hurt you, who hurt us! How can that not bother me? What do you expect of me?"

"What do I expect of you?" Her mother pulled her shoulders back and stood taller, looking Danica in the eye with a serious gaze. "How about a little respect? This is my life, and I make mistakes just like everyone else does. You can't blame me for that."

"Can't I?" Danica asked, then walked away.

Treat came around the corner and raised his hands. If his height and good looks were not enough to command the attention of everyone in the room, when he spoke, his deep, soothing voice drew the rest of them in. "Shall we try this again?" He led them toward a bank of elevators in the back of the hotel. They rode the elevators to the top floor, where Treat led them down a wide hallway, then up a set of private stairs to the roof. The room on the roof was fully encased by glass and functional windows. Not only did the room boast glorious views of the water, but Danica was surprised to smell the salty sea filtering through the open windows, as if they were on ground level rather than thirteen stories up. Fresh flowers decorated every table, and a beautiful altar had been constructed, much like the one on the beach. Danica couldn't help but wonder if Treat had multiple altars stored in a basement, ready to go. How else could he have them constructed in the blink of an eye?

Before Danica could thank him, Treat excused himself, ducking back down the stairs. *Where is he running off to?*

Danica watched her mother like a hawk. Hopefully, she wouldn't reveal her digression here and now, but she could hardly slow her racing pulse with the thought of it.

"Oh no, where's Max?" Kaylie asked.

"How should I know?" Danica snapped.

"Geez, Danica. What's with you?"

Danica shifted her eyes to the elevator. *Shit.* The thought of

Max avoiding Treat sent her nerves over the edge. She didn't know what was going on with them, but she didn't want to take any more chances. "I'll ask Blake to find Max." *Please make this nightmare stop.*

With Blake looking for Max and her mother safely talking to Nancy and Blake's father, Danica took advantage of her two free minutes to catch up with Sally.

"That was an insane day, huh? Rusty and Chase really pulled through for Kaylie."

"They love Trevor," Sally said while watching Gage and Rusty.

"How's everything going?" Danica asked, nodding toward Gage.

Sally sighed. "I should have ridden that ship when I had the chance. I'm afraid that being just friends for two years has thoroughly solidified me into the *just friends* category."

Danica had been referring to Rusty and Gage's friendship, but given how Sally felt about Gage, she wasn't surprised by her misguided, though honest, answer.

"I hear weddings can be aphrodisiacs for some people," Danica joked, then cringed as she thought of her mother and father kissing.

"Yeah? Hmm. What do I have to give him to make that happen?"

Just then, Gage turned and caught Sally's eye. Danica watched the way his lips lifted up at the ends and his eyes warmed and darkened. *Just friends, huh? Right.*

Blake stepped through the door, and Danica couldn't take her eyes off of the way his sun-kissed skin shimmered against his white shirt. Butterflies danced in her stomach, and she hoped those feelings would never diminish. She reminded herself that he was about to become her husband and she, his wife. *We'll never grow apart.* Even as she thought it, she knew the odds of divorce were high. She knew that no one intended on hurting his or her partner two, three, or five years down the line. And as he took her hand in his and drew her to her feet, she silently hoped that they would be one of the lucky couples who stayed together.

"I found her," Blake whispered. "She was getting your shoes and she got sidetracked."

Danica's eyes grew wide. "I'm barefoot at my own wedding and Max is sidetracked?"

Before Blake could answer, Max entered the room. Moonlight streamed through the glass ceiling and shone on her like a spotlight. Her cheeks were flushed and her face was pinched.

"Is she okay?" Danica asked Blake.

"Fine. I think she and Treat have a bit of a contentious relationship."

"What does that mean?"

He stepped behind her and whispered, "I think they're a bit frustrated with each other."

"Here are your shoes." Max handed Danica her shoes. "Sorry it took me so long. I had to...I...um. I had to find them." She turned on her heels and headed for Kaylie.

A minute later, Treat came through the door. He scanned the room, his eyes settling on Max. Again.

Just one more hour. One more nonconfrontational hour is all we need.

Chapter Thirty-One

Danica stood at the back of the room, watching everyone fall into place for their ceremony. Her mother looked gorgeous in her peach and gold dress, with her hair wavy and full, framing her face, and still, even with her beauty on this magical evening, Danica's stomach revolted against her secret. *Why, oh why, did you have to kiss Dad?* That's when it hit her. How could she have forgotten about her mother walking them down the aisle? Every time she looked at her, she felt sick. How could she walk down the aisle with her? And she never gave her father an answer, either. She felt her thin veil of sanity tearing away.

Get a grip before you ruin the wedding for everyone. She looked at Blake, standing beside Chaz at the altar, like two schoolboys ready for their first-grade graduation, their eyes anticipating, their hands fidgeting. She took a deep breath and closed her eyes for a second. *Pull it together.* When she opened them, Kaylie was elbowing her and nodding at Chaz and Blake.

"Look at him," Kaylie said. "Could I have gotten any luckier?" She didn't take her eyes off of Chaz.

"I'm not sure luck had anything to do with it," Danica answered.

"I know you believe in fate and all that higher power spiritual stuff, but for me, I'm pretty sure it was just dumb luck that I was in the bar at exactly the right time to meet him."

"I guess all that matters is that we're here now." Danica took Kaylie's hand. "Let's never let each other screw things up with our husbands, okay?" *Please?*

"Okay, but why do I think that I got the easy end of that bargain? You never screw up anything," Kaylie teased.

Wanna bet? Kaylie was a handful, but in her heart, Danica knew she'd never cheat on Chaz, or leave him for any of the hundred nonsensical reasons couples split up, like, *He doesn't understand me* or *I need more space.* She looked at her mother, then back at Kaylie. And that sinking feeling settled back into her stomach.

The bridesmaids and groomsmen readied themselves for the walk down the aisle. Blake's father and Chaz's mother joined them at some point. They were white noise to Danica's otherwise occupied mind. She searched the front row for her father. He sat tall and proud next to Madeline. Lacy slouched on Madeline's other side. Danica looked at the row behind them, where Sally sat next to Rusty, and Danica thought of the husband that Sally lost. If Dave hadn't passed away, would he be there today? Would she and Blake have found each other? Her eyes moved to Chase, Dave's other son, the product of a high school romance. That thought brought her back to Lacy. Was it inevitable? Did every marriage carry some sort of heavy drama that forced couples to sink or swim? Were they all doomed to carry heavy burdens? What would their test of strength be? Would she and Blake be able to weather it, or would it strike them down, too?

"Danica?"

Kaylie pulled at her arm.

"What?" she snapped.

"I asked you if you noticed the way Treat was staring at Max."

"What? No, sorry." *Treat and Max? I'm still on Mom and Dad and that goddamned kiss. It's looming over me like a villain waiting to pounce.* Danica inhaled deeply and blew it out slowly.

"You look green. Are you sure you're okay?" Kaylie asked.

"Yeah, yeah. Fine." *No. I want to pass out again and escape this mess. I want Mom and Dad to leave the room so no one says anything—and I want them to take Lacy with them. I'm afraid to get married. I don't want to end up like everyone else's nightmare. I want the happily ever after. I want the happily ever after. I want the happily ever after.*

The music began, and all eyes turned to the back of the room.

Chelsea dropped rose petals from a basket as she led the procession down the aisle. The groomsmen and bridesmaids made their way behind her. Camille and Weston walked side by side.

Danica felt like she was watching a movie of someone else's wedding.

Gage's tall, thick body dwarfed Marie's slim figure as they walked side by side.

Blake's father was handsome in his dark suit as he escorted Chaz's mother down the aisle, settled her into a seat in the front row, then took his place in the same row.

The Bridal Chorus began, and Danica's heart leapt.

Their mother appeared between Kaylie and Danica and silently offered an arm to each of her daughters. "Shall we do this, ladies?"

Danica froze, her eyes darting to her father, then back to her mother again. *This is all wrong.* How could she let her mother give her away any more than she could let her father? She didn't do anything any less wrong, at least not in Danica's eyes.

"Danica," Kaylie said through gritted teeth.

"I can't," was all she could manage. The man she loved was just a few feet away from her, waiting to become her husband, and she couldn't take her mother's arm and walk down the aisle. Kaylie was the drama queen—why was she thinking about poking the hornets' nest? This was so unlike her. Was she looking for an excuse not to walk down the aisle? Did she not want to get married?

One look at Blake, and she knew that wasn't the reason for her hesitation. *Damn it.* She glanced at her mother. *I love Mom.* She just hadn't had time to process what her mother had done yet, and it was still messing with her head.

"Are you okay, honey?" her mother asked.

Honey. The way her mother said it brought back a rush of memories from her youth: her mother bringing cupcakes to her second grade class. Her father running multiplication tables with them at the dinner table. Lying in the backyard on a blanket, studying in the sun, her mother right next to her with a Danielle Steel novel, her father flipping burgers while music played in the background and Kaylie sang and danced. Her mother and father helping her move into her first dorm room and out of her last.

He was there. In every memory, her father had been right there with them. Even if he was gone, spending time with Madeline and Lacy and pretending to be on a work trip, she couldn't retrieve the memories of him missing. In her mind, he was always there. He was her family. *Family knows no boundaries.*

Danica's pulse raced as the seconds turned to minutes and whispers filtered back to her.

It was a kiss. One kiss.

She looked at her father. His dark eyes caught hers, and there was so much pride and so much love in them that she could not turn away.

Danica knew what she had to do. She dropped her mother's arm. "One second," she said, and dragged Kaylie away from her mother.

"What are you doing? You're ruining the wedding."

"Listen to me. Just listen and don't freak out." Danica didn't give her a chance to react. "Dad wants to walk us down the aisle. I know we said just Mom, but, Kaylie, he's our father. He spent years taking care of us, and I don't care if he wasn't there after you graduated college, or if he missed a few days of our lives because he was with Lacy. I love Lacy. I love Madeline. I want him to walk us down the aisle, too."

A collective gasp told Danica that she was not whispering, as she thought she'd been. Every person in the room had heard her confession. She felt the heat of flush rise to the surface of her skin, and this time, she didn't care. All she cared about was Kaylie's answer, and from the appalled look on her sister's face, she was sure she'd never live down the moment she ruined her sister's wedding.

Chapter Thirty-Two

Kaylie's jaw hung open.

"I didn't mean to be so loud." This time Danica was certain she was whispering.

"Couldn't you have said something, I don't know, an hour ago? Twenty minutes ago?" Kaylie finally asked.

"I didn't know then. It just hit me as I was standing there."

"It just hit you. Really? How the hell does that just hit you? I have been thinking about it nonstop for months, and it just hit you?" Kaylie's limbs trembled; her face was red with anger.

"Kaylie, listen to me. I'm not saying this to stop the wedding or to ruin it. If you don't want him to walk us down the aisle, we'll just go with Mom, as planned, but"—she looked up at her father and felt Kaylie's eyes follow—"he didn't do what he did to us, really. I mean, he did, but…how can I explain it?"

"Damn it, Danica." Kaylie turned away and covered her eyes with her hand. "I love Lacy, too. And I don't even hate Madeline."

"So?"

"So? I don't know. I just…Dad? Really? Do you have any idea how much I *do* hate him?"

"Yes. I think everyone in this room knows just how much

you think you hate him." Danica couldn't have stopped her therapist's reasoning if she wore a muzzle. "But do you really hate him, or do you hate what he did? Think about it. Because once we walk down that aisle, once we say *I do*, there will be no do overs. There's only now. This. Right this very second. We have one chance, and it doesn't mean you love what he did to you or even that you forgive him. It just means that he's your father and you…" *Shit, what did it mean?* Danica felt the eyes of everyone upon her, and under the pressure of their gaze, she couldn't reason with her sister.

"It means that he's your father, and he loves you," her mother said.

Both girls looked at her, dumbfounded by her invasion into their private conversation. A second later, Danica realized that this part of their conversation wasn't private either, but that they were debating in front of everyone, and that realization brought another; her father must be mortified, knowing they were arguing over him and his affair.

Danica turned her back to everyone except Kaylie. She put her arm protectively around her sister's shoulder. "It was unfair of me to spring it on you, and it wasn't intentional. Whatever you decide, I'll be fine with it. You tell me, Kay. What does your heart tell you to do?"

Kaylie turned around slowly. Her gaze shifted from her mother, to Madeline, to her father, then to Lacy, where they remained for at least a full fifteen seconds.

"Okay," she whispered. "I'll do it for Lacy."

"Okay?"

"Okay."

"Thank you!" She hugged Kaylie. "Dad?" She hadn't meant to yell for him.

Her father stood, walking tentatively around the chairs, all eyes now upon him.

Danica motioned for him to come forward. *I did the right thing.* "You did the right thing," she said to Kaylie.

Kaylie moved to her mother's side.

Her father stood up straighter, walked a little taller. He straightened his tie, then ran a hand over his short hair as his nervousness gave way to pride.

A lump formed wide and painful in Danica's throat.

Her mother began to move away, and she reached for her and shook her head.

Suddenly he was there, standing next to Danica. She felt his presence like an embrace, though he didn't reach for her. He didn't touch her, or assume he should take charge. His eyes glistened, and in those tears that he held back, Danica saw the love in his heart and the appreciation for hers. He remained silent, waiting for instructions.

He simply came when she'd asked.

Like he always had.

Only she'd stopped asking long ago.

Chapter Thirty-Three

Danica looked at her parents standing side by side. Their indiscretion came rushing back to her. *It's not your business. It was just a kiss.* She couldn't allow their mistake to ruin her day.

Kaylie smiled shyly at her father, then stared straight ahead, as if she'd accept his arm, but refused to speak to him. The disappointment that washed through his eyes lasted only a second, for when Kaylie took his arm, his entire face lit up.

"Dan, how are we doing this now with both of them?" Anxiety thrust Kaylie's words, fast and panicked.

"I don't know. Um. Dad in the middle? Oh gosh, I'm not sure." *I'm ruining everything.*

"Girls, your father and I will walk Kaylie down the aisle, and then we'll return and walk you, Danica." It wasn't a question, and as her mother moved into place beside Kaylie, the Bridal Chorus began anew. Danica was glad her mother had the answer.

Doesn't she always?

No, she kissed Dad. Shut up.

Kaylie moved with the grace of a princess, and Danica wished she could see her face. Chaz looked at her with dreamy eyes. Pride drew his shoulders back, and nerves sent his fingers fidgeting against his thighs.

Danica's heart thundered in her chest as her parents placed a sweet kiss on Kaylie's cheek and deposited her across from her groom and headed back toward her.

She drew in a breath.

And looked at Blake.

This is it.

This is everything.

Her father and mother flanked her, and she must have taken their arms, though she had no recollection of guiding those muscles. Her legs carried her down the aisle—but how could they? They felt like rubber. So many years had passed since she'd held on to her father in any way that even this contact, her hand resting on his forearm, brought comfort. She tried to memorize the feel of him, the feel of walking beside him. Once she was certain she'd never forget the warmth of the moment, she lifted her gaze to Blake once again. As she neared her place beside Kaylie, she noticed the dampness in his eyes, causing an even larger lump in her throat.

She didn't feel her parents' kisses, or hear what Treat said as he started their service. She couldn't hear past the swelling of her heart as it raced toward the *I do* finish line.

She reached for Kaylie's hand and was surprised to find Kaylie'd been reaching for hers. Their fingertips touched, and Danica's heart slowed its frantic pace.

"Life doesn't get any sweeter than when you take a spouse." Treat's voice was laden with love. "There will be no one more tender and attentive to your needs, nor should there ever be, than the one you will take as your partner, your lover, your spouse. The union of marriage you are about to form will be your new home. It will house your strength, your love, your courage, and your fidelity. It will also house your sadness and the harshness that life bestows on you. The ability to heal and rebuild is within you, Kaylie Elizabeth and Chaz Michael, and within you, Danica Joy and Blake Earl. As you create this sacred union and accept these solemn vows, remember that your partner, your lover, your spouse will rely on, and trust in, your promise."

Kaylie's fingers trembled against Danica's and she held her hand tightly, letting her sister know that she was there and that the trust he spoke of was also within Danica for Kaylie.

"Do you understand this?" Treat asked.

In unison, they said, "Yes."

Treat nodded, using his hand to motion for the brides and grooms to face each other, and as they moved into place, a tear slipped down Blake's cheek.

Danica wanted to reach for him, but she could not move. Stilled by his emotions, she could only allow her own tears to fall, her eyes never leaving her future husband's sweet face.

"Who gives these couples in marriage?" Treat asked.

"I do." Danica couldn't decipher one parent's voice from the next, but she knew in her heart that all of their parents had responded.

Blake mouthed, *I love you.*

Danica's heart galloped again. She dropped Kaylie's hand and dabbed at her tears. *I love you, too*, she mouthed.

"Will you please join hands?" Treat asked.

Danica lifted her shaking hands and noticed that all of their hands were trembling. Blake took her hands in his and provided instant comfort. She blinked away her tears and looked at his strong hand, embracing hers with more than just love—with the promise of the trust that Treat had spoken of, and it sent a warm light right to her heart.

"Chaz," Treat began, "will you take Kaylie, and her alone, to be your wedded wife? Will you love, comfort, and adore her through good times and bad, in sickness and in health? Will you honor her feelings and cherish her emotions at all times? Will you promise to value her precious heart, to be faithful to her no matter what temptations come your way?"

"I do," Chaz said.

"Kaylie," Treat began again, "will you take Chaz, and he alone, to be your wedded husband? Will you love, comfort, and adore him through good times and bad, in sickness and in health? Will you honor his feelings and cherish his emotions at all times? Will you promise to value his precious heart, to be faithful to him no matter what temptations come your way?"

"I do," Kaylie said in a thin, shaky voice.

Treat asked the same of Blake, and Danica held her breath awaiting his response.

"I will not only do that," Blake began, "but I will also spend every waking hour in search of all things that bring joy to her life. I promise you, Danica Joy Snow, to never be less than the man you are marrying today."

Sobs billowed in her chest, and Danica swallowed against them. She saw raw emotion in Blake's eyes, love so deep and true that she could feel it blossoming like a rose between them. The gasp of the crowd reiterated what she felt but could not show. Her knees grew weak. She was sure her legs had turned to rubber, and she tightened the muscles in her thighs just to remain standing. *I promise you, Danica Joy Snow, to never be less than the man you are marrying today.* Her heart swooned, stealing her concentration. She blinked away tears of joy and took in a shaky breath, trying desperately to concentrate on the vows Treat was presenting her with.

As much as she wanted to give Blake the same beautiful promises that he gave her, when she opened her mouth, full of love and promises, her courage failed her. She feared something else might spew forth, pushed by the stress of the day. She didn't trust her own voice to follow her heart's path. Instead, she said, "I do," wishing she could have said so much more.

Blake's grin revealed that what she'd said was all he'd ever wanted.

"And who holds the rings to bind these unions?" Treat asked.

"Oh no!" Max jumped up. "Hold on just a minute. I'm so sorry." She ran out the door, and they waited with silly grins on their lips and love in their eyes, shadowed only by a fleeting thought: *Max never forgets anything.*

Max stormed through the door a few minutes later with two ring boxes in her hands. She stopped before approaching the altar and smoothed her dress back down. She ran her fingers through her dark, tousles locks, while Treat's gaze held her in place. Then, with grace and warmth, Max made her way up the aisle and presented the rings to the grooms.

"Sorry. They were still upstairs with the twins," she whispered. She shifted a quick glance to Kaylie. "Don't worry. They're sleeping like logs and doing fine."

Treat smiled and waited until she was seated before continuing. "Circles, and thereby these rings, are a token of love not to be broken. They are a token of the covenant between each of you, Kaylie and Chaz, Danica and Blake. Bless these rings and may you forever live in unity, with love and respect, joy and appreciation for one another. Amen."

Blake and Chaz held the rings before Danica and Kaylie's shaking hands.

"Please repeat after me." Treat nodded to both Chaz and Blake. "I choose you Kaylie, or Danica, and please choose the right one."

Everyone laughed while Chaz and Blake repeated Treat's words, each inserting the appropriate name.

Treat continued. "To be my wife, to love, honor, and cherish you from this day forward, in days and playful nights." They laughed again, and Blake and Chaz repeated his words.

Danica was thankful for the levity. She listened to every word Blake said, and when she thought of the playful nights they'd already enjoyed, goose bumps rose on her arms.

"And with this ring, I thee wed. Let it forever be a symbol of our love."

After the men slid the rings on their fingers, Danica and Kaylie repeated the same lovely vows. Danica slid the ring on Blake's finger, and when she reached the dip just below his knuckle, she ran her fingers gently over his hand. She wanted to pull his hand to her lips and kiss it, to feel his warmth against her cheek. Instead, she slid her finger back down the length of his and let her fingertips remain on his hands. He turned his hand over and took her hand in his.

With a smile that lit up his eyes, Treat brought his hands up high and said, "In the presence of those you have chosen, now, by the authority vested in me, I pronounce you husbands and wives!"

Blake didn't wait for the offer to kiss Danica, and Kaylie's impetuous side took over as well, as the couples came together in deep, passionate kisses, faster than Treat could take another breath.

With a hearty laugh, Treat said, "I now present Mr. and Mrs. Chaz Crew and Mr. and Mrs. Blake Carter."

Chapter Thirty-Four

Danica didn't know that heat from the moon could sear through her soul, but that's what it felt like when Blake drew her in to their first kiss as a married couple. He lifted her feet off the ground, holding her against his muscular chest. Through the thickness of his tuxedo and her dress, their heartbeats raced in unison. Right there, in front of everyone she loved so dearly, she felt herself floating up, looking down at a woman she was sure was the happiest girl in the world and at a man who could not keep his lips, or his eyes, off of her.

Suddenly her feet were back on the floor, and Kaylie was hugging her, laughing and trembling.

Blake took Danica's hand in his and faced their friends. Danica blinked away her dreamy state but could not quell her racing heart as Blake guided her down the aisle and rose petals flitted down upon them.

When they reached the end of the red carpet that Danica had somehow missed on her trip down the aisle, Blake looked into her eyes and said, "I meant every word I said. I will never hurt you, Danica Carter."

Danica Carter.

Danica Carter.

Oh my God, I'm Danica Carter!

She jumped into his arms and kissed him.

"Sheesh, there they go again," Kaylie teased. "Get a room already!"

Danica flashed a smile at her sister. "Excuse me, Mrs. Crew, but I'm Danica Carter now, and I'd like to enjoy that for a moment. In public."

The fatigue of the day was lost on the excitement of the reception. Treat had arranged for a full-course meal, a band that played tropical music, and he'd even managed to have a wedding cake specially made, very similar to the one Max had originally ordered.

"Thank you, princess."

Danica turned at the term of endearment that she hadn't heard since her college graduation.

"Dad."

"Thank you for letting me be a part of your ceremony. I can't tell you how much that meant to me." He looked down at his hands, then back up at her.

Danica still wasn't used to her father's new, less confident demeanor, though she realized that if he'd shown up with the same confidence he once held, she'd have thought less of him for it.

"I'm glad, Dad," she said. She scanned the crowed for Kaylie, then asked, "Has Kaylie spoken to you yet?"

He shook his head.

She thought of her mother. The kiss. "Probably just as well. Baby steps," she said.

"Thank you, for all those things you said about Lacy and Madeline. That was…they were…"

"Dad?"

He lifted his eyes.

"I meant them. I love Lacy, and I think I'm even finding a place for Madeline in my heart." She watched Blake hovering nearby, and she knew he'd jump in and rescue her if she so much as turned in his direction. His presence gave her strength to continue on. "Dad, we do need to talk. About Mom."

His eyes narrowed. His lips pressed into a tight, serious line.

"I know you two kissed," she said. *Why am I doing this now?*

"Danica—"

"Don't," she said.

He took a step forward, and Danica stepped out of his grasp. "But—"

She cut him off again. "I don't want to talk about it right now. I just want you to know that Kaylie doesn't know, and I don't want her to find out right now, tonight. Maybe not even on this trip."

"Find what out?" Kaylie asked from over her shoulder.

Chapter Thirty-Five

Danica tried to dissuade Kaylie from pushing for an answer, but Kaylie would have no part of it.

"Tell me, Danica. He's my father, too, and whatever you're withholding can't make me feel any more bad about who he is."

Wanna bet?

Thankfully, her father had melted into the crowd when Danica asked him to, so she had Kaylie all to herself.

"Drop it, Kay. Please?"

"Why do I always feel like you keep me in the dark until you deem it's time to bring me into the light? That's so unfair, and it's really kinda mean."

Kaylie stuck her lower lip out, looking so pitifully cute that Danica pulled her into her arms without thinking. "Come on. Our husbands are waiting."

With Kaylie safely smothered by Chaz, Weston, Camille, and Jeff, Danica went to do some recon with Max, who was sitting next to Sally.

"You're amazing, Max. You pulled this off beautifully."

"I forgot the rings," Max said.

"Yes, but that's so little. I mean, come on. You made two perfect weddings. Two!"

Max smiled. "Thanks, but it wasn't really me." She looked across the room at Treat, who stood with his arm around Blake.

"God, he's cute," Sally said.

"So handsome," Danica agreed.

"I'm talking about Treat." Sally laughed.

"Oh, yeah. He is too," Danica teased.

"He's arrogant and pushy," Max added.

"He is not. He's lovely." Sally picked up a glass of champagne and took a sip.

"Not really," Max mumbled.

Sally and Danica exchanged a curious glance.

"Did something happen, Max? Did he try something with you that we should know about? Because if he did—"

Max cut Danica off with a shake of her head. "No. Forget I said anything."

"Max?" Danica pushed.

"I'm gonna go to the ladies' room."

Treat watched every step Max took. Danica made a mental note to ask Blake about them later.

They drank, danced, and ate, and danced some more. Weston made a beautiful speech, as did Blake's father. When Danica's mother stood to speak half an hour later, the room hushed.

"There are certain days that a mother always remembers. The birth of her babies, their first steps, their first words. For me, two of the most magical days were when my daughters first told me that they found the men they were going to marry. Neither one delivered the news in a well presented phone call or even a clear letter. Not my girls. They delivered the news in bits and pieces. *I love him. He's everything I could ever hope for. He'll be a wonderful father.*"

Danica felt the strange pang she had noticed recently when thinking of Blake and parenthood in the same thought, and she looked at Blake's handsome face, allowing herself to wonder what their babies might look like. Would they have her springy hair and his strong jaw? Might their son be big and strong like him, athletically inclined, or might they have a daughter who was more academic minded, like her? She tucked away these new thoughts and focused on her mother, standing before them with tears welling in her eyes.

Her mother continued. "Now I'm forced to try to remember all those little messages at once. In time, I may forget each of those moments, and they'll likely become one general feeling. In fact, maybe they already have. But two things I'll never forget are the moments when I realized that you, Chaz and Blake, were the men my daughters had chosen to spend their lives with. I've loved each of you ever since that first realization occurred. They say that when your daughter marries, you don't lose her; you gain a son. I've gained two. I'm honored to have the two of you in our family."

Blake squeezed Danica's hand.

Perfect. Just perfect.

As they sipped champagne, Danica caught sight of Max at the next table with Abby. Max kept glancing at Treat, and when she wasn't looking at him, Treat was looking at her.

"What's up with Treat and Max?" she asked Blake.

"Nothing that I know of. Why?"

Danica shrugged. "You said things were contentious between them. She said he's arrogant, but he doesn't seem it."

Blake smiled, nodded.

"What?" She recognized the mischief in his eyes.

"I never would have put those two together, but if she says he's arrogant, she's probably right."

"Blake, what are you talking about?"

He lifted his eyebrows.

"Oh my God. You mean you think they slept together and…maybe he blew her off or something?" She looked at Max again. "No way, not Max. She's not that kind of girl."

"If Treat Braden sets his sights on you, even those girls that aren't turn into that kind of girl."

"No way. I mean, he's really handsome, but…"

"And rich, and a smooth talker, and very generous, you have to admit," Blake said.

"Yeah, but…" Danica felt like an idiot. It was all coming together. No girl would ignore advances by someone like Treat. She'd been viewing him as Blake's cousin, but if she removed that relationship, she saw Treat with entirely new eyes. That gleaming smile was suddenly smoldering. Those clear, direct eyes were hungry and lascivious. His masculine physique became ripped and thunderous.

Danica shook the thoughts away. "Oh my God. You might be right," she admitted.

"Might be? What did I tell you about the Braden boys?"

Danica remembered Dane's words. *We Braden boys are known for being ladies' men.* She tried not to think about his ten-inch comment.

An hour later, having shared their last congratulatory hugs, Danica and Blake made their way upstairs with Chaz and Kaylie.

"Where are you guys sleeping tonight?" Danica asked.

Kaylie bit her lower lip and looked up at Chaz with heat in her eyes.

"Your mom said she'd stay with the kids. We're staying in another room, thanks to Treat." He pulled Kaylie close and kissed her more passionately than Danica had ever witnessed.

"Yes!" Kaylie said with a playful fist pump.

"Go. Get in your room," Danica teased.

The two couples headed in different directions. Blake opened the hotel room door and swooped Danica up into his arms.

"I'm way too heavy for this." She laughed.

"You're just perfect." He kissed her as he carried her across the threshold.

Danica was sure that somewhere between saying good night to Kaylie and Blake sweeping her into his arms and carrying her into their room, which smelled like roses, she'd died and gone to heaven.

Blake set her down and flicked on the light. Danica gasped. The bedspread had been changed to a thick, white, velvety comforter. Red rose petals were strewn across it in the shape of a heart, and vases full of fresh red roses covered every surface, bringing the sweet aroma to every breath they took.

"Did you do this?" Danica asked.

Blake shook his head. "It must have been Treat."

"If Max and Treat did hook up, and she's avoiding him because of it, then he must have done something awful. I mean, the man obviously knows about romance." She took Blake's face in her hands, feeling the beginnings of prickly whiskers against her palms, and she kissed him with all the feelings she'd been holding back during the ceremony, then pulled away with a nip at his tongue.

"Whoa," Blake whispered.

"I want to take a bath," she said.

"A bath?" Blake cocked his head.

"With you." She trailed her finger along his chin, then motioned for him to follow her into the bathroom. Danica had been playing the evening over in her mind the whole way up the elevator. Everyone talked about their wedding night, the sex they did or didn't have. Camille and Jeff had been too drunk to do anything. He'd passed out on their wedding night, and Camille always joked that she was thankful that he had. But Danica imagined that the joke was to spare Camille's true feelings. Didn't every woman want something special to remember about their wedding night?

Danica definitely wanted a wedding night to remember—and one that would erase the discontent of the afternoon. She didn't have a plan, and she wasn't sure what *a wedding night to remember* really even meant, but when she saw what Treat had done, she realized that she wanted romance, and the one thing—no, more accurately, *one of the things*—she and Blake hadn't yet done together was to take a bubble bath. That was a start.

She started the bath and poured half of the bottle of bubbles into the water. She was suddenly nervous, unsure of how to make a perfect romantic night. *Maybe expectations aren't a good thing after all. Maybe Camille hadn't been joking. Maybe—*

Blake unzipped her dress and slipped his hands around from

behind before it had even fallen to the ground. Danica shivered beneath his touch, her worries forgotten. He kissed the back of her neck, trailing kisses down her spine, while he caressed her stomach, her hips, her—*oh yes*—

She closed her eyes, listening to the water pouring from the faucet, breathing in the thick floral scent and trembling beneath Blake's hand as his hand slid between her legs.

His tongue moved slowly up the center of her spine and she gasped, grabbing for the wall as he touched the heated folds of her flesh. One hand disappeared and she felt him unbuttoning his shirt, then shaking his chest free, never pausing in his rubbing, caressing the bundle of nerves between her legs. Fast, then agonizingly slowly, as she arched against his hand.

His pants fell to the floor, and she felt him step out of them; then his chest was against her, prickly against her back. His hardness pressed against the flesh of her bottom while his fingers worked their magic. His other hand came around and pinched her nipple. She sucked in a breath, and he quickly released her, dropped his hand to her hip, thrusting her back against him. A sexy little moan escaped her lips.

Everything fell away—the sound of the water, the light in the room. There was only her and Blake and the incredible heights he was drawing her toward. He took the muscle between her neck and shoulder in his teeth, biting just hard and fast enough to send searing streaks of lightning through her body. He did it again, and at the same time, his fingers slid inside of her, taking her up and over the edge as he lapped at the nip he'd taken, then took her in his teeth again.

"Blake," she cried out, curling her toes under and reaching behind her and grasping his hips as her muscles squeezed and contracted around his thrusting fingers.

"That's it, baby. Come for me," he said.

No one had ever spoken to her like that before. In all her years of dating—not that she'd slept with many men, but she'd had enough—and none, not one, had made her feel so wanted, so sexy.

"You're so beautiful when you let me love you," he said.

Danica couldn't catch her breath as her body rode out the convulsions like mini aftershocks. She gasped when he slid his fingers out of her and turned her slowly toward him, covered her mouth with his. Her senses were on fire. Each thrust of his tongue sent new shocks through her loins.

"Better turn off that bathtub," he whispered.

Danica reached for the tub, not wanting to leave his arms, his lips, his God-like hands. She felt drunk, though she hadn't had enough to drink to send her mind into the sexual haze that possessed it.

With his hands gently placed upon her hips, he guided her into the oversized bathtub and helped her down, until her body was submerged in warm bubbles.

"God, you're beautiful," he said as he climbed into the tub, facing her. "I just want to look at you."

Danica felt her face flush again. She hadn't blushed this much since she was a teenager. Blake made her feel beautiful and sexy, shy and incredibly desirous. Naughty. He definitely made her feel naughty. He continually awakened new parts of her that she didn't know existed, and the more he did, the more she allowed herself to enjoy it.

He touched her cheek, and she closed her eyes, pressing her cheek against his palm. If they did nothing else the entire night, she wouldn't care. The closeness they'd already experienced was more romantic than anything she'd ever dreamed of.

He slid his hand from her cheek, and she relaxed her head back against the tub. He ran his hands down her calves, and she moaned. She'd never experienced anything as luxurious as her husband's—*husband's*—tender touch. He squeezed each calf until her sore muscles relaxed; then he moved to her foot. Why did it feel so erotic to have his hands massaging her feet? Danica had never experienced a man touching her foot with so much love that it was as if he were making love to her.

He moved to the other foot, both of his thumbs pushing on the tender pressure points in her arch, caressing the pads of her feet with his strong thumbs. Tension drained from her—tension she didn't even realize had taken hold of her.

He set her feet on either side of his hips and inched himself closer, then went to work loving, massaging, the muscles in her thighs. His strength pushed and squeezed in all the right places, stealing the stress from all the way up her torso and drawing it out through the release in the tight muscles of her thighs.

She was being spoiled, she realized, and lifted her head. She should be giving him just as much love as he was giving her.

"Uh-uh. I want to take care of you. Every inch of you," he said.

Danica didn't have the energy to argue. She gave in to his desire and relaxed back into the decadent role of her willing and able body.

He took her hips in his hands and squeezed the tension out. His hands moved inch by inch along her body, gently massaging his way across the taut skin of her stomach and up her rib cage.

Danica's body tingled in anticipation of his touch to turn more desirous, but he continued loving every inch of her with his hands, not taking her, not doing anything overly sexual, just bringing all those muscles that had clenched around him, and for him, to a relaxed state.

He slid his hands up to her breasts, stroking them. She felt the prickling of her nipples hardening. He worked around their hard peaks until Danica's breathing became shallow, and she craved more. His hands slid to the flat area above her breasts. She felt the prickling of his pubic hair against the flesh of her bottom as he moved in closer to reach every possible piece of her. He slid his hands up and down her arm, squeezing each muscle. His sensual touch had her so close to the edge that she debated slipping down, making him take her. No, she didn't dare break the erotic feel of his hands on her flesh.

"I want to love every bit of you. Forever," he whispered.

"Love me," she responded. He moved to her other arm, then took each finger between the knuckles of his index and second fingers and drew the tension from them, too. Danica had never imagined such a feeling of sheer pleasure, such heightened erotica from the sensation in one little finger.

He cradled her hand in his, using his thumbs to drive the tension up and out of her palm. She bit her lower lip to keep from calling out his name.

"What?" he whispered.

She shook her head, afraid to break the delicious arousal that he had built. She felt his hard shaft against her, making her insides pull down toward him, against the warm and bubbly water.

"Tell me," he said.

Danica shivered. She knew what he wanted. She'd been thinking of *Tell Me* ever since he'd first coerced her to tell him what she wanted. She didn't want to respond. She wanted him to do just what he was doing, nothing more, nothing less.

He brought both hands to her neck, raising her to a sitting position, rubbing, stroking, his fingers digging under her hair to the base of her skull, kneading her muscles into submission.

Danica's head fell back with a moan, and he moved his thumbs to the soft divot behind her ears. His touch was like a drug she couldn't get enough of, like a dream she never wanted to wake up from.

"Touch me," he said.

Danica opened her eyes and blinked away the haze of her arousal. Blake's dark, desirous eyes pleaded with her. He was telling her. *Tell me*, she thought.

"Where?" she whispered, hardly believing she was asking him.

"Anywhere," he said, then closed his eyes as she rubbed his thighs in the same slow, sensual way that he'd touched her. She worked her way down to his knees, spending extra time on the soft, delicate skin behind them.

She caressed her way back up his legs to his strong, wide hips. Oh, his delicious hips. She was so close. One slip of her hand and he was hers. Her hands seemed impossibly small against his body. She kneaded her fingers deep into the tension hidden in the fibers of his muscles. The movement pushed the bubbles to the side, and she dropped her eyes to his impressive erection. She was surprised at the surge she felt within her loins; the desire to lift herself onto him was almost too much to resist. But no, she held back. She gave his body every bit of loving attention that he'd given hers, touching, loving every inch of his flesh. Kneading, massaging, caressing him, until she knew there was no doubt in his mind that she loved him as much as he loved her.

When she reached his neck, Blake opened his eyes, and the

sleepy, lusty look he gave her made it almost impossible for her to finish what she'd started. She tried her damnedest to blink away the heat of attraction, rubbing his neck, pushing her fingers up along his hairline, until she grasped his skull as he'd done to her and applied pressure with her fingertips and thumb. The motion pulled her forward, out of the water.

The cool air hit her wet breasts, sending a shock through her. She gasped, closing her eyes while she regained control. If he could touch all of her and not take her, she could be just as strong. She slid her hands to his shoulders, pushing and pressing with all of her might. His eyes were open now, watching her breasts sway with her efforts. Just knowing he was watching her heightened her arousal. His warm breath mingled with the cool air, and her body responded instantly, aching for his mouth to touch her, taste her.

She opened her eyes and met his heated stare, slowly lowering herself back into the tepid water.

Blake grabbed her arms before she could settle all the way down into the tub. Her body trembled from the cold. He pulled her against him, chest to chest, eye to eye, then kissed her softly.

Danica thought she might just melt into him, until her body and his became one gooey mess of love. He stole her thoughts with another soft kiss, then guided her back down into the tub while he stood, grabbing a thick white towel, and then helped her up to her feet.

He wrapped her lovingly in the towel, then, still naked, his erection never faltering, he took another towel from the rack and bent to dry her feet, moving up her calves slowly, careful to dry every spec of her shivering skin. He took tender care as he dried her hips, her belly, and the low curve of her back, working his way up her chest and down her arms.

Every nerve in her body felt electrified. Every breath a shallow, careful movement. She kept waiting, wanting, hoping he would take her to the next level, touch her in the ways he had before the bath. He'd created a fire within her that craved him.

He tucked the dry towel around her and dried himself, then took her hand and led her to the bed, where he laid her back upon the rose petals.

Blake rolled her over and hung the towel over the chair. She lay on her stomach, naked; even the warm air of the room felt erotic as it danced across her skin. She felt the bed dip by her knees as he positioned himself with one knee on either side of her. He kissed her spine to the curve of her shoulder.

"Blake," she whispered.

"Tell me," he said.

"Take me. Love me."

Blake took something from the nightstand drawer, then resumed kneeling above her. She heard a cap unscrew, then winced as liquid dribbled along her backside and spine. The cap screwed on, and then something landed on the bed. She opened her eyes and saw a dark bottle beside her.

Blake's strong palms worked the oil along her shoulders and down her back, slipping, sliding, gliding up the curve of her ass, where he worked it along her backside, then down the slope of her inner thighs. The oil warmed beneath his touch, leaving a trail of fire behind.

She moaned, unable to restrain the pleasure from escaping her lips. She gripped the bedspread in her fists as he spread the oil along her inner thighs, so close to her sensitive skin that she could feel her body tugging toward him, wanting him.

"Blake, please," she pleaded.

He slid his hands up along her sides, spending extra time on the sides of her breasts, then lowered his body on top of hers.

"Please what?" he asked.

The weight of him was too much. She needed him, every inch of him.

"Please…" She heard herself begging for sex, and the embarrassment she expected never came. She had to have him, and now they were husband and wife. She didn't need to be cautious or shy.

"Please make love to me," she said, and closed her eyes again, waiting for him to flip her over. When he didn't, she felt his heat filling the space between them.

He slid his hand down her side and drew her legs farther apart. He held himself up with one elbow, his arm shaking as much as Danica's body trembled. She closed her eyes, waiting for him to take what any man would with a naked, spread-eagle woman lying facedown beneath him in a sex-induced coma. Part of her hoped he wouldn't, and another part of her hoped he would. She bit her lower lip, gripping the edge of the mattress. She was ready. Whatever he wanted to take, she'd give; whatever he wanted to give, she'd receive.

She didn't expect his fingers to slip beneath her hips and touch her in fast, expertly positioned strokes. She didn't expect to buck into him as she pinned his hand beneath her grinding hips. And she surely didn't expect to be begging him to be inside her.

"Now. Please. I need you. Inside. Put it inside."

He slipped his fingers in and out until the teasing escalated and her body was in the throes of the most intense orgasm she'd ever experienced. Her nerves clenched, her toes curled under, every muscle in her body constricted, and her breathing caught and held. She squeezed her eyes shut, waiting for the waves of thunder to pass. Just as she opened her eyes, he slid his fingers out and she released her breath in one loud rush of air.

"Tell me," he whispered.

"Can't," she huffed.

"Tell me, pretty girl."

She couldn't imagine enduring any more than her body had. She knew it was selfish not to tell him what he wanted to hear. She forced the words from her mouth, certain she'd disappoint him. She had no energy left. She lay still beneath him. Spent. She wasn't even sure she'd said the words aloud.

"Take me. Love me. Become one with me."

She felt his hand on her bottom and held her breath.

When he slipped deep inside of her, she felt it all the way to her core, slow at first, then harder, deeper. He didn't take her from behind. He entered her center, and before she had time to wonder why he hadn't taken what any other guy would have felt was his to claim, she was peaking again, arching up as he met her clenching body, thrust for thrust, in his own beautiful orgasm.

Their bodies glistened with sweat and oil. They panted, their fingers intertwined, as they lay beside each other.

"Why didn't you…you know?" Danica asked in the wee hours of the morning.

"Hmm?"

Danica closed her eyes. He had to be kidding. "You know. I was there for the taking. Oiled up, ready."

"Yeah."

She turned her face toward him.

It was then, eye to eye, no pretenses, no hidden agendas, no barriers, that he said the words that swept away any concerns that might have crept in.

"I wasn't even sure I'd enter you at all tonight. You filled me so full of love, your touch made me feel so close to you, that I didn't need more." He lifted her hand to his lips and kissed it. "You said to become one with you. I did the only thing that could bring us closer than we already were. I'll never take anything from you that you don't want to give."

Her voice failed her.

As she drifted off to sleep, Danica realized that the romance she wanted had been right there all along—in Blake's eyes, in his touch, in his words. All she had to do was open herself to him.

Chapter Thirty-Six

Danica couldn't stop looking at her wedding ring. *Wedding ring!* She'd been up for an hour, had already showered, dried her hair, and dressed. She watched Blake step out of his towel and into his jeans. The shyness she'd felt just two nights earlier no longer plagued her. Something inside her changed. She felt it from the tip of her head to the ends of her toes and in all the naughty places in between.

"I love you," Blake said as he pulled a white polo shirt over his head.

"I love you, too."

"I know you do." He kissed her on her forehead. "We leave tomorrow. You know, there's still time to book a honeymoon."

In the last few hours, when it was just the two of them in their room, without the chaos of her parents or the outside influence of Mother Nature, Danica had felt like they were already on their honeymoon.

"I thought we agreed that we'd take our honeymoon after the bliss of the wedding had passed." She loved the idea of traveling with Blake, but she knew that the wedding wouldn't be easy with Kaylie, their mother and father, Lacy and Madeline all in one room, and the idea that they'd go from one whirlwind event directly into another without time to process or breathe made Danica a little nervous. She worried that the honeymoon might be dampened by the stress of the wedding.

"We did, and I'm fine with that. I'll go wherever you want, whenever you want." Blake's ski shop had really taken off the previous year, and her youth center was also doing well. They could easily afford a honeymoon at any destination they chose.

"Greece is still looking good," Blake said with a grin.

"Australia, too," Danica added. "I don't know where I want to go. I only know that I feel like I spent a full week away with you in the last twenty-four hours, so everything else is just gravy."

"Whipped cream."

"Dirty boy."

He pulled her against him. "Only with you, babe. Only with you."

They found everyone lounging around the pool. Some looking a little worse for wear than others. Kaylie and Chaz sat at the edge of the baby pool while Trevor and Lexi splashed in the knee-high water.

"There they are," Kaylie teased. "I thought Blake might have done you in."

"Ha-ha," Danica sneered. "How did my favorite niece and nephew do last night?"

"Great. Mom's at the gift shop with Madeline."

"What?"

"I know, right? Who would have ever thought that they'd

get along?" Kaylie patted the space beside her. "Sit."

Danica sat in her shorts with her feet in the water.

"So?" Kaylie whispered. "Was it everything you ever dreamed of?"

For the hundredth time since they'd arrived in Nassau, heat flushed her cheeks. "I never dreamed about my wedding night. But if I had, I can guarantee you that it wouldn't have come anywhere close to last night."

Kaylie squealed and hugged her.

Blake gave her a knowing look, and she licked her lips, feeling the rush of anticipation from the evening before like a tickling of fingers along her spine.

"How about you?"

Kaylie leaned forward and whispered, "Un-freakin'-believable." She tossed a toy in the water for Lexi. "I swear, I never remember my boyfriends being that hot." She screwed up her face like she was thinking. "Maybe you have to marry a man to really get him to put in effort."

They both laughed.

"Everyone leaves tonight but us," Kaylie said.

"I know. But that's good. We'll have a nice, quiet evening."

"I still can't believe you're not going on a honeymoon."

"We will. I'm in no hurry." Danica looked at Blake and knew that no matter where they were, their love would carry them through. They could live in a cardboard box, and she wouldn't love him any less.

"Well, I am. I love my kids, but a week in Las Vegas without them? Sleeping in, having a drink once in a while. Going dancing? Gosh, it's been forever since I've done those things. Last night was like a dream." She poked Danica in the ribs. "Even with your last-minute guilt trip."

"Sorry about that."

Kaylie shrugged. "No worries. The drama is all over now, and we made it through unscathed."

Danica spotted her mother and Madeline headed their way, with Lacy trailing behind them.

I'm not so sure about that.

"Look what we got for the kids!" Their mother pulled out an inner tube with a Mickey Mouse head. "Chaz, can you blow this up? We got Donald for Trevor, too."

Danica watched Lacy take off her gauzy cover-up, lay a towel down, and relax into the lounge chair in her bikini. She had sunglasses on, but Danica could feel her eyes on her mother. Why did everything have to be so painful? Danica wished she could just throw her hands up and say, *Mom kissed Dad. Okay? But since you've already done that to her, it shouldn't matter, right, Madeline? No hard feelings?* And in this fictitious world of hers, Madeline would look at her mother and smile. She might even touch her arm thoughtfully and say, *Oh, Helen, it's okay. Whatever happens, happens, right?* And then they could all go back to their happy little bubbles of life where none of this ever came into play again.

But that would never happen.

And Danica knew from the scowl on Lacy's face that she'd never drop it from her memory bank until it had been dealt with. She took a deep breath and went to Lacy.

"Move over," she said, pushing Lacy's legs over with her butt. She took the glasses from Lacy's eyes and felt like she was replaying the scene with Kaylie the day her father had arrived. Why were her sisters so stubborn?

"Hey," Lacy said. She had heavy bags under her eyes.

"Ugh." Danica put the glasses back on her. "Why do you

look so tired?"

Lacy shrugged.

"Drink too much last night?"

Lacy lowered her shades and looked at Danica over them. "I wish." She righted them again.

"Then what's up? You're following Mom like you're ready to pounce."

"I wasn't following them. I just came out of the hotel after them."

"Lacy."

"Danica."

How could someone she just met already feel so much like a *real* sister? "Look, Kaylie doesn't know anything about what happened. Do you feel the need to tell her? Do you really want to hurt her like that?"

"Kaylie? How did this become about her?"

"Because once you bring something like this out in the open, it's going to affect everyone they're involved with."

"It doesn't have to. It only has to affect them." Lacy leaned forward and removed her glasses. "See that woman over there?" She pointed to Madeline. "She's my mother. How can I look at her and know that he—*our* father—pushed her feelings aside like that? Would you be able to? If the tables were turned, could you look at your mother every day and know she might find out one day? And that it might hurt her even more, finding out that you knew the whole time and could have told her, but you chose not to?"

"Okay, I get that. I really do. So, let's talk to them, but can we please do it without Kaylie and the rest of the family around?"

"You don't have to be involved. I just want my mom to

know."

Danica looked at Lacy then, really looked at her. She saw how the anger, or perhaps guilt, had stolen the spark from her eyes. "Lacy, we're sisters. If you want support, I want to be there."

"You do?"

"Yes, I really do."

Lacy slipped her glasses back on and embraced Danica, whispering a thank-you in her ear.

"Let me just tell Blake; then I'll ask Mom to go for a walk, and maybe you could ask your mom? We could meet down at the beach?"

Lacy nodded, slipping her fingers beneath her shades. Danica had a sneaking suspicion that she was wiping tears from her eyes.

Chapter Thirty-Seven

The sand was warm beneath Danica's bare feet as she and her mother walked toward the water's edge. A warm breeze blew through her hair, and she looked up at the cloud-free sky.

"I can't even believe that yesterday happened. Look at that sky, Mom. What are the chances that the one sudden storm during our trip would be on our wedding day?"

"That's Murphy's Law for you." Her mother had on a pair of dark blue capris and a white T-shirt, over which she wore an open navy blouse, which blew with the breeze.

"You look really nautical today." It was nice to spend a little time with her mother. She put her toes in the water and turned to look at the hotel. She wanted to remember every single detail of the hotel, the beach, even her mother, right then, at that very moment. As the minutes passed, she could almost forget about what her parents had done. She could almost forget that she was sneaking off behind Kaylie's back. And if Lacy hadn't been heading directly toward them, scowl still in place, she might have been able to pretend that she wasn't about to open a whole new can of worms.

"Madeline, Lacy, what a nice surprise," her mother said.

Guilt tightened around Danica's chest, and she had to work

hard to remember that it wasn't her who helped someone break a marriage vow.

"It's actually not really a surprise," Lacy said.

Way to jump right in. Danica was struck with an overwhelming drive to protect her mother. She inched closer to her, watching Lacy like a hawk.

"Why don't we walk," Danica suggested. Everything was easier when your body was busy.

They walked down the beach, Madeline and Helen between Lacy and Danica. Her chest tightened more with anticipation.

Her mother stopped to pick up something from the sand. She turned it over in her hand and held it out to Madeline. "This is that sea glass that you collect, isn't it?"

"Would you look at that? Look, Lacy." Madeline said to Lacy.

Lacy removed her sunglasses. Her feet moved anxiously from side to side. Her eyes darted from her mother to Danica, then back to her mother.

"Mom, I have something that I think you need to hear." Lacy drew in a long breath. "Helen, I'm really sorry, but I have to do this, and I know it's gonna hurt you." Before Danica could say a word, Lacy blurted out, "Helen kissed Dad. He kissed her. I saw it."

You could have been a bit more tactful. Danica stepped closer to her mother.

"Wha—" Madeline looked from Lacy to Helen.

A rascally grin spread across Helen's lips as her eyes widened at Madeline, then darkened at Danica.

Danica cringed.

Lacy narrowed her eyes.

"Yes, we did," Helen admitted. "We…had a momentary

indiscretion. And, Lacy, that was never meant to hurt you as much as it obviously has."

"Forget me. What about my mother? You owe her an apology."

"Oh, yes, you're damned right. And I gave her one earlier. Privately. A well thought out, meaningful, honest apology." She ignored the fact that Lacy and Danica's mouths were hanging open and turned to Madeline. "I detailed every single second that led up to that horrid kiss, and I detailed every waking minute since."

Madeline reached out and took Helen's hand.

"Mom? What is going on? She *kissed* Daddy!" Lacy crossed her arms.

"Yes, she did," Madeline said.

A smile passed between Madeline and Helen.

Time stood still. Danica couldn't reconcile what her mother had just said to the pleased look on the two women's faces.

"Lacy, I know this weekend has been anything but normal," Madeline began, "and I also know that meeting your sisters for the first time—and not hooking up with that handsome snorkeler—must have really been difficult for you."

Lacy clenched her jaw.

"But, Lacy, honey, I trust your father. And believe it or not, I trust Helen. If she were here to steal your father back, well, then I think we would have had quite a different situation here. Unfortunately, your father is not the type of man that women risk their lives for more than once."

"Mother!" Lacy fumed.

"Lacy, he's a good man. A loving man. But look at what Helen has been through. He's already left her once. He left her in a state of chaos. We, you and I, we had him all to ourselves, and he never looked back. He did that for us, and while I'm glad for that on one level, he did it at the expense of Helen and her girls—your sisters."

If a person could shrink right before your eyes, Danica would swear that Lacy was doing just that.

"I don't expect you to understand this. Not now, and maybe never, but what Helen was doing wasn't for your father. She was soothing her soul, healing an old, gaping wound."

"I have no idea what you could possibly mean." Lacy turned her back to her mother, whose eyes had filled with sadness as she watched her daughter cross her arms and put up an invisible wall between them.

Helen shook her head, and understanding dawned on Danica. "It wasn't a mistake," she said. Her mother had lied to her. To protect her? Why? She'd have to deal with that later. Right now, she had to help Lacy.

Danica stepped forward and took Lacy's hand. "I think I understand."

Lacy's eyes pleaded with her. *Tell me I'm not crazy* hovered behind the anger.

"Lacy, I think my mother was exacting a certain type of revenge."

"Revenge? Against my mother?"

Who knew a slim girl like you could puff up in all the right places to look threatening? Lacy reminded her so much of Kaylie that she had to swallow a smile. "Honey, not against your mother. Maybe inadvertently, but I doubt it was a conscious act against her as much as it was a conscious act against our father." She put her arm around Lacy and walked with her a few feet away from their mothers. "I think she wanted to prove to our father that she still had it. To show him that he'd lost something good—a worthy, attractive, vital woman—when he turned his back on her."

Lacy shook her head. "That's so childish."

Danica looked past Lacy at her mother, and for the first time since the whole situation unfolded, she saw pieces of the mother she'd been longing to see. "She was so broken when Dad left. I wasn't really sure she'd ever climb out of the rut he left her in. Between his leaving and Kaylie's anger toward her—"

"Kaylie was angry at your mom? Why? She didn't do anything wrong. At least not back then."

"Kaylie was angry because she stayed with Dad even after she knew about his affair with your mother."

"Oh." Lacy turned and looked at Helen with compassion in her eyes.

"She was basically saying *F-you* to our father. You know? I'm sure you've done it before. Given a guy who dumped you the old, *you don't know what you're missin'* treatment?"

Lacy smiled.

"And she told your mother, without the threat of you exposing the kiss. Not that I'm supporting what my mother did—although I have to tell you, after all she's been through, it is pretty impressive. But this isn't worth ruining our families over. We've only just found each other."

Lacy nodded. "Do you think Dad knows that we all know?"

She shrugged. "Let's go find out."

On the way back into the hotel, Lacy's phone rang. She looked at the number and told Danica that she had to take it in private.

Danica turned to her mother. "Why did you lie to me?"

"I thought it would be easier than the truth."

Okay, Danica could accept that. Didn't everyone take the easy way out? "So, Mom, you really told Madeline? Just like that?"

Her mother smiled. "Just like that. I told you that I'd sleep in my own mess. And really, what did I have to lose by telling her? Either she'd hate me, which maybe she already did—"

"Helen!" Madeline swatted her arm with a friendly smile.

"Well, you could have. You have to admit, it's a very strange thing that you and I are friendly after all these years."

"I want to know what Dad said when you told him that you told Madeline." Danica watched the women exchange another smile, this one loaded with mischief.

"I didn't." Her mother lowered her chin and held Danica's stare.

"But you just told Lacy that you did." Understanding dawned on Danica like a bee sting, fast and painful. "Oh my God. You are wicked. Really, really wicked. I have to tell Kaylie."

Her mother grabbed her arm. "Oh, no, you don't."

"Mom, she'll find out. You know she will."

"She will. You're right. But it doesn't have to be handed to her on a silver platter on the day after her wedding. She's already not speaking to your father. Do you really think he needs the wrath of Kaylie breathing down his back?"

Danica pulled her arm away from her mother's grasp. "You're not worried about Dad. You're saving your own hide. You're afraid she'll go back to being angry with you again."

"No, Danica, I'm not." Her mother pursed her lips and furrowed her brow. Then she drew her shoulders back and crossed her arms.

"Oh yeah, you are. You *so* are. And now that I know the truth behind the kiss, I can tell you with certainty that what you don't realize is that what you did is exactly what Kaylie would do. I can see her doing it. She won't be mad at you; she'll probably sing your praises." Danica headed toward the side doors that led to the pool, and her mother's voice drifted behind her.

"Danica, don't!"

Lacy ran right into Danica as she exited the building.

"Oh, sorry. I'm so sorry." Lacy fumbled with her phone.

"Why are you so flustered?"

"No reason." Lacy put her phone behind her back.

"Who called?"

"No one."

Danica shook her head. "Sisterhood Rule 101: Tell your sisters all the dirty deets of your love life."

Lacy rocked her shoulders back and forth. "Okay, sure. You tell me the details of your wedding night first."

"You witch."

"I'm the good witch, and don't you ever forget it." Lacy pulled open the doors, then turned back. "Where are you going, anyway? I thought we were all going to grab some lunch."

"We are. I want to talk to Kaylie."

"You aren't—"

Danica turned on her heels and headed down the path toward the pool. The *snap, snap, snap* of Lacy's flip-flops followed her.

She stood by the pool entrance and watched her sister with her babies and her husband. Kaylie's laugher filtered through the afternoon air. She picked up Trevor and rocked him in a tight hug before setting him back down on the pool deck. Chaz carried a sleepy Lexi in his arms. Behind them, Blake lay on a lounge chair, his arm casually draped over his eyes. By the tilt of his right foot, hanging loosely toward the sun, Danica guessed that he was sleeping.

She couldn't do it. The scene was too joyful to ruin with a rant about her parents—even if Kaylie might find something twisted and beautiful in what her mother had done. She turned back and bumped into Lacy.

"Geez," Danica said, having forgotten that Lacy had followed her out.

"You're not telling her?"

Danica shook her head. *Not now. Look at them. How could I? She's way too happy to take a chance of ruining it with something as stupid as this.*

"Hey, Dan! Lacy!"

"Busted," Lacy said as she waved to Kaylie.

Kaylie ran over to the entrance. "We were just gonna feed the kids and put them down for a quick nap before they leave with Mom. Where are you guys going?"

"Nowhere. I just came to see where you were," Danica lied.

"You must have worn your man out last night," Kaylie said with a wink. "He's been asleep since about five minutes after you left. Where's Mom?"

"She's inside. Have you seen Dad?" She didn't even know why she asked. Danica wasn't thinking about her mother or father. She was thinking about Kaylie's words: *You must have worn your man out last night.* Flashes of the evening before brought Danica's hand to her chest. Her heart raced just thinking about his touch.

"Hello? Earth to Danica." Kaylie was waving her hand in

front of Danica's dazed eyes.

"Yeah, what?"

"You asked where Dad was. He's in the restaurant. Everyone is. We're all meeting in about ten minutes before they have to take off for the airport. I'm gonna get the kids' pool stuff packed up. I'll meet you guys there."

Kaylie turned, and Danica said, "I'm gonna get Blake. I'll meet you there, Lacy."

Danica purposely waited to wake Blake until Kaylie and Chaz took the kids out of the pool area. She didn't want him sidetracked when he woke up. Danica didn't want to disturb the energy that they'd nurtured.

With Kaylie gone and the rest of the hotel guests nowhere near Blake's lounge chair, she leaned down and ran her tongue playfully along his lower lip. When he didn't respond, she did it again, this time letting her tongue slip into his parted lips, ever so lightly.

He remained still.

She put her hand up his shirt and ran her fingers across his chest.

"You wanna play?" he asked in a gravelly voice, heavy with sleep. Before Danica could respond, he'd pulled her onto his lap and tickled her ribs. She screamed out in surprise, playing right into his hands as he grabbed her ribs again and again. She kicked her legs, squirming to be set free.

"Stop! Stop!" she cried through tears of laughter.

He pulled her down beside him. "I wouldn't want you to get any crazy notions about being in control or anything," he said before kissing her so passionately that she came away breathless.

"Wanna play?" he asked.

Danica looked around, then turned back and shook her head. "Uh-uh. Not here."

"What's wrong? Public displays of affection suddenly aren't your thing?"

"Public playing isn't my thing," she said.

"Or maybe it is, but you just don't know it yet." He lifted his brows. "Mmm. A new game?"

Chapter Thirty-Eight

The restaurant smelled of coconut suntan oil, icy air-conditioning, and French fries. Danica touched her father's shoulder as she passed on the way to her seat. Danica was slowly realizing that she'd never fully understand what had happened between her parents and Madeline. Their lives were like tangled webs, and she didn't need to be the one to figure out how to undo the past. She could love her parents for who they'd always been to her and for raising her and loving her. Their mess really was their own mess, and maybe they didn't feel like it was a mess at all. For now she'd hold the memory of their walk down the aisle in her heart forever.

She could hardly believe that their bittersweet weekend had come to an end. She surveyed each of her friends and family members and realized that even with the storm and the drama, the weekend had brought them all closer together. Elise and Madeline were deep in conversation about the difference between today's writing and the classics. Gage was deep in conversation with Rusty, while Sally looked on with a torn expression—hovering somewhere between frustration and joy.

Kaylie lifted her glass at the same time their father did, and an uncomfortable lowering and lifting of the glasses ensued.

"Sorry," Kaylie said.

"No, go on," her father responded.

"No, Dad, go ahead."

Hearing her sister call their father *Dad* without tension, without restraint, like the word had once again become comfortable, Danica knew she had done the right thing by leaving Kaylie out of her parents' issues.

"Thank you." Her father stood, glass in hand. "I wasn't really sure if I'd be welcome at my own daughters' weddings." He looked at Kaylie, who dropped her eyes, then Danica.

Guilt pressed in on her, and she clenched her jaw to keep from letting her emotions take over. Blake took her hand, and she held on tight.

"I couldn't have been more pleased when the invitation came." He looked down the table. "Danica, Kaylie, Lacy. We all know that I'll never win a father-of-the-year award, but I do love you, all of you. Chaz, Blake, my daughters couldn't have found better men to be partners with for life." He put a gentle hand on Madeline's shoulder, and with his next words, his voice turned tender. "It took a great deal of strength for Madeline to face this crowd. Thank you, Maddy, for having the strength to come with me and for giving me the courage I needed to be where I really wanted to be but was afraid to go." He raised his glass higher. "To Danica, my dear sweet eldest daughter, you have chosen a perfect partner. May you and Blake enjoy a long and happy life together. Kaylie and Chaz..." He blinked away dampness from his eyes and opened his mouth to continue, then faltered and looked away.

Madeline reached up and touched his side.

Their eyes met, and he continued. "Kaylie and Chaz, I have watched the two of you these past few days. Chaz, Kaylie is one of a kind. She's smart, funny, and sometimes too stubborn for her own good, but you could never find a more loving, intelligent, and stable wife. She's already proven to be a wonderful mother. But she'll test you at every turn."

Kaylie's eyes grew wide. "Dad!"

He held up his hand. "Please, let me finish. She'll test you because she loves you and because she wants to make sure you'll always be there. That's my fault. I take full responsibility. From what I have witnessed in these few short days, you know how to love my daughter, and I have a feeling that the very love you give will eventually negate the worries that my actions stirred in her." He began to sit down, then stood up again and added, "And if either of you boys break my daughters' hearts, I won't hesitate to hunt you down like animals and tear you apart."

A collective laugh eased Danica and Kaylie's tears.

"Thank you, Daddy," Danica said.

Kaylie stood and tossed a sarcastic smile in her father's direction. "Drama queen here." She laughed.

Danica smiled. *Leave it to Kaylie to play up to her father's teasing.*

"All kidding aside, thank you all for coming so far to join us in our somewhat harried wedding. Mom, you're such a strong person. I know that now, and I'm so sorry that I spent so many years acting like a spoiled brat. Dad, you're right. It is your fault that I test every relationship that I've ever been in." She lowered her shoulders, and her eyes narrowed. "Do you know how long I've been waiting to tell you that? Gosh, that feels good."

"Kaylie," Danica warned.

"Don't worry. I'm not going to take down the toast. The truth is, Dad, by testing every man I've ever dated, I've found the one man I know will never let me down. So, in a way, I should probably thank you."

Who are *you?*

"Even if you and Mom did kiss and throw my entire life into a whirlpool of stress and anxiety that I couldn't even share with my sister because it was our damned wedding day."

How the hell do you know? Danica glared at her mother.

The guests grew uncomfortably silent.

Kaylie held her glass high. "To love!"

A quick glance down the table showed a mixture of shock and embarrassment as eyes dropped, hands fidgeted. Madeline and Helen shook their heads. Their father's jaw was lucky it didn't smack the table when it dropped open. Lacy's glare shot daggers at an oblivious Kaylie.

Danica sprang to her feet. "Nothing like a little joke to end the toasts. Um…" She lifted her glass and looked at her sister, who was deep in a heated whispering conversation with Chaz. "Kaylie, I love you, honey. I love everything about you, and that includes your poor timing. Chaz, more power to ya, sweetie. She's a firecracker, but the best kind of firecracker, and I wouldn't change her for the world." Danica breathed a sigh of relief when everyone laughed, including Chaz. "Mom." She wanted so badly to yell, *How does Kaylie know?* She had the sneaking suspicion that her mother had played her for a fool, but that was not something to be spoken of in public. No matter what Kaylie thought. "I love you," she said to her mother. She turned back to Blake and took his hand. "Blake, my dear, sweet Blake. I have just as many painful traits as my sister does, and I also have every faith that you'll find a way to love me despite them. I love you."

"Lacy." She waited until Lacy finally looked at her to continue. "You are everything I could have hoped for in another sister, and my only regret is that we didn't meet much sooner."

Lacy's smile couldn't quite camouflage the anger hovering in her eyes, aimed at Kaylie.

The food was brought to the table, and Danica walked as calmly as she could to her sister's side and grabbed her by the arm. "Come with me to the ladies' room?" she whispered.

"After I feed the kids," Kaylie said.

Danica yanked her from her seat. "Now." She smiled down at Chaz, whose nod told her that he understood completely what she was doing, and if Danica had read him right in that flash of a second before she pulled Kaylie down the hall, he was thankful that she was handling what he had tried unsuccessfully to handle himself. Sisters didn't have to watch their P's and Q's. There was no risk of divorce from a sister, and Danica was counting on that.

"What is wrong with you?" Kaylie asked as Danica dragged her down the corridor.

Danica fumed. She heard the fast footfalls behind her and could only guess at who was on her heels. Lacy? Her mother? Hell, at this point it could even be Madeline. And she was shocked that Camille and the girls hadn't come running after them yet. She knew that storming out of the restaurant was not a graceful move. But she didn't care. She wasn't going to play these games for one more minute.

Chapter Thirty-Nine

Danica barged into the ridiculously large sitting area of the ladies' room with Kaylie in tow, and before she could get her bearings, the door swung open and in walked her mother, Madeline, a very angry Lacy, Camille, Chelsea, and Marie.

"Oh my God. Is anyone left out there?" Danica said, exasperated.

"Not anymore," Sally said as she and Nancy walked in with Max behind them. "Unless you count teenagers, men, or Chaz's family, whom I assumed you didn't want involved, so I told them that sometimes you got sick, Danica, and we'd check on you."

"Thank you," Kaylie said, "but what the hell is going on?"

Her mother stormed into the bathroom and fumed. "Kaylie Elizabeth, what did you just do?"

"What is everyone so up in arms about?" Kaylie said, pulling away from the eyes that had her pinned beside Danica.

"Have you lost your filter?" Danica spat. "Do you know what you just said out there, in front of everyone we know and love?"

Kaylie wrinkled her brow. "I thanked Dad. His leaving did actually help me in the long run."

"Kaylie!" Danica and her mother said in unison.

Lacy broke through the group and faced Kaylie head-on. It was like looking at twins with opposite wigs. "How did you know they kissed?" she spat.

"Oh, is that what this is all about?" Kaylie said like she was talking about a new dress. "I thought I did something wrong. Mom told me."

"Mom told you?" Danica turned toward her mother, too angry to speak.

"Danica, calm down, please," her mother said.

Camille crossed her arms. "Wait, so it's true? You kissed your ex-husband at your daughter's wedding, with his wife right there? Oh, Mrs. S., this just keeps getting better and better. I mean, after seeing Max with hottie the other night—"

"Camille!" Max turned her back to the group.

"What? You gotta admit the guy's a total beefcake. I feel like the old married one here. Between Lacy's sexy calls from Dane and the way Sally and Gage were drooling over each other like two dogs in heat, and—"

Danica's jaw hung open. *How did I miss all of that?*

"Okay, okay, just stop." Madeline held her hands up to shush the murmurs. "Suffice it to say that weddings have a way of bringing love to the air. And revenge," she added.

Danica turned a hot glare on her mother. "This is why you told me not to tell Kaylie? It wasn't to protect her, or Dad, or Madeline, or Lacy. It was because *you* had already told her? Why wouldn't you just tell me that?"

"Oh, Danica." Her mother sank into one of the armchairs. "Huh, so this is why they call this a ladies' lounge instead of a ladies' room. God, these chairs are comfy."

"Mom!"

"Okay, okay. Danica, you're a smart woman. You can reason yourself in or out of anything, but you coddle Kaylie like she's still a little girl."

"Mm-hmm. You do," Camille said.

"Do you think? Not so much, maybe like a teenager?" Marie added.

"No, she's done it her whole life. She protects her from everything," Chelsea said with a roll of her eyes.

"Stop, okay. Just stop." Danica's head spun. "I was protecting Kaylie from having her wedding weekend ruined by something that you and Dad did. She just got over being angry at you two years ago and it still seems like it was yesterday. And as far as Dad's concerned. Kaylie"—she looked at her sister—"you can't tell me that when she told you, it didn't make you want to lash out at him."

"No, you're right. I wanted to lash out at both of them, but then Mom explained why she did it, and"—Kaylie shrugged—"I guess it just all made sense. She showed him what he was missing and threw it in his face. I was kinda proud of her. But I didn't know that you didn't want me to say anything to Danica or in front of anyone else," she said to her mother.

"That's kind of what *this is our little secret* means," her mother said.

Danica let out a breath and flopped into the other chair. "So, you didn't trust me to tell Kaylie? And you lied to me about the kiss?"

"No, that's not it. I knew that if I told Kaylie myself, she'd get it, and I thought that if I told you, you'd tear it apart like a therapist and we'd spend many hours debating the whys and wheres of it all before you realized that what I had told you was the real reason that I did it. It was easier to call it a mistake."

Her mother leaned forward and reached for Danica's hand. "Danica, honey."

Danica pulled away. "Easier doesn't make it right. I get that you thought I might overthink it, but you chose to tell Kaylie over me?" Had there been more secrets over the years? Of course, there must have been. What had ever made Danica feel like she was the one her parents trusted? Whatever it was, surely it was exactly why she felt the need to protect her sister.

"I can see your brain pulling apart this whole thing," her mother said.

"It's just, I'm not sure why, but I always thought it was me that you trusted, and that Kaylie was somehow more delicate, thin-skinned."

Kaylie piped up. "Thin-skinned? Do you have any idea how much of a beating girls like me get? I knew that everyone else thought that I was a dumb Barbie, but not you, Danica. You've never treated me like that. Is that what you've thought all along?"

How did things spiral this far out of control? "What? No. Kaylie, you are anything but a dumb Barbie."

Kaylie crossed her arms. "Thank you."

"I never thought you were a Barbie either," Chelsea added quietly.

"Me either," Marie said.

Kaylie smiled at them, then turned back to her sister. "Then what, Danica? Are you surprised that Mom and I have secrets?"

"Well, kinda, yeah," she admitted.

"I'm her daughter."

"I'm your sister," Danica said.

"Exactly," Kaylie added. "Look, Dan, I love you to pieces, but Mom's right. Sometimes you pick things to death, and you try to fix everything. It's who you are, and I love that about you. But there are times that I just want someone to listen and understand, not necessarily fix whatever's broken."

"I can do that," Danica said.

Kaylie laughed. "Of course you can, Miss Fixer."

Danica threw her head back. "Oh God, I am Miss Fixer, aren't I?"

"So am I," Lacy said with a wave as she moved to Kaylie's side. "I want everything neat and tidy and put onto organized little shelves."

"That's your father's influence," Madeline said.

Danica looked at her friends watching her with a mixture of pity and intrigue, and she began to laugh. A quiet, under-her-breath laugh, which grew louder as her friends watched her with what was definitely pity.

"What is so funny?" Kaylie asked, unable to keep the smile from her lips.

"Me. Us. You." Danica bent over, caught in another wave of laughter that suddenly became contagious. "My own mother didn't trust me enough to tell me what she did? And look at them." She waved toward her mother. "Mom and Madeline!" Danica blurted out. "What must Dad think? Both his wives are now friends? What the hell is that all about?"

"You think your mom doesn't trust you to tell you things? My mother tells me everything." Lacy's voice became animated. "*Oh, now that was a night to remember*," she mocked. "And when she stumbles out of the bedroom with Dad, thinking I'm not in the room, and they're all over each other. *Forget you ever saw that, but oh my, was that the best kiss ever!*" She laughed until tears fell from her eyes.

"Wait, wait, I've got one," Camille added. "How about my

drunken mother?" She lowered her voice to a husky tone. "*Hey, sugar, pour Mama Bear another vodka, and bring one to the naked man in my bedroom, too.*"

The room silenced.

Camille threw her hands up. "Kidding! Duh!"

Danica fell back into fits of laughter once again, and as she finally tried to regain control, her stomach muscles clenching in pain, she looked at her mother and thought, *You were protecting me, and I just never realized that I needed protecting.*

Chapter Forty

"You and Gage? Dogs in heat?" Danica said as she hugged Sally goodbye.

"Trust me, if there were anything going on there, you'd be the first to know." Sally glanced at Gage and Rusty. "I have to admit, he's great with Rusty."

"You can't fool me. Now that everyone else sees it, maybe it's time we pushed things along a little."

They said goodbye to their guests, helping them into the airport shuttle.

Her father set Trevor down by Kaylie's feet and opened his arms. "Honey?"

Please hug him.

Kaylie walked into his arms, and as her father embraced her sister, Danica saw the tension in Kaylie's muscles ease, replaced with comfort. She slowly drew her arms around her father's waist and settled her head against his chest.

"You smell like you always did," Kaylie said.

"I'm the same person, princess. I'm not sure if that's good or bad, but I'm still your old dad, and I love you." He moved from Kaylie to Danica and turned her chin toward him, the way he had when she was a stubborn teenager. "You're something else,

Danica."

There it was, the moment of impact. It was his little compliments, the ones he didn't bestow on Kaylie, the way he always made her feel one step above anyone else in the room, that made her feel like she was just that—and that because of her position, she had to protect her sister. *Like she always had.*

"I love you, Dad."

"I love you, too."

Max appeared behind him, and Danica thanked her for everything she had done for them.

"Really, it's okay. I didn't do that much." Max's cheeks flushed.

"Whatever. Come here." Danica hugged her close and whispered in her ear, "Is there something I should know about you and Treat?"

Max took a step back and looked Danica right in the eye. Without so much as a hesitation, she said, "Not a chance on your life."

"Wow. I'd think any woman would be crazy not to go after him. He's handsome, wealthy, and so incredibly generous."

"Don't forget arrogant," Max added.

"You keep saying that, but why? I haven't seen him do one arrogant thing."

"Just something he did."

"What?" Danica knew they were holding up the others, but she'd seen the way Treat eyed Max, and it was anything but arrogant.

Max shook her head. "Remember the night I was with that other guy?"

"Yeah." *You were really with Treat?*

"Oh, never mind. I just think he thinks a lot of himself.

Listen, this isn't important. Say goodbye to your friends. We'll catch up when you get back."

Max climbed into the shuttle, taking one last long look in the direction of Treat's office. Danica was sure she caught a whiff of disappointment when Treat failed to appear.

"If you ask me, she's just fooling herself," Lacy said, nodding at Max.

"Yeah, I don't know what to think. Kaylie says she never even hears Max talking about guys, so…" Danica shrugged. "Wanna tell me about this thing with Dane that everyone but me seems to know about?"

"There's nothing to tell."

"Sisters, remember? We share the deets. Hell, even Sally knew something was up with you two."

Lacy watched Trevor pulling at Kaylie's leg. "Those two are so cute, aren't they?"

"Yes, cutest little spawns ever, but don't think they'll distract me from you and Dane."

"So this is what it's really like to have sisters? They badger you until you finally cave?" Lacy smiled.

"Pretty much, yeah."

"Well, there's really nothing to tell. He's got a life zooming around the world and I've got a life behind my very nice desk at World Geographic. I can't see myself leaving to chase whale sharks, and you saw him. He's not a guy who would be happy sitting around in one place." She blew out a tired breath. "Besides, I don't even know the guy, really, so all this speculation is just that—speculation."

"If you say so. I thought I saw something more between you two."

"No, you're right. There is something between us. Ten

inches of something." Lacy winked.

Danica gasped. "So it's true?"

Lacy flashed a devious smile.

"Oh, honey, we'll have to plan a girls' week this summer so we can hear all about your…so we can catch up. You, me, and Kaylie."

"That sounds more perfect than you could ever imagine. A sister weekend. I've waited my whole life for that." Lacy's eyes grew wide. "Oh, Kaylie, Danica, I almost forgot!" She dug into her purse. "We got these for you that day we went into town." She handed them each a silver necklace with a silver charm. Each one had one third of an engraved heart.

"S-I?" Danica asked.

"S-T?" Kaylie said, scrunching her face in confusion.

Lacy held up hers. "Yup, and mine says "E-R." She stood next to Kaylie and they held them up in a line. "Sister," Lacy said proudly.

"This is what you and Dad bought in that shop? In the glass case?" Kaylie asked.

Lacy beamed. "Mm-hmm. I know they're kind of corny, and it's kind of presumptuous, but I was just so overjoyed that we'd finally met. You don't have to wear them." She dropped her eyes.

"Are you kidding?" Kaylie lifted her hair off of her neck and handed it to Lacy. "Put it on me. I'll never take it off!"

She embraced Lacy, and the three of them promised to stay in touch.

Danica watched her mother juggle Lexi in one arm while holding on to Trevor's hand with the other, and she immediately remembered the feeling of holding on to her mother's hand so her mother could hold Kaylie safe within her arms when they were young girls. She'd always protected Kaylie, and as she watched Kaylie say goodbye to her children, she knew she always would. Even if her sister didn't need her to. It was what big sisters did.

"Give Twevor one!" Lexi said to Kaylie, as Kaylie dug another lollipop out of her purse and handed it to Trevor.

It's just what big sisters do.

Danica waved as the shuttle pulled away from the curb. The sun showered them with midafternoon laze-inducing warmth. Blake wrapped his arms around her from behind and nuzzled against her neck.

"Sad to see them go?" he asked.

"Maybe a little." Danica turned to face him.

"A whole week. Seven whole days!" Kaylie was doing a happy little dance around Chaz. "No babies, no diapers, no sleepless nights."

Chaz picked her up and twirled her in his arms. "I'm making no promises about sleepless nights," he teased.

Kaylie threw her head back and laughed.

"I rather like my sleepless nights," Danica whispered to Blake.

Chaz set Kaylie down on the sidewalk and she ran over to Danica. "We leave tomorrow. Are you sure you don't want to come with us? Think about it. A honeymoon in Las Vegas. Never a dull moment."

Even the thought of Las Vegas, the noise, the lights, and the need for nonstop energy, made Danica cringe. The look in

Blake's eyes told her that he had no interest in a wild week in Vegas either.

"Nope. I think we'll go back to our little house, on our quiet little mountain, and enjoy being Mr. and Mrs. Blake Carter for a while."

**Ready to meet the hot, wealthy,
and wickedly naughty Bradens?**

Fall in love with Treat and Max in
LOVERS AT HEART, REIMAGINED

Chapter One

TREAT BRADEN DIDN'T usually charter planes. It wasn't his style to flash his wealth. But today he needed to be anywhere but his Nassau resort, and missing his commercial flight had just plain pissed him off. He owned upscale resorts all over the world, and he'd been featured on travel shows so many times that it turned his stomach to have to play those ridiculous media games. Lately, the pomp and circumstance surrounding him had begun to irk him in ways that it never had before meeting Max Armstrong. It had been too many long, lonely weeks since he'd seen her standing in the lobby of his Nassau resort, since his heart first thundered in a way that threw him completely off-kilter—and since they'd spent one incredible evening together. Treat wasn't a Neanderthal. He'd known he had no claim on her, even after their intimate evening. Hell, they hadn't even slept together. But that hadn't stopped his blood from boiling or kept him from acting like a jerk the next morning when he'd seen her with another man in front of the elevators, wearing the same clothes she'd had on when Treat had left her the night before.

He hadn't been able to stop thinking about Max since the moment he'd first met her, despite the uncomfortable encounter, but he'd been burned before, and he wasn't into repeating his mistakes. Getting away from resorts altogether and spending a weekend with his father at his ranch in Weston, Colorado, a small ranch town with dusty streets, too many cowboy hats, and a main drag that had been built to replicate the Wild West, was just what he needed.

His rental SUV moved at a snail's pace behind a line of traffic that was not at all typical for his hometown. It wasn't until he crawled around the next curve and saw balloons and banners above the road announcing the annual Indie Film Festival that he realized what weekend it was. He uttered a curse. He wasn't in the mood to deal with crowds.

His cell phone rang, and his sister's name flashed on the screen. Before he could say hello, Savannah said, "I can't believe you didn't tell me you were coming to town."

"Hi, sis. I miss you, too." The only girl among his five siblings, Savannah was a cutthroat entertainment attorney, but to Treat she'd always be his baby sister.

"When will you get into Weston?"

"I'm here now, sitting in traffic on Main Street." He hadn't moved an inch in five minutes.

"I'm at the festival with a client. Come see me."

All he really wanted to do was reach his father's two-hundred-acre ranch just outside of town, but Treat knew that if he didn't see Savannah right away, she'd be disappointed. Disappointing his siblings was something he strived not to do. Having lost their mother when Treat was only eleven and his youngest sibling, Hugh, had been hardly more than a baby, his siblings had already faced enough disappointment for one lifetime.

"You're with a client. Sure you can get away?" he asked.

"For you? Of course. Besides, I'm with Connor Dean. He can handle things for a little while. Come in the back gate. I'll wait there." Connor was an actor who was quickly climbing the ranks of fame. Savannah had been his attorney for two years, and whenever he had a public engagement, he brought her along. It wasn't a typical attorney-client relationship, but for all of Connor's bravado, he'd been slandered one too many times. Savannah kept track of what was and wasn't said at most events—by both Connor and the media.

"I'll be there as soon as traffic allows." After he ended the call with Savannah he called his father.

"Hey there, son."

Hal's slow, deep drawl tugged at Treat's heart. He'd missed him. Hal had always been a calming influence on Treat. After his mother passed away, his father had pulled him and his siblings through those tumultuous years. But Hal wasn't a coddler. He had instilled a strong work ethic and sense of loyalty into their heads, and that had enabled each of them to be successful in their endeavors.

"Dad, I'm here in town, but I'm going to stop at the festival first to see Savannah, if you don't mind."

"Yup. Savannah called. She misses you, and I'd venture a guess that you could use a little extended family time, too."

He could say that again. Anything to keep his mind off Max.

TREAT PULLED UP to the rear gate behind a mass of media surrounding a number of cars. He rolled down his window and was met with too many shouts to decipher. It was obvious no one was going anywhere anytime soon. He pulled into the parking lot outside the fence and decided he'd run in, say hello to Savannah, and tell her he'd catch up with her later at their father's ranch. The last thing he needed was to deal with this type of headache.

He heard his sister's voice and swiftly scanned the crowd. If anyone was giving her a hard time, he'd set them straight. Savannah was standing with her body out of a limousine's sunroof, shouting who knew what as the media hollered questions at Connor through the slightly open tinted limousine window.

Treat leaned against the entrance to the gate, crossed one foot over the other, and watched his little sister in action. Her long auburn hair looked like fire against her serious more-green-than-hazel eyes. She'd inherited their mother's spitfire personality and was the only one to have their mother's coloring, while he and his brothers took after their dark-haired father.

Savannah's gaze shifted in his direction, and her scowl morphed into an excited smile as she hoisted herself through the sunroof like she climbed mountains for a living.

Treat pushed away from the fence and headed toward his sister in full protective mode. She might be tough, but those media animals pushing their way forward could easily injure her. He plowed through the crowd. His six-foot-six frame naturally commanded more space, and the sea of paparazzi parted for him. He gently persuaded the few that remained in his path with a domineering stare—a stare he hadn't needed to rely upon since Savannah was a teenager, when he and his brothers had spent countless hours keeping horny boys away from their precious sister.

He reached up and caught Savannah as she jumped down from the roof of the limo. He spun her around and, as he lowered her to the ground, his eyes landed on a woman standing at the front of the line of cars waving her hands. Her dark hair was pulled back in a ponytail, her red-framed glasses perched on her perky nose. She looked fierce and beautiful, and Treat's breath caught in his throat. *Max.*

MAX ARMSTRONG STOOD beside her car waving her hands, hoping to create a long enough break in the excitement to gain control of the crowd. Chaz Crew, Max's boss and founder of the Indie Film Festival, had created so much buzz over the past few years that they were expecting more than forty thousand attendees. The festival grounds covered one hundred acres a few blocks from Main Street and boasted five new theaters, restaurants, gift shops, and a high-class hotel. Hotels in neighboring towns were booked a full year in advance of the festival. Whether there were twenty thousand or fifty thousand attendees, Max was ready. She'd been handling the festival sponsors and logistics for almost eight years, and nothing could throw her off her game. Not even the ruckus between the celeb's entourage and the media, which was creating a tornado of confusion.

Photographers surrounded Connor Dean's limousine and the two accompanying SUVs. Max should have known this might happen. Dean was a local actor turned millionaire whose reputation had exploded since they'd booked him ten months earlier. She'd been wrong to think the Hulk-like security guards could manage a little drama. Shouts and threats were tossed around like candy to children, and no one was making any headway. *What on earth is that woman doing with her body halfway out of the sunroof on that limo? And what is she shouting? Legal jargon?*

The heck with this. It was time for Plan B. She climbed onto the roof of her car, which she'd strategically parked in front of the first SUV. *This* was why she wore jeans and her usual festival T-shirt. Because crazy shit happened at festivals.

With a quick flip of a switch on the control panel on her belt, she turned on the intercom mounted above the gate. "Okay, the show is over." Her voice boomed from the loud-speakers. "Let's give Mr. Dean some space to continue driving through. He'll be signing autographs and answering questions after his appearance." She scanned the area, her gaze landing on a man towering above the crowd with a gorgeous woman in his arms. He spun the woman to the side and his face came into view.

Max froze.

Treat?

Her pulse soared, and the butterflies in her stomach she thought she'd annihilated weeks ago swarmed to life with a vengeance. She had worked with Treat's assistant, Scarlet, for months coordinating logistics for Chaz's double wedding, which had taken place at Treat's Nassau resort. The other groom in the wedding was Treat's cousin, Blake Carter. She'd dealt with Treat so many times over the phone that he'd become the object of her late-night fantasies. But even her fantasies hadn't prepared her for meeting the impossibly tall, darkly handsome god that was Treat Braden, with his seductive voice and the way every inch of him screamed of adrenaline-pumping, heart-fluttering masculinity. She'd thought herself unflappable, but Treat had proved her wrong.

Her entire body heated up just thinking about the magical evening they'd spent in each other's arms. She could still feel his eager arousal pressed against her as they danced, still taste his warm, sensuous lips, and she could still see him gazing at her as though she were the only woman on earth. He hadn't even pushed when, after hours of dancing and walking on the beach, kissing like they'd been lovers forever, she'd turned down his offer to return to his suite and extend their evening into morning. Seeing him now, she had a hard time reconciling that incredibly romantic, thoughtful man with the arrogant one who had blown her off the next morning. Sure, she'd been in the same clothes she'd worn the night before, and yes, she'd been out for the remainder of that evening with a man named Justin, but Treat's assumption about what they'd done pissed her off. And the look he'd given her was too reminiscent of the painful relationship she'd escaped years earlier to chase him down and explain. She had every right to do whatever she wanted to do with whomever she wanted, without judgment. Even if she hadn't done anything at all.

She shouldn't care what he thought.

But she did, and that hurt because that awful look he'd given her was in such stark contrast to the impeccable manners he'd otherwise exuded, holding doors, thinking of the needs of her and his other guests before himself, taking extra steps to ensure that every little detail of his cousin's wedding had been taken care of. The truth was, she'd fallen hard for Treat within a few hours of being with him. But Max knew she shouldn't let those feelings sway her resolve. She'd been mistreated, demeaned, and judged by a previous boyfriend, and she swore she'd never go down that road again—not even for too-sexy-for-his-own-good Treat Braden.

She stumbled backward. One of the security guards reached for her across the roof of the car, and she grabbed his arm, finding her footing.

"Max! You okay?"

The security guard's voice wrenched her back to the ensuing chaos. She tore her eyes from Treat and whoever the woman was that he was holding as if she meant everything in the world to him and tried to blink away the unexpected sting of hurt slicing through her.

"Clear a path or you'll be removed from the premises for the rest of the festival." Even she could hear the difference in her voice, the weakness. Her gaze darted back to Treat, who was staring at her with an incredulous expression. Suddenly painfully aware of her jeans and T-shirt, the ponytail in her hair—and how she must look like a crazy woman standing on top of the car—she clambered down to the ground as the crowd surprisingly obeyed her orders and began to dissipate. Threats of eviction usually worked.

She turned off the intercom and fumbled for her keys. Treat was heading her way, but she didn't want to speak to him, *couldn't* speak to him, after the way he'd looked at her.

"Max," he called.

His rich, deep voice was enough to make her body ache. She cursed under her breath as she started the car and navigated around the crowd. She glanced in her rearview mirror. Treat stood alone in his dark suit, staring after her, while his beautiful companion looked on with a confused expression on her face. Max's hands trembled as she gripped the steering wheel tighter and drove away.

To continue reading, please buy
LOVERS AT HEART, REIMAGINED

SHOP.MELISSAFOSTER.COM

More Books By Melissa Foster

LOVE IN BLOOM BIG-FAMILY ROMANCE COLLECTION

SNOW SISTERS
Sisters in Love
Sisters in Bloom
Sisters in White

THE BRADENS at Weston
Lovers at Heart, Reimagined
Destined for Love
Friendship on Fire
Sea of Love
Bursting with Love
Hearts at Play

THE BRADENS at Trusty
Taken by Love
Fated for Love
Romancing My Love
Flirting with Love
Dreaming of Love
Crashing into Love

THE BRADENS at Peaceful Harbor
Healed by Love
Surrender My Love
River of Love
Crushing on Love
Whisper of Love
Thrill of Love

THE BRADENS & MONTGOMERYS at Pleasant Hill – Oak Falls
Embracing Her Heart
Anything for Love

Trails of Love
Wild Crazy Hearts
Making You Mine
Searching for Love
Hot for Love
Sweet Sexy Heart
Then Came Love
Rocked by Love
Falling for Mr. Bad

THE BRADENS at Ridgeport
Playing Mr. Perfect
Sincerely, Mr. Braden

THE BRADEN NOVELLAS
Promise My Love
Our New Love
Daring Her Love
Story of Love
Love at Last
A Very Braden Christmas

THE REMINGTONS
Game of Love
Stroke of Love
Flames of Love
Slope of Love
Read, Write, Love
Touched by Love

THE RYDERS
Seized by Love
Claimed by Love
Chased by Love
Rescued by Love
Swept Into Love

SEASIDE SUMMERS

Seaside Dreams
Seaside Hearts
Seaside Sunsets
Seaside Secrets
Seaside Nights
Seaside Embrace
Seaside Lovers
Seaside Whispers
Seaside Serenade

BAYSIDE SUMMERS

Bayside Desires
Bayside Passions
Bayside Heat
Bayside Escape
Bayside Romance
Bayside Fantasies

THE STEELES AT SILVER ISLAND

Tempted by Love
My True Love
Caught by Love
Always Her Love
Wild Island Love
Enticing Her Love

THE SILVERS AT SILVER ISLAND

Flirting with Trouble

THE WHISKEYS: DARK KNIGHTS AT PEACEFUL HARBOR

Tru Blue
Truly, Madly, Whiskey
Driving Whiskey Wild
Wicked Whiskey Love
Mad About Moon

Only for You
Love Like Ours
Finding My Girl (Graphic Companion Booklet)

HARMONY POINTE
Call Her Mine
This is Love
She Loves Me

SILVER HARBOR
Maybe We Will
Maybe We Should
Maybe We Won't

STANDALONE ROMANTIC COMEDIES
Hot Mess Summer
The Mr. Right Checklist

HARBORSIDE NIGHTS SERIES
Includes characters from the Love in Bloom series
Catching Cassidy
Discovering Delilah (F/F)
Tempting Tristan (M/M)

More Books by Melissa
Chasing Amanda (mystery/suspense)
Come Back to Me (mystery/suspense)
Have No Shame (historical fiction/romance)
Love, Lies & Mystery (3-book bundle)
Megan's Way (literary fiction)
Traces of Kara (psychological thriller)
Where Petals Fall (suspense)

Acknowledgments

The *Snow Sisters* series has been a joy to write, and not only will there be more *Snow Sisters* books, but you can follow Danica, Kaylie, Lacy, Max and their friends in the remaining six books under the *Love in Bloom* series umbrella, *The Bradens*.

I grew up with six brothers, and as the only girl my competitive nature drove me toward being able to do all that my brothers could do, rather than the more feminine things on which other young girls focused. Creating the *Snow Sisters* was a fun and interesting process, and I am indebted to all of my girlfriends for sharing their lives with me, through which I've learned—and parlayed into my writing—about friendship, sisters, and the differences in the way women and men approach life. There are so many friends who have become my sisters at heart, and instead of trying to name each of them, I'll say this: You know who you are. When you read this, you'll feel it in your heart, or maybe you'll get that chill up your back that we laugh about, or perhaps you'll remember when we talked on the phone and laughed, cried, screamed, or cursed. Or the emails we've shared, the Facebook messages, the quick tweets, or the handwritten notes. Yup, it's you, sweetie, every one of you, and I love you all. And of course I cannot skip my brothers, because without each of you I would not have a clue about how to be a strong woman or how the minds of men work. I'm still a little confused there, but you each have helped tremendously. Thank you.

I cannot give enough praise and gratitude to my patient and dedicated editors, Kristen Weber, and Penina Lopez.

Writing the *Love in Bloom* series in such an expedient fashion would not have been possible without the support of my family. My kids have endured months of kissing me goodnight while I'm at my keyboard, and listening to me hash out story lines over dinner or on their rides to school, and my mother has learned to call after my "writing hours," and although she hates it, she never complains. Kids, Mom, I adore you, I appreciate you, and I would not write with such strong emotion if it were not for each of you.

Last, but never least, my gratitude goes out to my readers. Thank you for picking up my stories and sharing them with your friends. Thank you for your emails and messages on social media. I hope you will continue to send them. You inspire me on a daily basis.

www.MelissaFoster.com

Melissa Foster is a *New York Times* and *USA Today* bestselling and award-winning author. Her books have been recommended by *USA Today's* book blog, *Hagerstown* magazine, *The Patriot*, and several other print venues. Melissa has painted and donated several murals to the Hospital for Sick Children in Washington, DC.

Visit Melissa on her website or chat with her on social media. Melissa enjoys discussing her books with book clubs and reader groups and welcomes an invitation to your event.

Melissa also writes sweet romance under the pen name Addison Cole.